The Journals of An Invisible Man Trouble in Venice

1

Hello Reader, seems we are off again. Some people never learn and the majority seem to be happy to stand by and do nothing. Well it is 9am and I have managed to get a room overlooking Vesna and Ana's Boutique Hotel on Calle del Teatro. Short walk from the Grand Canal and all the usual sites. It looks like any ordinary, but beautiful building in the area. No signs as all guests are from recommendations. I have an old friend who gave it a great revue staying as she is in town for the film festival. Yes my darling Antonella Salvucci. She is actually using her suite as a TV station to interview the stars and once she had a few lined up, those stars looked to see the hotel and started booking out the rooms. I did not stay as wanted to have a vantage point to watch front door and saw my old friend Jimmy, the concierge come Night Manager, walking in and out and directing traffic. Traffic being those allowed in and those that are coming out. I think Jimmy's Invisible Man skills are so adapt as he seamlessly arranges the most complicated of itineraries and does it so effortlessly. It seems his skill made him talked of in high circles, his services wanted, and therefore his invisibility lost. He often comes out and in, checking movement in the street and once saw him come out looking like a street cleaner from a door that cannot be seen to anyone without prior knowledge it is there.

Sorry, rambling Reader. So why in Venice? And during the Film Festival? Firstly, if you remember after exposing New Order in Parliament I received a call from Jimmy saying trouble in Venice? Well I came and to be honest was in a rush and forgot the festival was on. I managed to find this apartment last minute as used links to a property baron here in Italy who has the flat for himself when he needs it. He intended to stay, but someone told him that there was a situation in Sicily he had to urgently attend to and that a man called Philippe was to come sort out problem in Venice and would stay at the apartment. So I managed to make a diversion, get my man to Sicily and here I am, Philippe, a fixer.

Yes a fixer for the Mafia. Laughable, but fixing problems for them for years. They think I am a hitman making people disappear without consequences for them, and I have been. I manage to move people at risk, fake their deaths and set them up in countries miles away and keep the Mafia happy and me safe from the Mafia, as those that escape with their lives never want to be seen again. This also gets me cover and connections worldwide when in really tricky situations and I also am known as the Baron.

By now Reader you are as confused as me with my life, but just to say, here in Venice in amazing apartment, across from Vesna and Ana's Hotel, nobody knows I am here, and Mafia think I am working for them as the Baron, their most celebrated hitman, that they have never actually met.

I leave a note for Jimmy in the crack of the secret door to the side unnoticed and watch now as Jimmy finds it. He does not see me watching, but knows I am close by. I watch him tug on his left ear and re-enter the hotel.

I look to collect my Italian Mobile and the keys to the apartment to meet Jimmy in St Paul's Square. There is a small café on the corner of one of the streets leading into the square and we had shared a drink there before. I watch Jimmy leave and he disappears within seconds. Smiling I leave as really looking forward to seeing my old friend and yet apprehensive as I still have no idea what the trouble in Venice is. I also realise in watching the hotel I had not seen Vesna or Ana.

Sat at the back of the coffee bar drinking an espresso with a shot of whiskey was Jimmy. He saw me enter and immediately exits. I take his table and collect the note he left as the waitress asks me what I would like. A one shot latte, wet. Well that is the way I drink it. Being a good Italian girl she looks at me and smiles hiding her contempt for another Englishman who basically orders hot milk with a hint of coffee.

The coffee culture is so different in Italy. People walk in order double espresso that is made with incredible care and attention to detail. The coffee grinder set to a certain grind for perfect thickness and hold aroma. The cup is warm not cold. The coffee served, customer knocks back in one or two gulps and pays three euros and leaves.

My coffee arrives and I pay with a hefty three-euro tip and she smiles even more. Such a pretty girl and I read the message from Jimmy as now no one sees me in the corner.

Message reads as follows,

"Thanks for coming. Girls in hiding as Eastern Europeans found us via leak in UK. I am working at hotel best not come there. Word is hit out on them and they have hired Philippe. Meet at 7pm and stand in casino, I will find you. PS. Thanks again."

It seemed funny that Jimmy and I were actually going to be saving one of us as well as the girls. But funnier is he is worried as the hitman is Philippe and that is me, yet I received no message of any such thing so there must be a leak in the Sicilian MAFIA for him to know I was in town.

All getting complicated and all I know is the Eastern Europeans are pissed at us for having their team in UK shot dead and the girls disappearing, but how did they trace the girls to Venice? Again another leak at UK parliament. So all we have to go on is we are living in a security sieve where anyone can find out anything without really trying. I think that there is obviously something more happening in Venice than previously thought.

I return to my apartment to see a hand left note for the occupant in the hallway. I take the letter and open it. It has a number to call on it. I exit and call from a pretty girl having photos done by the Grand Canal on her mobile; told her needed for a second. She was most happy to help. I call the number.

Marco, an Argentinian fixer for the Mob, who is confused, as does not recognize the mobile number, answers the phone. I answer.

"I got your note at the apartment. I am calling from a gorgeous young models phone so keep the number and call her up next time in Venice."

" Hi, I am in Venice", he replies.

"Well if I ever see you or you see me you know you'll disappear?"

I hear Marco on the other end of the line breath.

"It is OK Marco, I know you will not be curious enough to die for meeting me."

Marco starts to mumble.

"The message Marco?"

"Told you are to clean the hotel opposite as the place is full of rats. Orders from New Order." I listen to Marco tell me to kill Vesna, Ana and Jimmy.

"It will be done, but do not interfere or expect instant notice. I want to make sure all happens and no one is the wiser. I need info on the extermination and my usual fee to be agreed. You know where to contact me." And with that I hung up.

Jimmy was right there was trouble in Venice, but why was the MAFIA interested in a hit on three people that were of no threat to them. I fear a bigger pact was being made with an alliance of countries underworld, which to date, had been carefully steered away from by all who knew the bloodbaths that would follow.

I return to the apartment over the rooftop and in through the skylight so no one saw me enter. I was going to have to be much more careful and this was going to be no picnic. Still ringing in my ears was the line from Marco 'the New Order'.

Sat in the kitchen making a cup of tea I start to write up links to all that I knew.

>   Leak from UK
>   Leak from MAFIA
>   New Order here in Venice

What the heck was all this? Thank heavens for tea. In times of true confusion have a cup of tea Reader as nothing brings the mind together, better focused than a cup of tea.

2

I spent the night drinking more tea and trying to focus on all that had happened and remembered to meet Jimmy at 7pm.

So there I am in my black tie and playing Blackjack when sat next to me is Jimmy. He has a weird moustache and a really good disguise except he has a glass of his favourite scotch.

"You should try not to drink too much scotch my friend," I say and Jimmy smiles as he thought I had not realised it was him.

I place all my chips on the table; the dealer tells me that I have exceeded the maximum. I ask the dealer to talk to the pit boss and he calls the manager and he then nods that it is OK to deal. By now everybody is watching me as Jimmy slinks off unseen. I win and the crowd claps.

"Let it ride," I casually say and manager again nods. Dealer has a two and I have twelve. I motion no card and dealer draws a jack and has to take another card. It is a queen, he busts I win. I cash up my chips and realise I have somehow won so much I am being watched. I walk to a roulette table to hear a commotion by the entrance as a waste bin has a small fire in it. As all look to see the casino staff deal with the fire I disappear, invisible again. Back at the café in the square Jimmy and I are laughing as we loved playing the old games together of being seen then working out how to become invisible whilst all eyes are on you. We were a good team it seemed.

I told Jimmy I knew Philippe had been employed, but not to worry he was not going to hit them. Jimmy seemed curious how I was so sure, but I did not divulge I was Philippe at that point. It was best Jimmy acted naturally so my actions would not be compromised.

It would appear that the New Order I unearthed in Parliament was more than a few Tory MP's vying for power; it was a global organization that was linking all groups in Europe and Russia forming a super power. A Super Power headed by Heads of State being funded by the underworld and much was not as it seemed.

We had just seen Brexit in the UK. Bought about by policy from the leave campaign fuelling hatred for immigrants and anyone of colour as an excuse for their pathetic lives not being what they felt that have a right to expect even though they do nothing. Millions of morons had rallied round the make Britain great again slogan and once the deal was done all those at the top ran like rats leaving a sinking ship. With the country about to go into meltdown, the underworld would find seizing power much easier. Why even that prat of a media mogul who wanted us to leave the EU as they never did his bidding soon realised his days and that of his money grabbing trashy model were shortened. He was now in the hands of the mob.

Even during the campaigns it was highlighted that the BNP (British National Party) had funded the exit camps campaign. Yes a nasty little group of fascists had funded a huge political campaign. Where did they get the money? Seems with the UK out the right wing in France were to try a similar coup. The fascist rise in France was truly scary as the French seemed even lazier to stand up for themselves and loved even more than the Brits to blame others for their failures. It was only now as I listened to Jimmy that there was a New Order rampaging through Europe that was more dangerous than even Hitler and his Third Reich. Yes, Reader the New Order was a new master race, where career hungry and easily led politicians were being bought by a fascist group that would soon control Europe and beyond.

I realised that if they linked with the MAFIA then the mission we found ourselves in was an almost impossible one; with the likelihood we would not survive. Jimmy and I looked at each other and it was then we decided that no matter what we would fight. But at this point we have absolutely no idea who we would be fighting or how?

Jimmy and I hugged and went our separate ways. Although I was running along the rooftops into my apartment, Jimmy was walking in the shadows unseen and into his secret side door of the hotel.

At 3am I collected the message left by Marco and went back to the apartment. I opened the envelope to find pictures of the girls and Jimmy, although Jimmy was hard to recognize from the picture, and details that they were to be hit as a favour to the New Order.

I heard the kettle boil and made my cup of tea and retired to my secret flat. Sorry Reader, forgot to mention. When I first used this flat I was here for six months on a mission for the Mob cleaning out rats from a villa close by. A group of Jewish jewelers who would not hand over a priceless diamond to the mob and had to be eradicated. The mob thought, as they were made invisible that others in the Jewish family would hand over the diamond.

I had the family give me the stone that was sold to the British Royal Family and made as part of the jewel of HM Queen Elizabeth' 90th birthday tiara. I then convinced the mob that the diamond was indeed a fake and that the real diamond was hundreds of small diamonds that I sent them. It seemed the Jewish family had a secret stash of diamonds they handed to me. I disposed of them with new identities and in new countries, where they live happily ever after, and the mob get their diamond(s), reputation of not to be argued with, and no dead bodies to explain as no one has a mess to clear up. You see Philippe really is the best rat exterminator the mob has ever had. All other operatives they use leave trails that lead back to the mob and Philippe never does that.

So during the six weeks in this apartment I had the Jewish family hidden here. With a clever redesign and fake wall there was a massive space above I was able to build as a safe haven. I even stayed here once and had a party whilst the owner was in bed below and he had no idea. I have a lift in a building next door that moves at an angle so those using it have no idea they are in the building next door. I have a lovely three-bedroom apartment fitted out to the highest standards and all for nothing. It is mine, but worthless, as there can never be a deed etc.

I nip into mine upstairs, but use the kitchen downstairs so if anyone did come they would see that the apartment had been used. The secret entrance from the flat is in the bathroom en suite from the main bedroom. Well I also use the bed now and again, well did before Megstar. I was thinking of her recently and decided to call her tomorrow to see how her mother was and if she fancied meeting in Venice.

Sadly the cup of tea did not clear the mind and decided to sleep on it all until tomorrow. I awoke the next morning at noon. I had blacked out again. There was someone knocking at the door.

I turn on my mobile and see two Eastern European heavies outside. Seems the MAFIA leak was worse than I feared. I put on some plumbers overalls I kept in the cupboard and out of the pocket a false moustache and fake scar. Pop on fake glasses and shout to the door.

"Hold on Hold on I am coming."

I open the door and the two men look confused.

"Hello, I am Fritz the plumber," I say in my poor Italian. "Are you from downstairs, has the leak entered your flat?"

Bewildered both unsure what to answer.

"Well the guy staying here will be back in about three hours."

"We'll wait." And with that both entered.

I raised my hands as if to say 'please yourself', and went back into the en suite bathroom through the secret entrance and up to my flat. On my Italian mobile I called my MAFIA boss who asked me to sort out the problem. I explained what was going on and he was furious. MAFIA bosses are like that when people do things without asking on their patch. I was told to sit tight, do not exterminate, he wanted that pleasure himself.

I decided to chance going back to the flat below and saw my two New Order hitmen waiting playing cards. I offered to make them a drink whilst they waited and they both asked for espresso. Seemed they had been in Italy a while. I make the drinks and ask if it is alright if I finish up in the bathroom. They seem to not care and I go to leave when my mobile rings. It is Megstar. Not great timing, I thought, but it was perfect timing.

"Hello darling, I am at the flat on my job list in the office, so call you back in a moment."

I saw one of the goons starting to reach for his gun in his jacket and then on hearing someone knew where I was stopped as he had to think about a hit on me and then how to dispose of two bodies.

"She is Polish so speaks no Italian and I have to talk to her in English, so confusing, but she will be here soon too," I kept walking to the en suite.

As I passed out of sight I rushed to the bathroom to escape. I looked at the mobile app that showed the two deciding to come and kill me, and then quickly shouted from the bathroom,

"My friends my boss is coming."

They stop and I switch to the mobile app to see the MAFIA arrive outside in the street, then back to the main room where my two goons get ready to shoot whoever walks in the door. I text on mobile my Italian Boss the situation and send video link. Suddenly, one of the goon's mobile rings and he answers. He looks to the other and both rush out of the apartment. As they exit they are both shot and bodies in body bags and thrown down an old laundry shoot. There is silence. My mobile rings and it is Megstar. She got my message and will be in Venice in an hour.

Must have arranged something then blacked out and things now getting more difficult by the minute. I exit into my flat above and remove disguise then call my MAFIA boss. A brief thank you and told him that we need to meet. I told him he will have to come to Venice, as the rats he wants cleaned are best as bait to clean the rats in his offices. Her agrees and I realise I have a few days clear to relax with Megstar.

3

As I stand at the train station I see my beloved step off the train onto the platform. It is funny as I am invisible to all there except her. Megstar is radiant and smiles back at me. I walk over, we kiss and I collect her suitcase. It seems as no time has passed since we last met except I notice a new glow to her.

Well reader, you may of guessed where this is going. Yes, she is pregnant. I am to be a father. I am overjoyed, but say nothing as want her to tell me. I would not want to take that moment away from her. I love her. Sometimes life deals us a partner that is a soul mate. The cards may be stacked against you, but no matter what you cannot stop yourself holding your cards close to your chest and believing you can beat the other players. This is what it was when I first saw Megstar and it is the same today. Yes, the sex is amazing and she is breathtakingly beautiful, but to others she is just another sort of pretty woman. Horses for courses and to stay on track you just have to realise that the other runners and riders will never give you the same feeling of completeness.

I take Megstar to stay with Vesna and Ana. First to see me arrive is Jimmy, whose look of shock is as joyous as his hug he gives me.

"This is too dangerous my friend."

"Not at all I reply as be good to see the girls again also."

We enter the hotel. It is beautifully decorated and the modernistic style meets the old world Venetian chic of the 17th century. Ana and Vesna truly have a gifted eye for this sort of thing.

In reception we are greeted by Tulisa (Ana whose name was changed by UK Government) who rushes to us all excited only to slightly recoil as I open armed say,

"My darling Tulisa where is Camilla?"

"Camilla, come quickly," Tulisa calls to the small back office behind the reception desk, "Old friends have arrived."

Tulisa hugs me as Camilla (Ana) arrives and starts to cry as we all embrace. I pull back and smile at which point I see Jimmy motioning with his head Megstar.

"Ladies, good friends, meets Megstar."

"Are you invisible too?" asks Camilla and then Tulisa digs her in the ribs as if to say quiet.

"Well it appears as if I was for a moment, but nice to meet you." Megstar then hugs the girls who over enthusiastically hug her back. Megstar looks at me and smiles.
"Alright, alright, put her down and you two get these two their room key," says Jimmy and the girls look as if to say what room key.

" We are under the name.."

"Warsaw," Jimmy interrupts. Jimmy smiles and the girls look as if they are confused and see my reservation in the book.

"Two nights I believe," continues Jimmy as he grabs our suite key and then leads us to an old Victorian elevator. I have made reservations for us all at Tony's for eight tonight. Tulisa, Camilla, I have Margot on tonight so you are both free."

The lift doors open and Jimmy, Megstar and I all enter. Megstar says nothing, but squeezes my hand and smiles. I am suddenly miles from the mission I am encountering with the four most important people in my life stuck right in the middle.

As we enter our room Jimmy hands me the keys and then whispers that I should look at the photographs by the front entrance. I realised our entrance has been watched and pictures taken. Action needed so shake Jimmy's hand and smile so he knows I will meet him in five. As Jimmy exits I see Megstar who is literally shattered from her train journey and needs to change so I suggest I give her thirty minutes to have a shower and freshen up while I sort out the day. We kiss and she suddenly feels hot and clammy and says the shower is just what she needs. I suggest that she unpack slowly then if she is in the shower in fifteen minutes I possible may join her to wash her back. Megstar smiles and winks, " Fifteen minutes and if you are not here will call room service for Jimmy to fill in." Then in one moment turns on her heels, her dress already unzipped falls to the floor and as she walks into the bathroom I see that incredible shapely bottom encased in suspenders and ..... Sorry Reader, more information than required. Need to see who was taking our photo.

I meet Jimmy by his obscured exit and we manage to catch up to the photographer. He is heavily built and more a contract killer than photographer. Within seconds Jimmy bumps into him from behind and knocks the camera off his shoulder that he catches and apologies as I pass and in a second collect the guys flash card Jimmy took from the camera without our new friend seeing me. Jimmy apologies and I see Jimmy back in the foyer. We look at the contents on the flash card and there are both the girls, Jimmy, me and Megstar, actually nice shots, but this is not funny. I cannot have Megstar or me exposed. I tell Jimmy sit tight and watch our friend. We hit him so quick he did not even register it was Jimmy that bumped into him. Like I say Reader, amazing how when we are often in front of someone we are invisible.

In the lift I make a call to Marco. I have lifted the train stationmasters mobile when meeting Megstar, well he was being a dick to two guys trying to find a trolley for their luggage.

"Marco seems we have a problem. You have another person casing for a hit. Either you take care of this or I will come hit you, do we understand?"

"Baron, I mean... I have no idea... who?"

"Sending you picture took on this phone lifted and hope sorted in next hour. Bye Marco, stay safe."

I hang up and walk into my room and hear the shower running. I have an hour before the situation outside is cleaned up.

Laying on the bed next to Megstar I realise how lucky I am. We have decided to spend the morning unpacking and if we can walk after all that unpacking we will hit the sites. I open the bar to see bottle of Champagne with card saying love J on it. I look out the hotel room window and see our friend with the camera being carried into a van and disappear. The mobile rings and I realise it is Marco.

"Marco, I see your road sweep has been successful, now who is he?"

"He is …"

"Eastern, possibly Croatian? Yes. I think that he works for the New Order and I believe so do you Marco. Now this is where it gets interesting. I think you are being played so we will protect these hits until we know the score before moving bodies. Do not call me again and see what info you can get from your new friend the photographer. Bye Marco." I hang up and return to popping the champagne cork.

Megstar walks into the room naked. "Oh Prosecco, lovely."

I look at the bottle and realise that this girl is more observant that I realised. Also she had a great body. I look at the bottle and smile.

As if reading the label, "To be drunk only whilst naked in bed," I smile at Megstar.

"I think that is one of my favourite bottles," replies Megstar and we again return to the bedroom of our suite holding aloft two glasses.

I had a sudden feeling that site seeing was not going to be able to be done this afternoon.

4

As I stand in the shower listening to Megstar getting ready I have a slight anxiety attack. I have these as well as blackouts, which knowing how I operate is not the best of attributes to possess. It is over Megstar. Has my love made me blind? You see I realise after the last incident with the 'photographer' I have really placed her life at risk. If Jimmy and I had not been alerted to his presence then there would have been photographs of her to connect her to me, or the girls in peril... and sorry Reader, but I am more than a little concerned. I have to take next two days with Megstar and concentrate on why the hotel in Venice was compromised?

I look to see if London has a trail and within moments trawling through the net it becomes clear. It was not the buffoon Head of the New Order, and I know the New Order is bigger then just that pillock, it seems he backed a Brexit pact to humiliate the Prime Minister for not giving him a top job. It seems his campaign of lies hoodwinked an already dumbed down nation to believe and the UK is out of the European Parliament. It seems in the wings the real assassin was orchestrating everything and plotted her way into the top job. No one suspected any foul play on her part as she already had the idiots dancing, unknowingly no doubt, to her tune. Yes, the New Order is a much bigger parasite and Britain's new Prime Minister is the Head of the UK Chapter. I know hysterical, as it may seem they call their groups chapters just like the Hell's Angels. It appears from Intel gathered through a reliable source that the New Order is indeed a right wing fascist movement whose allegiances are invisible to those around them. She exposed Venice to the New Order's secret army of henchmen massing all over Europe. The New Order has influenced right wing fascist groups and the underworld, that included the Mafia in Italy and why I, Philippe was drawn to here to sort out my friends Ana and Vesna quietly unnoticed.

So how can I find out all this in such a short space of time when others do not see it when happening right under their noses? Well Reader, what you don't see is what you are shown. Remember we never notice those we can see as not watching what is in the open. Hide it and when one person sees it the world sees it. We only see the things we want to see. In this case all happened out in plain view of the media and we saw the story we wanted to see. As an Invisible I see what you are not looking for.

Why is there again such hostility and poorly chosen rhetoric about the Germans not running the UK after they failed during two world wars? Well firstly, it was the Nazi's not the Germans, although they were complicit at the time or shot in many cases, and it is actually the German's of today who are prevent war in Europe and bailing out the other countries in order to keep peace. It seems using old wounds to divide a people looking for scapegoats for their own inadequacies is a long used device of those in power. You are all looking the wrong way.

I am standing in the magnificent St Marks and watching all around as Megstar sips her espresso at the café on the corner. I said I was looking to find somewhere to buy the girls and Jimmy a present. She was desperate for a caffeine hit and happy to sit watching people pass by.

I am relieved to see no one watching her. Apart from the local gigolos and lotharios who fancy their chances. She spots me across the square beckoning by a gondola and finishes her coffee and rushes over. I see the men watch her and see her take my hand and enter the gondola. They only see my back, they never see me, but in honesty looking back at Megstar, I wonder if ever anyone sees me next to such radiant beauty?

The ride on the canals is romantic, fascinating and awful all in one. Anyone doing the canal trip in a gondola in midsummer can confirm that the smell of the canal water, especially under the low bridges, is rank. The Gondolier steering our boat grimaces a little as the smell is too strong and makes a joke of how the tourists got drunk and puked from the bridge into the canal. What a joy this little idiot is and we both laugh as we see locals toss their rubbish into the canal.

Suddenly I am taken with a sudden urge to, not throw up, but sing. Now I have not a great voice, but decide to sing something from 'Into The Woods'. Now I am no John Barr, but I love that show so much and Megstar is looking at me with such love I do not care. No One is Alone seemed apt and as I sing people on the bridges and by the canal side look up and cheer. I realise I am drawing attention to myself and Megstar applauds and pulls me next to her to kiss me. I am an old romantic at heart.

We pull up at the place nearest the hotel and I pay the Gondolier and we run like two school kids back to the hotel laughing and very much in love. It is six o'clock and we have a date with the girls and Jimmy. I realise my suit is in the flat opposite for tonight and make excuses to climb over the roof into the apartment. I find notes waiting for me and suddenly back into reality.

Whilst fetching my suit I see that one of the motion detector cameras had been set off. I play back the footage and see a little mouse scurry past. I smile and realise that this camera covers the centre of the floor and nothing else triggered so I go to the kitchen and get what is needed. No Reader! Not a mousetrap. I fetch a nice piece of cheese and leave it out for my roommate.

With suit in hand I exit into the flat above again with the notes and read. It seems Marco is concerned that there is more importance on the girls than he had realised as there were other contractors coming. The note was a day old and he begged I realise it had nothing to do with him.

In the street I ask a nice Italian Boy if I can borrow his mobile and he says no worries. I call Marco.

"Just got your note as planning route out after job done. Listen no worries I know that there are bigger players at work. Ask your boss if he has been contacted by the New Order for this hit and if he replies, as I know he will, yes. Well then Marco we have a problem, as it is not only the hit, but your bosses are in danger. Tell him Philippe will call tomorrow with more news."

I hang up as the lad that gave me the phone is chatting to a lovely American girl. I delete the numbers called and tap him on the shoulder. The girl looks at me.

"Thanks, and Miss, this lad seems to be genuine and if he is not, well I will see you both again. Ciao."

I exit and return to the suite where Megstar is waiting. We all meet in the lobby and Camilla introduces Margot. I smile and shake her hand and see in her bag a brown file behind the reception chair. As we exit I see her pick up her mobile unawares I was watching. We exit and it seems Margot may not be all she seems.

Sat at Tony's we have a secluded table with the most magnificent of views. The wine flowed, the talk of imminent marriage of Camilla and Tulisa, and missing nobody in London. The girls are truly happy and I soon realise that Jimmy has not told them anything of the danger they are in. Jimmy looks at me and instantly I realise he called me to help sort without having the girls panic and create further problems.

"So tell me ladies, Margot seems a nice girl. Where did you find her?"

"Oh she found us." Replied Tulisa.

Jimmy's eye flits towards me as he had not realised and I smile.

"Well you all are lucky to of found each other I guess." I smile and I see Jimmy is uncomfortable.

Tulisa leans forward towards Megstar, "So how did you end up with this one here?"

"He was sleeping with my flatmate."

There is a sudden silence and then Tulisa gives at a mighty laugh and Camilla joins in.

"You are a lucky man, she is wonderful. Shame you're not gay." Camilla looks at me and laughs again.

Our food arrives and we enjoy laughter and stories from the girls of some of the weirdo's that have come and stayed as well as the story of local girl who lost her family in tragic car crash they have adopted and even though she is 19 they have paid all her school fees anomalously. Seems her mother was accused of being gay and her father was shot trying to protect her. The killers had no idea he was gay too, but his courage became a beacon, a symbol of strength for the gay communities around the world. The girl believes it was all mistaken identity and the girls wanted to support her, as they never received any support when they lost friends.

We toast Anna, the young girl, and then realise it was gone midnight. Well fed, girls all slightly drunk, Jimmy laughing and me sober, watching and realizing that I am happy and glad I was able to switch off for a few hours.

"Back to the hotel," says Megstar and Jimmy looks at me and smiles.

"Must see Margot is OK," I say and we order a taxi.

Back at the hotel Margot was sat at the desk and smiled as we entered. She gets up to greet us and forgets to turn off her laptop. Upon which I glance and see she had been online dating. It was some weird site called missingperson.com.

It seems if you are missing a person in your life then finding the perfect soulmate is shopped for online via missingperson.com or some other dating site. Margot saw me look and smiled embarrassed as I see her looking at a girl in Rome, Maria Santa. Well of course Margot was gay…..

Tonight was such a great night and as I make my way up to our room Megstar kisses me on the cheek and distracts me from my thougts.

5

I awoke the next morning and the sunlight was streaming into the room. It seems that I blacked out again and found myself in bed, naked and alone. I rise and dress after seeing Megstar is not here and go downstairs to see the woman of my dreams chatting to the girls. By the door is Jimmy watching the street, although he does seem a little agitated. Being an invisible you see what others do not.

I smile at Jimmy as I kiss Megstar and apologise for over sleeping.

"Please do not apologise, it was my fault, I think I wore you out." All laugh at Megstar's comment and I look a little embarrassed and realise why I love her so much, I also realise why I must get her out of danger. Each day here I am placing her life at peril.

Jimmy calls me over to him and I join him by the entrance, "We have another friend watching the hotel it seems." I look at the corner of the street and see a British looking three-piece suit guy and it is sweltering hot. I look to Jimmy and decide to walk out and confront my new admirer.

As soon as I walk out the man waves to me as if he was looking for me; I am slightly taken by surprise and walk straight towards him. He holds out his hand. My heart starts racing. Is this the killer, is this the time I am not invisible and there is nothing I can do. I feel Jimmy rooted to the spot, unable to move and yet I cannot stop walking towards my death.

Now forgive me Reader, I am not trying to over dramatise here, just as an invisible often we know once we are visible we are vulnerable. Yet at this moment I am completely unable to avoid what is about to happen. I hear the click of a gun being cocked as the man offers his hand to shake mine and know Jimmy is secretly aiming at my killer.

"Sir John, or are you someone else now?"

"I beg your pardon?" I reply as trying to remember when was I Sir John and then it hits me, back in Parliament.

"I am Bailey, Matthew Bailey, I work for the previous PM. He sent me. Well he sent me to say you may be in danger, well he actually sent me as he knows you are in danger, but I did not want to panic you."

It was like talking to Sergeant Wilson in Dad's Army. 'Awfully sorry old chap' or 'Dreadfully sorry to say this.' would be his opening line to the most dire situation and yet always hold himself with modest integrity.

I smile and ask him to join me in the hotel and have a cup of coffee. We walk back and Jimmy looks as confused as I am. As we enter the hotel Megstar is in the reception and she and the girls turn to watch us return.

"Oh there you are," smiled Megstar, "and you have an old friend with you?"

"Yes, this is Bailey, Matthew Bailey. He works with the old PM and just bumped into him on the street, well thought I recognised him and rushed out so not to miss him."

Jimmy looks at me and then shakes Matthew's hand. Tulisa then nervously walks towards Matthew.

"Hello Matthew how is the old PM?" I had forgotten that Tulisa as Ana knew Matthew or must of seen each other.

"Oh he sends his best and that is why I am here."

I cut Matthew off in mid-sentence. "It appears the 'old' PM is thinking of staying in Venice and would love to meet up."

Camilla looks at me as if she cannot believe what I just said and rushes to the diary, "When was he thinking?"

I looked to Matthew who is more than confused and in true British style starts to look to me as if not sure what to say. Tulisa looks to me and I smile reassuringly that all is OK. Camilla is still looking for a date for the diary.

"Well, if you block out a space during the Rome Film Festival, he was thinking of a stay after that." Matthew looks to me as if he surprised himself with his answer.

"When is the festival?" asks Tulisa.

I realise Tulisa knows that there is danger and Megstar answers, "October or November, is it not?"

"I think you are right, anyway, Matthew come have breakfast with us and let us know the gossip from Parliament and what your thoughts on new PM are." And as

I say this Megstar grabs Matthews arm and leads him into the dinning area of the hotel.

Jimmy takes reception and guides Camilla to follow as he will work the door and Tulisa places her hand in mine and looks to me as we walk slowly in for a coffee with Matthew.

"They know where we are, don't they?" she whispers.

I clench her hand tight and say that I have everything in hand as we enter. A young girl aged 19 is working as a waitress whilst studying at University nearby. Her name is Anna. She is completely unaware that she works for her benefactors. As Anna takes our order and goes to make coffee Tulisa smiles at me. Megstar motions ' Is that Anna from...' and Camilla nods 'yes'. Matthew sat in the centre of us all looks around completely confused. Then laughs.

"You know the PM sends his best regards and also warned me to expect not to understand anything that happens." To which we all laugh.

Over coffee Matthew is told how the PM helped Ana and Vesna, now Camilla and Tulisa, escape and become part of a new identity scheme. That Sir John had been involved in helping and that all had worked out wonderfully. Matthew was completely in awe of the story and also decided to tell us more.

"Well, since you left Ana... Tulisa, things have gone extremely dark in Parliament. It is like walking through the pages of a mix of Harry Potter and House of Cards. It seems that there is a much bigger New Order, well the New Order was much bigger than we thought and the bungling idiots unearthed by you guys were just pawns in a much bigger set up. Brexit vote came and the vote was lost. PM stood down, much against my advice, and new PM steps in. All seems really innocent until looking through the dossier you handed the PM Sir John, we see that the Head of the New Order was just a puppet and the woman behind him was the real Head. It seems this was an amazing coup de tard by her to steal top job. A real right wing zealot and we fear she is working with the right wing nationalists not just in the UK, but throughout Europe and even have a Russian group ready to move on their heads backed by Russian Mafia."

"So Mafia involved in New Order?" I ask.

"New Order seem to be now trying to mobilise all of Europe and the biggest problem they have to start this New Order of fascism is funnily enough the Germans. They are the ones keeping Europe safe."

With stories of decent British Citizens from Polish extraction being killed on UK streets it seems that the New Order is committing all kinds of atrocities in order to throw the public off the real scent.

Matthew wanted to let the girls to know that the PM is doing all he can, well the ex-PM, and that he still has a few friends that can help.

I smiled and started to think that it was only a matter of time before Philippe would be beaten to the bounty and the girls could be eliminated. It was time to make a call to Marco and I had a plan forming.

6

A room was fixed for Matthew to stay and be good to have visible a man from the UK government in high visibility at the hotel. That night as I lay cradling Megstar in my arms I watched her sleep and realised her leaving tomorrow was the best possible news.

It was eleven o'clock and I was waving goodbye to Megstar in the airport and turned to see two faces from the past. Two Russian secret policemen who were a direct line to Kremlin. They looked concerned and seemed ready to go to war. You can see it in a man's eyes and they were here to clean town.

The funny thing is I did not think they were here to work for the New Order, I had a sixth sense they were here to see who and what New Order up to. They were the Klutes. A killing machine, born in Serbia, and as hard as nails. They felt no pain and never stopped for a moment to show any emotion. There were three brothers, but one was injured in an operation so they just blew his head off and burnt his body to avoid detection.

Now Reader this is where an Invisible Man has the edge on assassins, top secret service men or James Bond-like characters as they all look like you would expect them to. We look like nobody in a crowd. I decide to go back to the apartment across the road from the hotel and there I would find the next part of my plan.

As I entered via the roof I saw that there had been a stream of people leaving packages for Philippe and monitoring them. Two faces caught my attention. They were part of the Croatian Mafia and obviously they had been tipped off by the Head of UK New Order, our new illustrious and truly evil new female Prime Minister. I climbed into the flat and called Marco.

The phone rang and suddenly Marco answered, "Hello, Philippe, sorry I was in the shower…"

"Relax Marco all is well and I think you should hire me to protect the hit rather than kill." The line went silent and a timid Philippe started to mumble as he was confused by what he heard me say.

"Marco, it seems you are being played. This New Order that has hired you is actually set to then use this hit to bring you down, but more importantly take your money and infrastructure to take over your business. Set up a conference call for tomorrow morning 10am Venice time and have all the bosses ready except the Eastern Block to listen, they are not with you as you think, I think they are setting you up to be killed in friendly fire."

I hang up and realise that by tomorrow at 10am I better have a good story for them and also have the Klutes on board.

I open the apartment door and look at the packages to see one suspicious looking object that I did not trust. I retreat and recall Marco.

"Yes Marco, me again…no not now, 10am tomorrow and for all to hear. Listen seems my cover compromised and parcel arrived that may be in need of defusing. I will find who sent it and have them killed, but if I need to do that then I will realise I need to clean your house too. I like you Marco so be a shame to send flowers to your funeral. Guess you'd better find out before me," and I hang up.

I knew that whoever did this, and I would not have resources or time to find out, would be found in under twenty-four hours by Marco. Very resourceful the Mafia as well as do a lot for charity. They are becoming more business and less gangster every year, but I feel if I suggest this they will look to make a mark to deter anyone crossing them and with this save the girls.

I enter the hotel and am met by a lovely smile from Tulisa. I give her a hug and tell her all will be fine. I also tell her I liked her as Vesna more and soon they will revert to their old names and be truly safe. Ana appears and looks worried, but smiles as if to not let me worry. I cannot find Jimmy and enquire if he is about?

"He never came back last night."

I am concerned and then Jimmy appears. He shakes my hand and asks me to go sight seeing with him. I guess Jimmy has news and needs me to see something that had spooked him.

Sat in a café in Venice Jimmy points to a door of a safe house owned by Russian Secret Police and out come the Klutes. I smile and tell him to go see the girls, act natural and meet him back there. Jimmy motions to me to say something, but cut him off and tell him that not now later as I follow the Klutes.

As we walk down the street I see them looking for a taxi, hard to find in Venice, but I then see a taxi driver stop, get out of his car and go into a shop to buy cigarettes. Such a bad habit and so I get into his cab and drive towards the Klutes who flag me down and give me an address to drop them off at. I see the satnav and put in our destination as we drive off.

Outside of Venice to a large villa the Klutes tell me to wait and I ask to use the toilet, they ask a guard to show me where to go. I tap a Klute on the arm and shake his hand and thank him. I managed to attach a mic to his sleeve. I sit in the toilet listening to what they are saying and then walk back to the car to listen to the end of the conversation.

The Klutes are in town to find out all Mafia connections for the New Order, as there is rumblings of a new syndicate forming that will run all the illegal gambling worth billions to the Mafia and they have been given orders to muscle in when it happens. I smile as I wait in the car and the two return. As they get in the car I manage to collect the mic by saying that he had something on his jacket, well he did, my mic. He looks annoyed, as did not liked being touched and yet I get away with it. I drive them back to their safe house drop them off, make two hundred Euros and then park the car from where I stole it. The police are taking down notes from the driver and they never see me park or return the car. It was like a comedy moment as the driver turns to see his car where he left it.

I tell Jimmy that he must call the Klutes to meet tonight and leave an Invisible Man style card for them to get the information.

Jimmy is still amazed how I found everything out and soon we are putting everything in place. I remember the look of a smile on Jimmy's face as he returned having got the message to the Klutes without them even seeing him in the room. Jimmy was the best and he had entered the safe house, walked in and given the message to the Klutes and walked out without anyone even stopping him or remembering his face. How did he do it? Easy, well easy for Jimmy. Firstly full of confidence he offers a Russian cigarette to the doorman and says hope he won't be in shit for being late. Enters as if all natural drawing no attention to him, and knowing that since the Klutes had arrived lots of unknown faces were coming in and out. Walks up to the main room and holds aloft an envelope so the guard opens the door to let him in and he hands the envelop to the Klutes and just exits and they think he is one of the safe house guards. Oh and of course Jimmy managed to call ahead to say messenger coming with information they needed from Kremlin.

Most spies, and secret police love the cloak and dagger so much that they never question something, even when obviously has no validity.

I sit in the apartment and my phone rings. All the envelope had in it was a new pay as you go mobile number. I answer in my best Russian.

"Gentlemen, listen carefully. The people you search are the Croatian and a splinter group of Mafia looking to overthrow the gaming cartel, but eliminate them and you eliminate the status quo; also there is a hit on two women in a hotel that will trigger off the biggest crime war starting in Russia. These women have to be protected and those that want to start the war need to be stopped. You know who they are and tomorrow morning you will have a call from the Mafia and have a house clean in all your houses. Then we will carry on with the same arrangements as before and life will continue for all, well except those that want to bring down our financial houses." With this I hang up and destroy the phone. I was on the phone for less time than a trace could be made.

I see a nice bottle of champagne in the fridge and decide to take to the girls and Jimmy to enjoy as we celebrate the success of the plan.

I call Marco one more time and he is now really frightened to answer, as Philippe has never called three times in one day.

"Marco, great news. Russians in town happy to assist cleaning house and tell everyone that anyone who touches the girls will pay dearly, in fact their life continuing unchallenged will be a testament to how order has been restored. Time to see if you guys really have any power anymore or has the New Order taken you over? Tomorrow Marco, tomorrow and be ready."

I hang up and see that packages had been removed.

7

I had seen an opportunity, as this is what all Invisibles do. We look to see where the vanity of the opponent, the hit, lies and then once attention is all on them, they have the spotlight, they never see what is right in front of them.

I was lying in bed smiling, yet apprehensive as to the day's events, and how they would unfold. Often things happen as planned; other times thinking on feet and quick thinking the way forward. This would be, well it would be like it would be. There is no point ever second-guessing. All that is needed is concentration and staying in front of hit invisible.

I call Marco and explain that I have seen the Klutes and they also know that the Croatian Mafia in town, who are his clients wanting girls killed are now on the wrong side of tracks. Helping them will strategically place him in line to be hunted as they are now.

I tell Marco that he must protect the girls and the hotel as a show of power for the Mafia. You see the Russians and Eastern Block Mafia are trying to take over. Their first strike will be to have the Italians do their dirty work and in doing so find their place in the New Order, at the bottom. Territories would be rewritten and as to the millions earned, sorry billions of dollars in illegal gambling, their empire that has stood for hundreds of years would crumble. The money, the drugs, the power would shift and they would be living in fear as second cousins to the New Order.

Marco asked me what to do. It was hilarious in a way as I was calling the shots. I sent a file from a shop early as part of a computer demo that had photos of all those that look to overthrow. The Klutes and the Croatians were of course the ringleaders. Clean house I said and make sure that the girls are safe as a symbol of Mafia power and strength for all to see.

He bought it! Of course he did. Marco runs the gambling in the whole of Italy for seven main houses. He called all of them and within minutes I called Jimmy to be alert and ready to take the girls for a meal in the main dining room of the hotel. Jimmy understood as it had three exits, to the reception, to the kitchen and to the lobby for the lifts. I knew Jimmy had cameras linked to his mobile on all three.

Jimmy was concerned Philippe would get through, but I assured him that Philippe is working for us. Jimmy trusted me, as always and now all we had to do was wait.

Wait, what was I thinking? In minutes I see seven carloads of recognizable Mafia Men surround the hotel. Time for Philippe to make himself scarce, I enter my secret flat above and set cameras on flat below to motion detectors. Linked these to my phone and then walked into the hotel. I was not going to sit and wait safe, I had to be there for the girls and Jimmy.

As I enter the hotel I see the receptionist, Margot, is looking pensive. I had looked for missingperson.com to find it did not exist other than a secret network for the Klutes. It seems with us as a diversion the Mafia would not see their empire raided until it was too late. I act naturally and smile.

"We are expecting guests, can you make sure you show them in?"

Margot smiles at me and replies, " Of course sir."

Then the unexpected happens. In walks the former PM and Matthew grinning. I see Margot react, as she knows who it is and then bows. It was quite surreal.

"Prime Minister, how lovely to see you."

"You too Sir John." The PM shakes my hand and as if in a covert movie looks to say to go somewhere private that we needed to talk.

I lead the PM, and Matthew in the dining room. As we enter I see Jimmy look even more confused and the girls rise to greet the PM. I look back to the reception to see Margot with her back to me furtively on her mobile. I feel her involvement in the hit is greater than I thought and she is warning those coming that the PM was here. It gave us a little more time to adjust to the situation.

Jimmy stands and shakes the PM's hand and without a chance to say hello Vesna gives him a warm hug.

"I am sorry to hear things compromised," he says and looks to Ana.

From behind I slowly take control and often as an Invisible you notice the things others do not notice and this often leads to assist later when needed. I refer to the seeing Margot on website, linked to Klutes, then making call. To the three vantage points of exit or enter in this case. The doors to the kitchen have porthole windows and the chefs are still happily working. I see Margot looking to collect her bag and leave via the front and the exit to the rooms upstairs and bar from front lobby are clear. Jimmy looks to me and we nod.

"It appears you come just an opportune moment sir, as things are about to be sorted and I feel we have a few moments to up date you on matters here, not only in Venice, but in Europe." The PM looks round as if curious to what I just said and how it fitted.

"Tell me, are you MI6?" asked the PM.

"If I was I could not say," I replied.

"You can tell the ex Prime Minister Sir John, I am sure he has clearance," says Matthew to which I grin and reply,

"I could not say."

Jimmy laughs to himself, as Matthew is full of excitement at the thought of me telling him in code I was MI6. The PM or ex PM as he is now grinned too and sat at the table.

"Prime Minister or is it ex-Prime Minister, I apologise, but not sure how to address you, anyway, if you want a quick catch up with the girls I will have our hotel manager and Matthew join me to secure the front desk."

Jimmy joins me and Matthew looks at the ex-PM excitedly as if he was part of a MI6 moment. We walk into the lobby joining the bar and the stairs to the rooms.

"Matthew, if you would be so good as to stand in the doorway of the hotel and wait for me to call you on your mobile. Keep looking at it so that you are seen to be monitoring it." Matthew nods and exits.

"What the feck is going on?" asked Jimmy.

"Well Philippe has contacted the Mafia doing the hit of the change of plans. Just in case I need you in the kitchen to divert any unwanted guests from coming in, but I truly do not think they will make it."

Looking at the entrance I see Matthew open the door to let Margo out and in walk two goons. Not sure of who they are I watch in amazement as Matthew then continues to pretend to be a spy. The goons look at Jimmy and he walks up to them.

"Gentlemen, can I help you?"

Both look at Jimmy and then as if covertly whisper," Sent by Marco, is Philippe about?"

Jimmy can see me, but they do not. I nod to Jimmy to say affirmative. Jimmy looks at me in mirror and I motion for him to send them upstairs. Jimmy does so and they walk up and take positions on the landing. Jimmy looks to me and I have gone. Jimmy walks to Matthew and taps him on the shoulder. Matthew lets out a shriek.

"Good grief old chap scared me to death!"

Jimmy just looked at Matthew and said," Do not let anyone else in, tell them clean up squad in the hotel so until all finished no one allowed in."

Matthew nodded as if to say all OK and Jimmy turned to see me in the reception.

"Let's rejoin the ladies and the PM and note that Mafia are taking out assassins as we speak. Any one comes here then they too will be cleaned up."

Jimmy looks baffled and I continue, "I will sit in chair facing the kitchen doors. Trust me if this works you will never has to worry about Mafia ever again."
I see Jimmy break into a smile and places his hand on my shoulder, "After you old chap."

I enter the dining room and sit in the chair wanted as Jimmy walks into the kitchen to return after noting door to rear locked. The ex PM looks to me and asks, "So Sir John? What is the solution? The solution to our little dilemma?"

I laugh inside, as we are about to have a full on Mafia style hit this guy, who knows that all is compromised still has no idea of the danger he and the girls are in.

"Well sir, ladies, here is the position and it affects us all. When we managed to take out the Croatians all was safe then you lost Brexit and it seems that the real power of the New Order was not the bozos we thought but another. Upon your exit the real head of the New Order took *her* place. Yes the whole incident in Parliament was just another subterfuge by the real power. It seems that there is a New Order trying to take power in not just the UK, but throughout Europe. Luckily their greed and as with most politicians, no offence sir, but power goes to their heads and they make mistakes. They align with the wrong arm of the Mafia. The thugs, not the family and muscle in trying to take the family over. In order to save time the family looked to see what they need to do and how to get their enemies close. They needed time for the New Order to show themselves in their ranks and in their quest for power and their greed they revealed their hand too soon. A hitman know as Philippe is hired to carry out revenge killing of two of the New Order Mafia's targets. They are protected by new identities and under UK government surveillance."

"Us you mean?" says Ana.

"Yes, I am afraid to say, but Philippe is working for the Invisbles, the MI6 over here, and has hatched a plan to sort all out in one swift move. The Mafia behind this is known as the Klutes."

"The Klutes?! I had dinner…"

"Yes sir, I am afraid they have been wielding power in parliament for many years making sure their organisation is not noticed or can warn themselves should the need arise. Well they were to establish themselves as the new head of the family, but when Philippe pointed this out to his Mafia contacts he gained their interest by explaining how their billion dollar operations in illegal gambling would be jeopardised. The Mafia can turn a blind eye to a small massacre or beheading as long as you do not touch their money. Right now the Klutes are being taken out as their whereabouts have been gifted to the family. Although hitmen have been dispensed to come here. All is in hand and we just need to sit tight a few more moments..."

Suddenly the sound of three bullets firing through a silencer are heard on the landing above. Followed by the thud of bodies hitting the floor. I see the chef through the kitchen porthole window look concerned and look to Jimmy as our two friends from earlier appear with black gloves on I motion the kitchen. They smile politely and look to each other and enter the kitchen. A few more shots heard and they both come out.

In deep Italian accents one says in polite English, "I do apologise, but you need to all stay here a few moments as we need to clean the landing and kitchen, also your chef has fainted, and then we clean up kitchen."

I stand and look at the Mafia hitmen. "And the Klutes?"

One looks at me as if I know too much, "Do not ask?"

"But I must call Philippe, he would not want to not hear and call on Marco."

One of the men takes out a mobile and talk as the other looks nervously at me.

"It seems the cleaner has already cleaned the whole of that villa. Marco asks that you tell Philippe as soon as possible and would like me to say to you ladies that you will never, ever have to worry ever again. The family is proud to know you." With this the two men exit. One via the kitchen and the other into the lobby.

We all stay completely still and Jimmy looks to me and I see the ex PM stand to shake my hand.

"So the outcome, Sir John?" he enquires.

"A deal has been done where the girls can call themselves by their real names, come out of hiding and never worry again. They have the full protection of the Family. You see Philippe convinced the Family that they needed to flex their muscle and in a show of strength regain power. The New Order would have to renegotiate any deals and things should get back to order for now."

Vesna hugs me and Ana hugs Jimmy. The ex PM as we now call him stands smiling as Matthew enters.

"Sorry Sir John, but you forgot to call me."

I can see the bodies of those being cleaned carried out in laundry baskets and the guy in the kitchen nod at me through the porthole window.

"No worries, Matthew, all a bit of a false alarm it seems," says the ex PM, "it seems we can continue our last few days enjoying the sights of the city with the wife. Ladies, I am so glad that went well and was here for you at least giving possible a little extra time whilst the New Order had to work out a different strategy."

I smiled, as it seems this ex PM was a shrewder character than given him credit before. Shaking my hand as he leaves he looks to me, and whispers, "Thank you Philippe."

We exchange a glance and I agree to meet up the next night for dinner with his wife and a follow up conversation about the New Order. He exits with a bewildered Matthew in tow.

My mobile rings as they exit and it is Marco. "Is everything alright?" he enquires.

"Tell the Family they have done well and have a new ally. Have the message sent to all Families and hopefully this New Order can be marginalised and this hotel and the girls can be a symbol of all to see that no one tries to mess with the family."

"Oh and Philippe, the Family want you to know that your fee is being paid and doubled for you have truly supplied once again the perfect solution. They want me to tell you how happy they are."

"Thank you Marco. You will always be my favourite, sleep tight," at which point I hang up and laugh thinking of how

Marco on the other end would be sweating thinking I was coming for him; well Philippe would be coming.

Later walking through the Calle de la Canonica I see sat nervously in the café on the outskirts of the Basilica di San Marco Margot. She is hiding in the shade and as you may of learnt readers to truly hide sit in the open. I casually walk over and sit at the table with her before she has chance to move.

"Hello Margo? You waiting for someone?"

"Oh please sir, I was forced to do it. They have my mother."

"Sorry, what the Klutes?"
I am taken aback and see genuine tears in the girl's eyes. I suddenly fear that in the clean up her mother was accidently eradicated as well. I hold her hand.

"Where were they holding her?"

Margot looks up at me and explains that her mother was working in a local laundry owned by the Klutes and feared that they had killed her. The laundry was only three hundred yards away and she was there hoping to make contact.

It seems funny how sometimes things work out and again money is not a motive for me, why I am saying all this in advance reader, well this is what happened next.

I walk with Margot to the laundry to find a Family member going through files. I merely mentioned Marco had sent me and access was given. In a courtyard all the staff had been held for the past day as they tried to work out what to do. It seemed it was a massive laundry for not just bed linen. I call on the laundry phone, as the money counters continued not even noticing me. Margot looks petrified.

I call and the phone is answered, "Marco, it is me. Now slight change of plans. Klute laundry to be owned and run by me, with my new business partner as a laundry. You keep part of the property with separate entrance for your needs and that of the Family and accept half of my fee as payment. What do you say and I will deal with workforce so your boys can go home. All good for you...thought so. Cheers Marco, Ciao."

I hold Margot's hand as one of the front door goons walks in. He is looking for Philippe.

"Hello, Philippe wants me to introduce you to his business partner and tomorrow will return with the workforce and start up laundry again." Margot looks confused and then smiles as the goon, a very handsome young man takes her by the hand and kisses it. Margot is smitten, all the pressure and fear gone as she looks lustily at the Italian Stallion.

"Philippe would also like you to be liaison between Margot and Family to ensure two businesses never meet."

The young man smiles, no beams and exits after one last look at Margot and walks back and kisses her as if he had to no matter what. I smiled and he exits a little embarrassed, but I see he is a young lad in his early twenties. He exits and Margot stands there transfixed on the door he exited.

"Shall we get your mother? Margot? Your mother?"

Margot suddenly turns and looks at me as suddenly confused even more as to what happened.

"Here is what just happened. You are now the owner and business partner on this laundry. Tomorrow you come in and will run the business and expect many new hotels wanting to use your services. That young man will be making sure you have no problems and will run part of the building you will never need to enter. You will give me a bank account, your bank account and I will deposit a million Euros over six months until the business is running smoothly. You will live in the accommodation here and make sure that you never overcharge the girls in their hotel. All Ok?"

Margot just nods and then leaps at me and hugs me crying.

"Come on let's go meet your new manager....your mother."

As we run into the courtyard Margot rushes over and hugs her mother. All the staff are confused and a little scared, but Margot manages to assure them all is fine, to go home and return tomorrow to work as normal. I explain that I work for someone who co-owns the laundry with Margot and that from tomorrow new management will be in place and workers will all benefit from new profit share.

I see the young man from earlier and see a cellar with a stock of wine inside. He looks to me and I nod back good idea, no words needed as he returns with crates of wine and champagne opening and offering to all staff as he turns up the music in the courtyard. I see Margot introduce him to her mother then turn to see I have disappeared, but I see her and she knows I am there, she senses my presence and turns to cry tears of joy with her mother.

As I exit unseen a man knocks into me and as I stop in my tracks I see it is Jimmy.

"So I guess you are now the new John Isaac?"

I smile and am flattered, as the greatest Invisible Man ever was the great John Isaac. A Devonshire man whose exploits within the Invisible Men were legendary. He saved more lives, gave the greatest happiness to more people than any other Invisible Man and lived the life of a poor man so no one ever knew who is really was. I met his son once, years ago, and he told me stories of how as a boy in poverty his father made their lives the most wonderful experience every day. He truly embodied the spirit of a word I love to this day; wonderment. No matter how difficult or how impossible a task was John Isaac or GJ as he was known managed to make all those around him prosper. Never have I heard a son talk with such love and affection for a father than GJ's son. If only he knew how great a man he was, but sometimes as an Invisible Man we live for others to never know.

"So I followed you here and what's the score?" asked Jimmy.

"Well Margot won't be working the front desk again, but she'll be supplying the laundry from her new business here."

"And Philippe?"

"Oh Philippe has long gone apparently and is leaving money for you."

"Are you?" Jimmy said and I put my arm around him saying how we needed to get back to the hotel as having dinner with the ex PM tonight. As we walked off I looked back at the laundry thinking, I think GJ would have been proud of me.

By now having read my journals you will see how often much is done by chance, but what an Invisible does is they see the chance and then from a motto derived from the greatest Invisible ever, GJ Isaac, you do it because you can.

To most GJ was just a father with major health problems who was left by his wife for greener grass and affairs, with four incredibly young children. I knew him. He was an inspirational father. He never let the stress or his pain become something the children had to deal with. He saw them all safe and although lived in meager surroundings from miles around the laughter from the household could be heard. Children, friends of GJ's children as well as their friends and family would call to play the games he devised and reinvented. He devised ways to make games new and fresh and applied to his Invisible work. He was ground breaking and taught me that you do not need to be seen to be the best person you can be. He will always be missed.

8

So there we were at the UK Embassy with the ex-PM, his wife, the opposition parties wife, the too are now firm friends even though their husbands still lock horns over policies, Ana and Vesna, as they return to be, Jimmy, who is feeling completely out of place, Matthew and his assistant, a young lad from Axminster called Jacob, and chatting about art, theatre and places to travel.

I say that I hope to pop to Poland to see Megstar soon and all wish her well, and of course the subject turns to how beautiful she is and how we all wished she could have been there etc. The deserts finished the ex-PM's wife looks to her husband and as if on cue rises and smiles.

"Ladies I think it is time for us ladies to retire to the other room and leave the boys, and I mean boys as I do not think one of these men, including my husband, will ever grow up, and leave them to chat 'men's talk'."

"My old fart grew up and peaked at 16! Poor sod," said the wife for the opposition and all laughed as the ladies exit. Last to leave was the Ex-PM's wife who smiles and closes the door.

'That woman will never cease to amaze me," says the ex-PM. "On our first date I never felt as if I was ever in control, and to this day no idea who is in charge."
"She's an amazing lady sir, she even took Jacob today to the museum as she knows he loves art."

"He's a nice lad Matthew, but keep an eye not to compromise yourself with unwanted rumours etc."

Matthew blushed and Jimmy jumped in, "Sadly, rumours are often all they are, rumours. But stock and trade for us....I mean, yes you're a great lad Jacob."

There was a moments silence and without warning Jacob asks, "So, Sir John, what do you know of this New Order?"

I looked as knew this what was to be discussed and all looked at Jacob as I replied slowly and direct. Often Reader you need to be precise and direct to ensure nothing is misconstrued. This is one of my greatest challenges as you can see I am a waffle at times. Blimey! I am even waffling now.

"Sir, what Jimmy and I have found is that there was a New Order, we thought the two idiots at Parliament were running, based in UK. It seems the real Head was more brilliant at disguising themselves than we have ever come across. During the Brexit vote, which again was a disgrace we lost, the real Head of the New Order, still under disguise, as even the two bozos had no idea who was in charge even though doing their bidding, sorry waffling.... Well your successor was the real Head. She moved into number 10 and was only a smaller clog in a bigger movement to seize power in and across Europe. You see the main move for power is a New Order rallying the masses through misinformation and fear, and the Fourth Reich of sorts, was run from a base started in Russia and then it's main base was in Italy. A future empire that is the new Neo-Nazism, being sold as a Third Rome, far-right politics being dispatched in the buildings outside the EU."

"So it was as you expected sir?" said Jacob.

"Jacob! I never said this to him sir." retorted Matthew.

"It is fine Matthew and I think Jacob is an astute young man, but careful Jacob who you say what and when to speak." The ex-PM looked at Matthew and smiled.

"So it seems Nazi Germany wants to rule again?"

"No sir," I replied, "Ironically the German Government are the ones fighting them to preserve Europe."

"Matthew get me a meeting on the QT with the German Chancellor. And Jacob, try to keep it to this room only." The ex-PM laughs and smiles; "Only kidding Jacob."

"I think that with the recent clean done by the Mafia things will be slowed down, but it seems the New Order is being set up all over the globe and heard that there is a group moving into Africa. I think now that you know of the British PM's agenda best she does not know you know, but are you no longer in politics?"

The ex-PM looks at me and smiles, "No I have moved into retirement, which means with no one watching me I have set up as head of new organisation monitoring movements of many secret groups. We thought ISIS was what we were to major in watching, but it seems they are secretly being funded by a rogue Russian group who are taking our eye off the New Order. Well thanks to you we know this, I am truly grateful."

"Excuse me sir? It seems our presence and holiday have not gone unnoticed." Matthew hands the ex-PM his mobile with a monitoring camera device.

"How extraordinary, look Sir John, there we are, Matthew, Ana, Vesna and look there's Jacob, but how is it there is no picture of you or Jimmy? Is that your real name Jimmy?"

As he hands me his mobile I smile. "Seems I am invisible sir." We all laugh and the doors open as the ladies come back into the room.

"Darling, we need to make tracks as promised the children we would catch first flight home."

The ex-PM stands and grins at us all as we all stand as the ladies enter.

"Sir, ma'am," say Jimmy and the ex-PM's wife laughs.

"Please I am Eleanor and call him Teddy, we all do."

"Well, Eleanor, it has been a pleasure and I wish you both a safe journey home." I look to Teddy who holds out his hand. "Teddy," we both laugh.

"I'll just get the car sir...Teddy?" says Matthew.

"I'll help him, Sir," says Jacob and both exit.

"I'll be in touch," I say, "I have your number."

"Somehow that doesn't surprise me." Says Teddy and exits smiling.

As they leave Ana, Vesna and Jimmy stand and look around the room.

"Do you think he got the bill?" asked Jimmy.

"Do politicians ever pay the bill?" I reply. "Listen I have this and also you'll find funds in your account for the refurbishments you wanted girls and Jimmy you too have been paid from a grateful benefactor."

"What?" asked Vesna.

"Before we leave note I am off tonight. Going to see Megstar as a surprise visit. Your front of house girl Margot will be running her new business of hotel and restaurant laundry that she came into recently. You will soon receive a favourable rate. She was in on the Croatians, but against her will, suffice to say all is forgiven. The hotel is now a symbol of the power against the New Order and they or any other fraction will never attempt to make any moves on you or the business. You have a benefactor whose worldwide reach is happy to make sure you have a totally stress free life. You will benefit from high level customers and I believe that amazing actress Antonella Salvucci is coming next week to interview Roberto Benigni, who will also stay at the hotel with his partner and you will have a full six page spread in the Italian Vogue. Seems you truly now can relax and go and do whatever you like ladies. Oh and Anna, your 'waitress' has had her tuition paid in full and she should of found out about you two about, well about right now."

I look at my watch and see Anna walking into the street we are at. She looks at her watch as she has just received my message. I watch as she looks around and then look to the house we are about to exit. I walk out of the room and out of the front door past Anna who does not see me. Anna then sees Vesna come out and rushes and hugs her tight crying.

"Why, why did you not tell me you help me?" she cries.

Vesna looks to me and in her beautiful Croatian accent says in Italian, "Because we can." I smile and we decide to walk home through the beauty of Venice.

As we reach the hotel I receive another call and it is from Margot, she is at the hotel.

I walk in to see a very scared Margot with her new Mafia boyfriend standing by her side. He stands tall and with courage, but I sense he is nervous.

Margot starts to cry and sees Ana and Vesna enter, then in walks Anna who is confused.

"I did not know, I did not know, I am so sorry."

"Sir, Margot had no idea, please tell Philippe she did not know," says the young man. He stands bold and ready to defend Margot knowing his life is possibly over.

"Sorry who are you?" asks Jimmy.

"I am Constantine. I.... I look after laundry for new owner Margot."

"What's going on Margot, we hold no grudge," says Ana.

"It is lady friend, she have a heart attack. I never knew," cries Margot.

"What are you talking about?" asks Vesna.

Constantine stands erect and ready to take what he thinks is coming and looks straight at me. In that sudden moment I realise he means Megstar.

"Megstar!?" I cry. I am full of disbelief and try to call, but no answer. I call again. I cannot use the buttons and drop the phone.

"In the paperwork I found these pictures and note from Klutes." Constantine hands Jimmy the file.

Jimmy opens the file to see pictures of Megstar and none of him or me. He then sees a note saying liquidate. Jimmy looks up at me he is fuelled with rage and stands right up to Constantine. Tears well up in Jimmy's eyes and Constantine looks to Margot and squeezes her hand tight. Constantine realises that Philippe will have them both killed or the Mafia will and does not resist or cower. Jimmy looks to me as I stand and walk to Margot. Margot is terrified and Ana hugs her. I shake Constntine's hand and then hug Margot as well.

You see reader I realised I had broken the golden rule and put a loved one into the line of fire. I was full of guilt and yet could not blame my two young lovers in front of me.

"It is OK. It is OK. I will talk to Marco and Philippe. It was not your fault, it was not your fault."

I walk into the bar and young Anna is the only one to follow me in.

"Can I get you a drink, sir?" she asks.

"Yes, why not, American Champagne…. A coca cola," I reply. I have never touched a drop of drink, ever.

Anna pours me the coke and gives me a hug. The others walk in and all are silent.

"I will avenge you sir, please tell Philippe I will avenge," says Constantine.

I see Jimmy slipping off. I knew he too was going to avenge Megstar's death.

"Jimmy wait." I called after him and he stops in his tracks. "No one is avenging anyone. Megstar would not want death to come from her death. She was the purest, most beautiful soul I have ever loved and as a tribute to her, Constantine, you will love, protect and honour Margot always. Keep her and yourself safe. Jimmy, Megstar loved you too. She would want you to retire here and take care of her two best friends Vesna and Ana. Come on, all of you join me, raise a glass to my love, to my Megstar."

All stand in the bar silence descends and we toast. I am a complete shell. How I managed to stand to this day belies belief. But Megstar I think was with me. She was there in my heart making sure I made the right decisions.

In life Reader we often say things or do things we know we will regret, but as the great GJ Isaac once said to me was 'Do Nothing and Achieve Everything'. Often in a row if your girlfriend says in anger awful things, say nothing, because if in anger you reply something like you think she has a fat ass, she will remember that in ten years time and never forget. Do nothing, say nothing then there is nothing to recall. Just ten years later all forgiven and love flows strong.

I hug the girls and Jimmy, shake Constantine's hand and he hugs me. He is built like a brick shit house. I laughed later thinking of Megstar that night as I cried alone in my bed. There I was trying to hold it together and Constantine hugs me and I think something funny and she made me strong. That may not make sense, but it does to me reader.

I am lying on the bed in the apartment of mine above the Baron's across from the hotel. My mobile rings, which of course is strange as no one has the number. It is Jimmy of course.

"I love you my friend, just call anytime. Be safe."

As he goes to hang up I ask him, "How did you get this number?"

"Picked pocket, called mine, deleted and replaced. Did in less than fifteen seconds. One question for you? Why do you have a phone that no one has the number for?"

"I have no idea," I reply.

Jimmy hangs up and I look at the phone. I cannot sleep and decide to go to Megstar's, driving from Venice to Poland in my new Aston Martin. Why an Aston, well, if you could have a Ferrari or a Veyron or Chiron, they would be amazing, but they would not be an Aston.

In no time at all I am driving out of Venice and into the countryside. On the dash is a picture of Megstar at the bar in Parliament. God she was beautiful. She was just perfect.

9

Driving through the night streets and motorways of European towns there is an eerie quiet. Every now and again I would put my foot down to hear the melodic sound of the Aston roar.

I was driving for days unable to point the car in the direction of Poland and unable to come to terms that I may have been the reason Megstar was killed.

I had been given new mobile with the car and it rang. Even I did not know the number, but I knew it was Jimmy. Of course it was Jimmy, Only Jimmy knew the numbers of people who no one, not even the owners of the phone, knew their number, would have this number. From the steering wheel I answer and sit for a second in silence then the voice speaks on the other end.

"Pull over, I can tell you're driving."

"What is it Jimmy? All OK with the girls and the laundry?"

"All is fine with us, just thought I'd catch up with an old mate and need you to pull over as got some news you need to know." Jimmy seemed direct and impassive, if that is even the right word reader. I seem to be chatting to myself so much I have no idea how to write as I recount this and write to you now.
I pull over and stop the car.

"OK Jimmy you have me."

"Constantine found more files. You remember the old couple that left just as you arrived and the Berkowitzces we said were straight out of a Woody Allen sketch that stayed at the hotel? Well it seems the Klutes were going to kill all them too, just to be sure a thorough clean sweep was done. My friend you are not responsible for Megstar's death, she had a freak coronary, heart attack. They found traces of Troponin, which is a protein found in all heart disease related deaths. Seems she went to the doctor before she flew out to Venice complaining of chest pains and the doctor told her it was indigestion."

I sat there and started to cry. It was an enormous release and I just sat there crying. There was no one else on the road and so no one saw me have what was a monumental breakdown. Jimmy sat with me on the other end of the phone. He said nothing just sat there so I was not alone.

After what must have seemed like an eternity for Jimmy I looked up and saw the sunrise through the car windscreen.

"Thank-you Jimmy," and I hung up.

In a small farmhouse where I managed to find a quiet room to rent on the Polish borders I looked up Troponin to find it can be detected with a small blood test created by the British Heart Foundation, but was still not widely known on the medical circuit. Seems governments too busy on trips to foreign lands on jollies discussing things that none of us care about and therefore no funding to get this test out there. It seems women are more at risk than men from heart attacks as women are often told they have indigestion, or given a couple of paracetemol and sent to bed early, some never rise from bed again. Readers, please, get onto your GP and get this test out there. The pain feeling for this loss is as bad as losing my father recently.

Yes every now and again I open myself up in my journal Reader. You see when I was travelling I got news my father was unwell, dizzy spells and falling. He was elderly and visited him in hospital. He was having trouble remembering, so they put him on a dementia ward. He was in pain and was in the dementia ward as nowhere else was there a bed for him. He was going slowly mad.

Every morning the other inmates in the ward would wake look at him and say, "Who are you?" They would drop off to sleep for ten minutes in the day wake look to Dad and say, "Who are you?" We laughed at it together and then found out he had two huge tumors on his brain. Two falls in the hospital and a failed scan he had a stroke. It was a blessing when he died and in the moments that passed I remembered the man who was and see that I am because of the man he made me be.

You see Reader we are the role models for our children and only the strong can rebel against the poor parents they have to be different.

My father was just the greatest man I ever knew. We had little and yet we had everything. My friends all had all the latest gadgets and toys and yet they all wanted to come to our house and play the games that he made up. Our house was always full of laughter and when people were down he would lift them, yet he was seriously unwell himself. Left alone with four very young children, four slipped discs at the base of his spine, his ex-wife ran off in a van with her lovers and he had to cope. He did not just cope he excelled. He may not of been a great man, but he was the most incredible father.

I remember the day he died I was driving to the hospital as heard he had taken a turn for the worst and had pulled over as tears streamed down my face. I remember a sudden calm coming over me and a deep breath as knew that it was a blessing, he was no longer in pain, and at that very moment through the windscreen of the car I saw the most beautiful sunrise.

I turned the ignition key and headed to Poland and drove non-stop, except for fuel, to where they were laying my beloved Megstar to rest.

Just as I was wondering where to go a text comes into my mobile in the car. Jimmy of course. Directions to Megstar's funeral and where it was being held.

The sound of the engine roared as I drove off as if on a mission to get there in time. My mind racing as to what I would say, who would know who I was? I was getting panicked, scared even, but realised that this was one of the great loves of my life and yet no one knew I existed apart from a small gathering, well no one from her family, or had she told them about me or…. I am sorry Reader rambling as I have no idea how I should feel or behave even when I do reach her grave.

I see a sign. I had driven through Austria, through the Czech Republic, and saw sign Ostrava ten miles. It was a short distance from the Polish border.

As we drive we truly only concentrate fully for the first fifteen minutes driving and then seem to continue on autopilot. This was the case for me as my head was full of ideas that I would arrive and somehow Megstar would of made a miracle recovery, but then the pain of heartache knowing I will never see her again hits home. She often said that a broken heart was a good way to remind ourselves that we are alive.

Krakow twenty kilometers. I was close and the sun was high in the sky. As I turned the car through the city streets the people stopped and stared. It was the Aston. It had made me visible. I saw an underground garage and made my way in.

Parked I sit for a second as the sounds of the city start to become louder. The inside of the car is silent and yet all I hear is the muffled noises of a world continuing without hesitation, people living their lives, life carries on. I grab my wallet from the glove compartment and as I go to check cash I see a photo of Megstar.

This may not seem strange for a man who loves a woman to have her photo in his wallet, well unless of course he was not connected, but the significance was that I was an Invisible. We never carry photos that can connect us and yet here, in my wallet, for all to see, was Megstar, the woman that made me realise how much life meant. I start to think how I placed her at risk and a tear forms in my eye as I see a pretty young girl look at me and smile.

I get out of the car and see that the funeral is in the centre of the city and not for another five hours. They are having an early evening service.

I get out of the car to see the pretty young girl still standing waiting for me and I am tired and a little confused. Then I realise it is the Aston. I realise that pretty women often are drawn to fast cars and men that drive them. I realise I am invisible; she has ideas of me having wealth and being her ticket to another life out of Krakow.

I lock the doors and still standing there she smiles and I smile back.

"Boston Tea Party..Exeter?" she says.

"It's me Flo, Flo from the Boston Tea Party."

Suddenly, I look to realise that thousands of miles from anywhere anyone knows you, you often see a familiar face. I had not recognized Flo as she was different. Her hair was different, she was beautiful and a little make up. Wearing a stunning summer dress that emphasised her petite figure, it was no wonder I did not recognise her. I realised I was looking at the peripherals and not the person. You see Reader we all are perceptible to not see what is truly in front of us.

I held out my hand and smiled back.

"Of course, Flo," and I act as if caught off guard. I laugh at myself feeling awkward and yet why? "So what brings you to Krakow?"

"Holiday, well love visiting cities and never been to Poland so got a week here, just arrived two days ago. You live here?"

I looked a little lost as stumbled to think what to say. Do I say yes here to bury the love of my life or make up an identity, become Invisible and move on?

"No," I said. "I am here to say goodbye to a friend, well, someone I loved very much. She had a heart attack and passed a few days ago."

" I am so sorry," said Flo.

There was a slightly awkward silence and I realised it had been eight days since I left Venice. I had lost time, days gone by and I was just in limbo. I suddenly came back to Flo in conversation.

"Sorry, been driving. Looking for a place to stay and freshen up, then go to the funeral tonight."

"Well there was a complete cock up with my hotel and they placed me in some apartments close by at no extra charge, and they may have something."

" Perfect Flo, thank you. Sorry, have you time to….?"

"Loads of time, came on my own and nice to see a face I recognize," she said and I grabbed my small case from the car.

Well, actually I went to grab my case, forgot I had just locked it, set off the alarms, dropped the keys, and then managed to turn off and open the boot and retrieve case. As I set off to walk with Flo she looked at me and smiled, " Do you want to lock the car?"

I had forgotten to lock the car and she smiled and squeezed my hand. "It's OK. Let's get you a coffee and place to relax."

With that she took control and walked me out of the car park to a stunning building, one of the oldest in the city not flattened from the second world war, and introduced me to Aleksy. The owner and manager of his apartments. Within seconds I was whisked to apartment on the top floor, the penthouse, that was free and in the conversation introducing me Flo had mentioned the Aston, so Aleksy thought I could easily afford it, and as it happens I can, and then heard the door click shut and I was there at the window looking out over Poland.

"I'll see you downstairs? Or later?"

I turn and realise Aleksy had left and Flo was still in the room.

"No, one sec, quick pop to the loo and freshen up then let's go have a coffee."

"OK," Flo said coyly, "in that case meet you downstairs." I smiled and in an awkward moment Flo exited and the door shut behind her. I looked out the window and saw a church steeple in the distance. As I started to blackout the urge to pee bought me back into the room and I headed to the bathroom.

Actually headed to the kitchen first, I realised I had no idea where the bathroom was and found out that in the bedroom was the bath and WC was in a room the other side of the apartment off the lounge. I thought I was going to wet myself, as it seemed life had given me an apartment with no toilet. As I managed to make it in time I laughed at myself, and standing there, peeing, saw myself, well my face, smiling in the mirror. I continued to pee smiling and thought of Megstar. She had bought Flo to me I thought to help ease the pain.

Standing there peeing I looked up and grinned as if grinning to my darling girl in heaven, and then started to laugh as I realised I do not believe in heaven and again it was Megstar making me laugh. I was crying and laughing and peeing all at the same time. Could it be Reader the first true record of a man multi tasking?

With humour back in place I washed my hands and set off to take my young friend from Exeter to a coffee and find out why she was there at this time. Walking out the apartment I turn to see I had Megstar's photo lying on the sofa. It seemed as if she was smiling at me. I placed her in the wallet and placed the wallet in my jacket pocket.

"Of all the gin joints in all the towns, in all the world, she walks into mine." Megstar is with me always.

10

Men, honestly are we so easily distracted? What seems like a moment ago I was sat in the Aston unable to move, unable to get out, and yet here I am an hour later sat with the exquisite Flo. Her long dark hair cascading down her back and shaping her face, extenuating her deep down eyes that are big enough to fall into and be lost in her world.

Forgive me Reader, for a moment I am laughing and chatting, and enjoying the company of a friend, well someone I never knew apart from a distant glance in a café I once drank in, and realizing how small the world is. And as from the start of this chapter you may think I have sexual designs on my new beautiful friend, I have not, well not really as we chat and I am telling her all about Megstar; how wonderful she was, her smile and the way she knew me better than I knew myself. At last I was honoring the woman I loved by remembering her and sharing her with the world, well one person at a time. I was able to realise just how much I loved her. Even as sadness hit me as I realised she was gone it was as if her presence was with me always and a momentary low was hit by an explosion of enzymes as I clearly saw her smile. I would see Megstar in everything I looked at. She was Poland, and Poland defined her as well as gave her the character and beauty I fell in love with.

Flo was an amazing young lady. Young being the operative word folks and I am now too old to be chasing young girls. Not that I would not of liked to, but the more we chatted the more I got to know her and the more I started to feel at ease. In no time we had had coffee lunch and it was four in the afternoon.

Flo and I had a lot in common, a love for travel, adventure, love of family, loved all music, dancing badly, but not caring, and the company of others, yet happy with our own company not needy or looking to find someone else to live our lives.

Flo reached across the table and gently grabbed my arm, looked at my watch, and said, "Time to go. Would you like me to accompany you?"

I smiled and said that I did not want to impose, but thought about it and said that I would like to be there with a friend.

Back at the apartment I put on my dark blue suit; I could not wear black. Not for Megstar, not my love. For by not wearing the black suit of death she would always be alive in me. My apartment phone rings. I gingerly pick it up and answer. It is Flo, she is calling as apologizing for not having a black dress.

"Neither have I," I said placing her at ease, "Please do not worry, I am in a dark blue suit.."

"Wonderful," came her reply and I waited for her in the reception area. 'Ding', the lift door opens and out steps Flo. Dressed in a rich navy blue dress.

"I cannot believe you do not have a little black dress, all women have a little black dress."

"Well, I am not all women, and from our talk of Megstar I feel she would like this dress, it is a classic, well that is what the dressmaker said."

"A classic," I said, "Who is this dressmaker?"

"Me," Flo replied and we walked out of the apartments and the church was just a short walk away.

As we walked the streets my heart started beating and I became a little nervous, this was my first funeral in many years. The nearer we got the slower my pace became and Flo slowly held my hand and whispered, "It's OK, I am here."

In that moment it was as if Megstar had said it and my heart swelled, as I wanted to get to the church as soon as possible to tell everyone how much I loved her.

We entered the church and there in the front row is Chastity and Henry. Chastity sees me, and smiles, she has been crying. I walk up and introduce Flo and we join them. We all just sat there not saying a word.

Suddenly without warning music starts and six men carrying Megstar in in her coffin. I stood and felt myself shaking. I was hyperventilating and Chastity squeezed my hand. For the first time as the coffin was bought in I noticed that the church was packed. There were literally hundreds of people crammed in to say goodbye.

As the coffin passed an elderly lady and gentleman following stopped and looked at me.

"My son, she loved you." Said the old lady. It was Megstar's mother. She had the same piercing eyes and I started to feel a tear in my eye. Her father came and hugged me as all the church watched. Flo was in tears as was Chastity and everything happened in such a surreal way. There were songs, stories in Polish and English and then her father stood to talk. As he spoke with great pride in Polish of his daughter I felt myself drifting off as if I wanted to stop the world and make it all go away. Then I hear, "Fred". It was what Megstar called me. I look up and her father is addressing me and takes out an envelope from his pocket.

"She asked me to give you this, to read her words. She gave it to me few days ago when she know she sick."

The entire congregation look to me and I slowly stand. My tears running down my face and unable to control the grief I had been holding back.

"Today, you no invisible Fred," her father continued to say.

I started to laugh as even beyond the grave she had the ability to make me feel in awe of her. I walked to the alter, and as I passed the coffin stopped and kissed the plaque on which was etched her name.

Her father gave me a strong embrace and then went to sit next to his wife. Megstar had placed me in complete view of everybody there. People I never knew and made me visible. I look to the letter, which is still sealed.

"Read it, read my daughter's letter," said her mother smiling and crying.

I look to the letter again and open it. I could smell her perfume and she had left a kiss mark on the back in her rich red lipstick. I take out the letter and look to all the faces in front of me. Some looking to each other as if to say 'who is this guy?'

I open the folded letter and start to read.

"My darling Fred,

I am sorry not to have told you about my heart problems, but I wanted to live my life with you not sit waiting for this moment. I am sorry it seems so selfish, but I smile as I write this knowing for once in your life you are the only person people see."

I smile as I read through the tears, as she truly was my one true love.

"I knew you would come and glad you finally met my parents. Please tell them how much I loved them. Mummy, you were the most beautiful person I ever met and Daddy, you were my rock. With you in my life I knew I could achieve anything. To my Doctor, and the wonderful nurses, apologies for not obeying your orders, but please forgive me, but I had to be with this man one last time, Fred, Venice was incredible and know you were there for the girls and Jimmy, as always you were there for others, you were there for me, well today I want you to know I am here with you. I will always be with you until we meet again in some other existence."

I could not read further and looked to the faces in the church to see Flo rise and walk to me. Flo took the letter from me and continued to read.

"Tell Chastity that I will always be grateful to her for bringing you into my life and find Serg, my old school friend and hug him from me. He was the other man in my life that I adored without question."

A man stands in the church and starts to walk to the coffin. He is crying and from his demeanor I realise he is a gay man, but in Poland not easy to be, and as he walks to the coffin he stumbles and I find myself catching him. We hug and we openly embrace as I whisper to him that it was OK to cry.

Flo continues, "I am happy to leave, although I do not want to, but when I do please note that parting was easier as you had given me all I could want from life with your love Fred and I will miss you and your bad humour, farting in bed, yes folks this man farts in bed, and just your breathtakingly unselfish ways in putting all others first. Just know that if you ever find religion it will be a place you can find me. I'll be the one in the corner with the dodgy heart and a gin and tonic. My darling Fred, please take care and be safe, live your life, move on continuing with what you do, and I know a little, but never stop being you, for as long as you do I will stay alive in your heart with you as you were always in my heart, well the good bit anyway, and gave me happiness that I hope you will experience again. So check up on my folks and friends every now and again and remember they all know who you are now, my beautiful, wonderful, loving, and visible friend.

I will love you always

Megstar."

Flo walks forward and hands me the letter. I look to the congregation and we all cry in unison. I shake the priest's hand and from beside her coffin I raise my hand.

"My darling Megstar, thank you for your life force will always live on in my heart…. And thanks for the farting in bed line, I will get you back one day for that. You will never be out of any of our hearts here today. In fact I can prove it to everyone here now. This was taught to me by the great GJ Isaac, a great man, who told me so many wise things like, if you want to keep a secret the first mouth to keep shut is your own', but if you all here would like to close your eyes and think of Megstar, a moment that was dear to you, of a time you spent together, smile, and as you do you will see her in your smile. She is with us all always."

Megstar's mother walks up to me and hugs me.

I know not why or what possessed me, but feel if I ever have such a funeral this is what I would like to happen to me. The coffin was to be carried from the church to a side building where the body was to be cremated.

As the coffin bearers walked to carry the coffin out I asked them to wait.

"Everybody, there are so many of us that want to say goodbye and help Megstar off on her final journey. I ask that all those that would want to to form a line in the aisle and out of the church to the crematorium area and we all collectively pass the coffin over our heads to Megstar's last resting place."

Megstar's father started to explain in Polish and soon everyone able was standing in a long line ready to pass down the coffin. The six young men lifted the coffin and began to feed the coffin down the line as the men and women carried the coffin over their heads passing on the coffin to those behind them. Sort of coffin surfing. The women also able to place a hand on the coffin as if passed to say goodbye. As the coffin worked its way out of the church we all followed the possession and in the crematorium Megstar's father and I had managed to get to the front to take the coffin with the six men and place it onto the resting place that would convey the coffin into the fire behind the door.

The crematorium was packed and all stood as the coffin started to move into the fire burners.

One voice shouted, "I love you Megstar" and others in English and Polish all started calling out and cheering her name. The pride and love she had empowered in all she met was seen in that one final move to leave her mortal body.

After a four hours celebration of her life at her parents I made my way back to the apartment. With me Chastity, Henry, Serg and Flo. At the apartment I said goodnight to everyone and walked into my apartment and there on the bed was a photo of me, and Megstar. I looked to see the picture still in my wallet and realised Jimmy had been there for me. Invisible and keeping me safe.

The journey and the day had taken its toll. I looked out of the window and saw a couple kissing under a street lamp. I touched my own lips as they tingled. Was Megstar there with me?

Sorry Reader my mind is all over the shot as are my emotions, but to have loved someone so much was more than any man or woman should ever know, but to loose her seemed wrong, yet I felt grateful for the time we did have, albeit too short.

11

It is eleven in the morning and I wake hearing a knock at the apartment door. It is Flo. I rise to see I fell asleep in the armchair by the window. I blacked out again. It is happening more frequently and I rise to answer the door.

"One second...coming."

I realise I am in my dark blue suit. I quickly undress and throw clothes into bedroom and put on the robe on the door. Inadvertently I did not notice that there were two robes; one saying his and the other saying hers. I obviously have the 'hers' robe on.

I open the door and a smiling Flo greets me.

"Hi, just wondered if you OK?"

I looked at her and invited her in. She was a pretty young thing. Had the carefree look of youth and the personality of one beyond her years in as much as great manners, funny, listened as well as chatted, chatted interesting things and was just a joy to be with.

I join her for coffee again and we are sat in a bistro owned by Serg. Serg was in the corner looking really down and the loss of Megstar was as big a shock to him as me. Often we forget others and think that we are the only one suffering. As we entered I had not noticed him and it was Flo, smiling as always that walked up to Serg and shook his hand.

"I saw you here earlier and glad you are still here as thought we would join you."

I looked at Flo and realise that she had seen Serg earlier and had bought me to this bistro on purpose. Serg saw me and forced himself to smile and rose to come join us.

"I am glad to get to see you again Serg," I said as I stood to greet him. "This a local haunt of yours? Did you come here with Megstar?"

Serg was still raw with emotion. "I own the bistro and the lamb cutlets were her favourite. I will never take them off the menu."

I embrace my fellow brother in mourning. And the waitress comes over.

"Hello, I am Bella, can I get you something to drink? Serg, what would you like?"

Serg cannot speak as he starts to well up with emotion. I look to his table to see he was drinking vodka.

"Well no more vodka Serg," I smile, "How about three lattes and three lamb cutlets?"
The waitress nods and Serg looks up and says, "Espresso."

" I am happy with a latte too," says Flo.

I look at Flo and realise that she has the qualities of an angel. She had recognized Serg, come to see me, and got us together to help us both through the grief in a place

Megstar loved. I smile at Flo and she winks. It is funny we were thousands of miles from Queen Street and the Boston Tea Party in Exeter and yet that little meeting place served us well as we connect in Krakow. I never really had much more than a general, hello, how are you conversation with Flo in the months I used to go there, but here in Poland her lovely calm manner and pretty smile lit up the room. I suddenly thought I know absolutely nothing about Flo.

The coffees arrive and Bella looks to Flo to whisper thank you and smiles. "Lamb will be here in ten minutes, Chef's got them on now."

"Thank you Bella," I reply and Serg looks up to smile and drinks in one his espresso.

"So boys, tell me about Megstar, you both loved her so much and I want to know why?"

Serg and I looked at each other and then I smiled.

"She was just…..well, she would enter a room and suddenly you were filled with a feeling of awe," I said and was then interrupted by Serg.

"Yet what a wicked sense of humour? Once we were out at the opera and I see this young man look at me. I blushed and then became completely paranoid, as it is not easy being gay in Poland. I only survive here as locals once when suspicious, frightened to eat anywhere gay for fear of AIDS, dunderheads! Well my beautiful Megstar moved in with me as my lover. For years she was travelling and we were a couple, until she met you and dunderheads, that was her word, felt sorry for me as if I had been jilted. Anyway, this was after then we were at Opera and Megstar manages to slip the boy a note. The next day he turns up here to eat and we are sat over there at the corner table. I was gob smacked, as never saw here drop the note. She was sly, well you probably know, knew…anyway, the boy Manuel, was also into men too, so I was about to do up the restaurant and Megstar decided that if we told people he was new business partner people would see OK two men live and work together. This was only recently, and I think when she helped pay for the place to be done up as if from Manuel, it was a new leaf of life, I mean new lease of life."

"So what happened to Manuel?" asked Flo.

"Well he was so upset yesterday and feared being seen crying with me that he go today and is at the grave laying flowers and saying goodbye."

The lamb arrives and Serg is feeling better. I am feeling better and the lamb is exceptional. Over the meal Serg and I swapped stories and laughed. Yes we laughed, laughed out loud. I looked at Flo who was really interested in all our stories and suddenly Serg stopped and called Bella over.

"Bella, tell me who does she remind you of?"

Bella smiled and came to the table. "She has the soul of Megstar, I feel it."

Serg gives Flo a big hug and then me. Flo is smiling and sits back as if not sure what to say.

"He is right," I say, "Megstar would of seen two lost souls and bought them together. Just as you have done here, you wanted to know why we loved Megstar? She had your spirit and kindness. She was beautiful and funny, she was wise and protective. She was always doing the right thing. Just as you have done today. I think that today in honour of our beloved Megstar, to honour her spirit and truly beautiful nature we, Serg and I, will make this next two days Flo days."

"I love it!" shouted Serg.

"Dessert?" asked Bella.
"Flo, you came just as I needed someone, just as Megstar would have done. You came just as Serg needed this and made it happen, just as Megstar would of done. Now, lets celebrate the true essence of Megstar and her incredible lifeforce, find out what you want to do with your life and make it happen."

All three of us, Serg, Me and Bella look at Flo who looks as if she does not know what to say; and why would she Reader?

"How old you?" asks Serg.

"Twenty one," replies Flo.

"What you do?" asks Bella.

"I am waitress, I love art and sewing…"

"What do you really want to do?" I ask.

Flo looks at me as if she is not sure what to say.

"I waitress and want to sing," says Bella.

Serg looks at Bella, "Why you not say you silly girl? I get Manuel to play piano in restaurant for you to sing."

"That's what I want," says Flo, "I want to hear Bella sing."

"I organize big party at restaurant and in square with music and we celebrate, celebrate as Megstar would of wanted." Serg was now full of excitement and starting to mentally organise the event in his head.

I turn to Flo and in a calm voice take Flo's hand, "Now, what would you really want to do?"

Flo looked at me and the others then looked at Flo.

"Come on Flo, you're dream, my dream come true so your dream we make this day," says Bella really excited about singing. A nervous thought went through my head that what if Bella cannot sing. It would be a nightmare and all in honour of Megstar; then thought if it was a shambles Megstar would be the first to love it more.

"Well this is something I have always wanted to do… you are going to think I am daft, but I have always wanted to DJ."

"DJ?" says Serg.

"Yes, DJ. I have always thought it looked great fun," said Flo. This was her dream this is what she wanted to do. She smiled and then we all burst into laughter as she said, "I never have done it, do not even know how to DJ, just want to do it."

I laughed and Serg decides that it will be disco and Flo DJ with his friend Alberto who plays the local club. That Flo will go have a few lessons and this Saturday she will play to the crowds.

Now Reader I can see the fear hit Flo as well as the concerned smiled forced, as she does not want to offend Serg.

Saturday was just four days away, but Serg was like an unstoppable force. At that moment Manuel walks in looking down and sad as he returns from Megstar's grave. Serg jumps up and shouts, "Manuel we have a big party here Saturday for Megstar, Bella is singing and DJ from UK playing Flo."

Manuel looks at me with a look of confusion and exhaustion.

"Manuel this is Fred!"

Manuel looks up and smiles, a tear fills his eye and I stand to greet him. Manuel looks around unsure of what to do, as he is completely confused. I walk to Manuel and embrace him. At first Manuel is unsure then hugs me tight and starts to talk through his tears, "I miss her."

I find myself crying, Serg crying, Bella crying and Flo watching on smiling.

"We all miss her, but she is with us always, eh?" I say.

As we all embrace we realise Flo is standing outside the four-way hug. Serg looks to me and sees me acknowledge Flo with a wink and Manuel looks to Flo, "So you the UK DJ playing here Saturday?" asks Manuel.

Unable to answer we hear Bella as she hugs Flo, "And I am singing."

Manuel looks to Serg as if he is unsure. I think Bella may not be the performance artist we are hoping for. What am I talking about? She is full of life and a beautiful passionate young woman and that is all that matters. I start to laugh and raise my water glass and toast Megstar.

Bella starts to shriek, well that was her singing, and all start to dance. I am dancing to the music Serg had turned up in the restaurant with Flo. As we salsa badly Flo looks to me and starts laughing.

"I fear my DJing may be as bad as Bella's singing."

I laugh and I see the locals looking in. Serg goes to the entrance, "Everybody, this Saturday we have big party and dancing in the square, tell everyone, we have big UK DJ and Alberto playing as well as live singing from Bella."

I suddenly feel exhausted and at last in this little enclave bought about by Megstar I am finally at peace ready to celebrate her life, mourning was short lived, self pity was gone, Megstar had delivered an angel and she was called Flo. Flo walked over to me seeing me stretch and says that we should make a move so the others can sort out the restaurant and I nodded in agreement.

Hugging, saying goodbye, more hugging, more repeat goodbyes, Bella exchanging numbers with Flo, more hugging, more goodbyes finally Flo and I walking down the street waving goodbye to have Serg chase after us and give us both one more hug.

"We say nothing, we know, we love her always." And with this he rushes back to usher the others back into the restaurant, "Bella come on inside we have to practice what you sing."

"What you sing Bella...?" asked Manuel, "What can you sing?" we hear him say as they all enter back into the bistro.

Flo and I turn and laugh as we both have the same thought, Bella sounded awful. Suddenly Flo stops dead in her tracks.
"But I have never even DJ'd, I do not even know how to work the decks, they are called decks aren't they?"

I laugh and told her how years ago I was a DJ. I used to play mixes and by a few tricks would mix the unmixable with ways no one would know I was not that good. You see Reader in all things we do, as long as we do them with confidence no one is any the wiser. Learn enough to be able to do what you set out to do then enjoy and practice until you get better.

We passed an art shop and I stopped and went inside to buy some water paints and a couple of canvasses. With brushes and all needed to paint, including easels we exit and I told Flo after purchased that I could not paint, but we will sit somewhere and paint with confidence.

Sat in a square we set up the canvasses and began to paint. I was confident, full of strong brush strokes and watched Flo nervously look round as if being watched. An old man came over looked at my canvas and the bold strokes I had made, smiled then looked at the tentative beginnings of Flo's canvas.

"What do you think?" I asked him.

Smiling the old man in broken English replies, "Well she looks as if she knows what she is doing." And with that he exits. We both laugh and together sat speechless for an hour just painting. Mine was more putting paint on the canvas and what slowly became an abstract piece of art; Flo had painted a beautiful piece capturing the light falling on the square's clock tower.

As we finished I smiled at Flo and we saw people had been watching us. I started to pack up the paints and I told Flo to leave the easels and canvases exactly where they were. We walked away leaving our art, 'Our Art', what an idiot. We left Flo's wonderful piece and my daubed atrocity for the locals to come peak at once we had left.

Walking away I saw a woman wearing a very smart outfit look over both. We watched her reactions that looked as if she was seriously considering the paintings as works of art. She smiled and nodded appreciatively as she looked at Flo's. Then as she gazed upon my masterpiece I saw her eyebrows raise and a slight grimace enter her face. Flo and I laughed and walked back to the apartments.

As we entered the apartment Flo's phone rang. It was Bella who wanted Flo to join her at a party tonight. It was in a barn a few miles out of town. I could see Flo wondering how to get there. Bella than asked if I would like to come also. Flo said that we would call her back for details if both able to get there.

I looked at Flo and asked her whether she was on a budget trip and her face replied yes. I asked her to get ready to go out again in fifteen minutes, and that we should have time. Of course this confused Flo completely, but I really wanted to return her kindness.

"Quick, quick, go use the loo or whatever it is you need to do and see you here in fifteen."

Flo went off from reception to her room and I stood in the reception of the apartments with a plan. You see we Invisibles can also operate in many ways that are not mission related. I knock on the office door and there is Aleksy. I enter his office and within moments the deed is done.

The deed is done you ask reader, well yes from a moment in Aleksy office I was able to ascertain all the bank details required of Flo and make arrangements via the internet in under ten minutes, which was good as I was busting for a pee. Sorry too much information again reader.

In fifteen minutes there I was in reception as Flo arrived looking concerned and confused.

"So let's go to the barn party tonight and need you to help me buy a few things."

Flo looked and said OK and followed me out of the apartment building. It was five o'clock and shops stayed open until six. Not far from the apartments on the way to the bistro I noticed Flo look, just a glance, but to an Invisible enough to make a call, at a beautiful red dress in a couture shop window.

Before Flo could know what was afoot we were in the shop and I was organizing the shop assistant to find the dress in Flo's size and we would need shoes and clutch bag to match.

"I cannot afford this.." Flo said concerned.

"But I can, and in fact so can you." I replied.
Flo was in love. With the dress that is Reader. And she looked incredible. Across from the shop was a beauticians store with make up, facials and all that female stuff. As Flo changed I rushed across and back.

We bought the dress, the shoes and a stunning clutch bag. As we left the young lady in the beautician shop opposite was at the door to welcome us. Flo looked even more confused as I showed the assistant the dress and colours with Flo sat in the chair. The assistant then starts to bring out a full range of make up to compliment Flo's skin tones and the dress. We buy and rush to a local off license and I buy three cases of champagne to be delivered to the apartments in half an hour.

On the way back a speechless Flo looks to me and I place my finger to my lips to say hush.

"My dearest Flo. What you did today cannot be measured in words or gifts, but you have to know that you are an exceptional young lady. Now accept the dress and gifts from me with grace. I will not have any arguments. We will drive to the party tonight and I shall be there as your chauffeur and walker. I want you to do whatever you wish, to indulge and make friends and know that this is just the beginning of many adventures."

"What are you talking about, I cannot.."

"Refuse, correct," I say. "You cannot and will not refuse. I want nothing more than to know you will enjoy life and be safe in the knowledge you have a guardian happy to help if help is ever needed."

We enter the apartments where I pile the dress and bags onto Flo.

"Right call Bella, get the address and tell her we will be there and bring drink to say thank you for the kind invite. Oh and see you in ninety minutes. That should be enough time for me to have a bath and get ready and hopefully you too."

With this I rush up the stairs to my room and smiling all the way within no time I am at my apartment, open the door and see the picture of Megstar by the bed, just where I had left it. I feel alive and feel I am doing exactly what my love would of wanted me to do, carry on, help others as she did and live my life.

Megstar knew I did not believe in God or afterlife etc, but I feel here in Poland that those that we loose never leave us. They remain always in our hearts. Tonight I was going to be Flo's chaperone and then tomorrow help with the party to celebrate her life before exit somewhere to find out what I am to do with the rest of my life.

12

In the Aston Flo and I drive to the party being held in an old barn with water wheel. It had been beautifully restore by two brothers from England who had settled in Poland.

Well Reader. When I say two brothers, they have actually married in UK and as they have same name assume the identity of brothers as still in Poland gay men would be at serious risk. They have a thriving print business and in an adjourning barn are the press offices and machinery powered by the water wheel. They are charming and once we arrive everyone relaxes and the champagne is a great hit.

I sit on the sofa in the middle of the room watching everybody interact and the joy of the friendships is overwhelming. I mean to say that there are people from all over Poland, Brits, an American Girl disillusioned with America and an activist who felt threatened from the past election, as well as a group of Danish boys and Girls, all gay and outside of this safe enclave posing as students working for the press, and a German Professor completely unaware of everything around him as he just likes to eye up the girls and flirt. His family moved to Poland after the war and they were survivors of the Jewish concentration camps.

The music is an eclectic mix of house, old standards and show music. Everyone taking their turn to mix a record, but suddenly there is no music. Everyone so into their own conversations no one taking care of the mixing desk set up in the corner.

Flo is having a wonderful chat with the Danish Girls and Bella. They are so deep in conversation it seems only I, the observer notice that we have no music. I rise and walk to the decks. I see much is loaded from laptop and see someone was about to load the Cure. So I play my favourite, A Forest. I suddenly have the urge to play all night as a few look and nod in approval. Flo looks to me and smiles.

In no time at all everyone is dancing and see Bella, a little too pissed on champagne hugging Flo and see Flo suddenly realising that Bella is more than friendly. I smile, as Flo was totally unaware of the fact anyone was gay. She had not just a naivety, but also a purity of heart where she seems to have been untouched by cynicism and is truly pure of heart joy to be with. I motion for her to join me.

Standing next to Flo I motion for her to pick the next track and slowly show her how to operate the decks. She is a natural and being nearer the age of the audience I soon notice her song choices are better received than mine. I step back and marvel at what a natural she is. Inside I am smiling.

I think of Megstar and feel no sadness and realise I have to move on. I know I did not blackout, but the next few days the preparation for the Saturday night rushed by and it was as if I came back in the room as found myself in the square standing behind Flo, who is on the decks and has over 500 people in the square dancing. I look out at the love of everyone there and realise that most of the funeral congregation had turned up. It seems Megstar was loved and lives on in all our lives. I knew tomorrow I would move on.

Aleksy was there dancing with his wife and I saw children dancing with Serg and he waves to me. I sort of wave salute him and he looks to all the people and back to me. Manuel dances next to Serg and looks to me and smiles. Then a very drunk Mayor stands to say something and falls back drunk. Serg and Manuel rush to help him back to his chair.

Then I see Bella next to me and I squeeze her hand. Flo looks and if instinctively manages to mix a song that then lends itself to fade and Manuel at a baby grand on a stage next to DJ set up start to play. Manuel looks to Bella who looks terrified. I start to applaud and the audience start to clap as I lead Bella onto the stage.

On the microphone Bella still holding my hand tight looks to me, "Tonight I sing for my beautiful friend to the man and people she loved so much."

I am suddenly swept with emotion as beyond everyone's delight Bella sings like an angel. All are standing in unison crying and hugging each other. As the song ends the crowd go berserk, literally cheering and hugging and chanting 'Bella' 'Bella' 'Bella'. Bella acknowledges Manuel and another huge cheer with wolf whistles from Serg and Flo starts to play Heaven Knows by Donna Summer and on the mic Bella sings at full belt. At the end Bella and Flo stand side by side triumphant.

Serg takes the stage and says a few words and introduces DJ Alberto and he is a bit of a local God. Before he starts he offers Flo to go to Ibiza with him and support. Seems Flo is a natural and all cheers as I laugh with Alberto's first song being a huge gay anthem 'Pride'.

Flo hugs me and I tell her to go dance with everyone. Serg stands beside me saying nothing. We both look out at the packed square.

"She was love," says Serg, "wasn't she?"

"She was more than just love," I reply.

"You go tomorrow don't you? It's Ok I see it in your eyes."

"Yes Serg, I think I need to move on."
"I will make sure Flo has best time she not go until next Wednesday I think, anyway she will want for nothing."

I look at Serg and we hug.

"We both owe Flo a lot eh?"

"I agree Serg," and as I look out I realise that from the Boston Tea Party in Exeter to a square in Krakow people are all the same. There are no differences except what we are taught and inbred into us. We are not born with racism, homophobia, hatred; we are pure of heart and thirst knowledge. Let's make sure the knowledge we dispense is worthy of imparting on those we love.

"I have left Flo something so she will be fine and tell her tomorrow when she wakes that I will always be there if she needs me."

Serg looks at me. "I get it, I know why she loved you above all others. I am not jealous just glad she was able to experience such love before she moved on."
Again I am speechless and hug this wonderful man and suddenly without warning Flo and Bell with Manuel are pulling us to the dance floor, well area of square everyone is dancing in. Flo laughs and points as the children all are dancing around pilling faces at the Mayor fast asleep at a table outside the restaurant.

I find myself walking back to the apartment alone and can still hear the music and party from the square in full swing. I open the apartment door and walk to the window looking out over the street.

I call Jimmy, it is 2am, but he is awake.

"Hello my old friend, how are the girls and is all Ok?"

"All is Ok here, how is Krakow?"

"Full of love. Sorry to call late, but on the move."

"Well I think we may be needed at the Haig. I see our friend in need of support. Tuesday good for you?"

"Sure send me info, no I will look up, seems I need to get back into the real world."

"See you Tuesday," says Jimmy, "and be careful the New Order is still with us. Sadly our last outing merely sent them underground."

Jimmy hangs up and I see the ex-PM has been put in the spotlight for not openly showing support to the new PM. She is angry and he knows she is the Head of the British New Order, but does she know he knows. He goes to the Haig to challenge a bill as a peace ambassador regarding funding and research in third world countries. Seem he has started to look into funding cancer research and may have unintentionally uncovered a nerve of the New Order.

14

As I exit the apartment and lock the door I see a note that was attempted to be slide under the door, but sadly stuck half under carpet. It was from Flo. From the handwriting I guessed she was quite drunk and also it was only a few hours ago. I smile as I read.

'Dear Mystery Man, thank you for the most wonderful experience ever. I am drunk yes, but would write to say thank you even sober. You are a lovely man and want to show you my appreciation. I want to but late breakfast, no will miss that, let's do late lunch. Flo – DJ, with a bad smiley face drawing'

I look to my watch and it is 8am. I look at the note and part of me wants to stay, but I have to go see what is going on with the ex-PM in Brussels and see that on Tuesday he will be giving a speech at the Haig. Jimmy is meeting me there, as all is unbelievably fine in Venice.

With clothes in case and keys to the Aston in my hand I set off to leave Poland. I had approximately 1,200 miles to cover and this is no James Bond novel where a Teletype comes up on screen and Bond is instantly there. This is real folks; this is a Journal and what happens, happens. You have it to make you aware of all the things you often do not see or know. OK, I often right up later in the night or whilst having some lunch en-route, but the information you have could be life or death in reality for me or Jimmy or any of the people contained within.

As I drive over the Polish German border I whisk through customs as everybody looks at the car, not me, I think of the irony I am facing. The irony the world faces, especially in Europe. I am off to see the superpowers head quarters and the only true bastion of the right and good against the evil forces in Europe are the Germans.

Yes as I pass through this magnificent country, beautifully rebuilt and restored to former glory after Hitler, I see a new Reich, a New Order rising and threaten European peace, it is there for all to see, but we look away as we have to confront our own issues it seems, I have a new mission to keep friends safe and out of reach as always of those that place them in harms way.

I stop off in Berlin and stay in my favourite hotel, The Regent Berlin, and I have managed to get the Presidential Suite. I have money and believe we should live life not save for a rainy day and at just under four thousand euros for the night, which includes a magnificent meal, I think to myself, 'I am worth it'.

I stand by on the balcony looking out over the Gendarmenmarkt Square, I look at the diverse history of the city. The hotel is a short walk from many major attractions, built by Albert Speer for Hitler, and yet the new Germany that inhabits I truly feel would of stood up to Hitler had they been around. My suite manager arrives with the food and her staff. She is very efficient and very attractive. She sees the picture of Megstar by the mirror, "Your wife?"

"Sadly not," I replied, "she died before I had the chance."

Why did I say that? To a complete stranger? I write now in my Journal Reader as often we do and say things we wonder why did we etc etc etc, but before I can say anything else the beautiful young woman and her people had gone. I was alone in the suite. I felt very alone.

I sat at the table prepared with the food and placed the photo of Megstar opposite me so I did not dine alone.

I could not sleep so went downstairs to the bar and found myself surrounded by smart lawyer looking types and took a table near the centre. I ordered my usual, a coke with no ice. I seem to of caught the attention of a beautiful young woman at the bar, who asked my waiter what I had ordered. She watched him pour it and then smiled. I had my back to her, but could see everything in the mirror on the wall.

As the drink is delivered I see the woman adjust her top and begin to walk towards me. Just as she came behind me I stood, turned on my heel and smiled at her.

"Would you care to join me?" I asked.

I enjoyed the look on her face, as she to this day no doubt has no idea how I knew she was behind me. Timing is everything. Just watch the old comedies with Paul Eddington or David Jason to know how timing is everything. Yes that has dated me Reader, but if you do not know them look up 'Yes Minister' or 'Only Fools and Horses' to fully understand and experience some incredible comedic timing.

As she sits on the sofa beside me she angles her body so I can see her beautiful legs and if wanted to her panties as well as arching her back making sure her ample cleavage is just right, for maximum effect.

"I am grateful for the company," I say and then offer to buy her a drink. "Let me guess Champagne? No, sorry being facetious, vodka martini? No, I know, how about an espresso martini?"

"I would love one," she replied.

"My pleasure," I said holding out my hand, "The name is Fondle, Ivor Fondle."

She smiles and is not sure how to react. Obviously I have a daft name, but she is motionless in her position waiting to see if I glance at her beautiful breast or try to sneak a peak to see if she is wearing knickers. Of course I do neither. Partly because I am a gentleman, but mainly because I wanted, quite naughtily to see how long she could pose in that position. Yes Reader she is a hooker, high class and possibly works with the barman, but I wanted company and the cost of a cocktail, about twenty euros I had an attentive, attractive, ready for sex companion to talk to. I am sure she nearly always has people talk at her so I decide to have fun.

"Come with me," I say and stand and offer my hand and she stands and walks to the bar with me. The waiter comes to greet us and I see from the look that they know each other.

"My friend," I say to the barman, "as I am in the Presidential suite would it be OK for me to make my new friend here a drink?"

"Pardon, sir?"

I sit my new female companion on the bar stool and proceed to enter behind the bar. I do this with speed and confidence so there is no chance to halt my advances. Within a few seconds I am the other side of the bar and ask the barman to fetch me a boston shaker and I want a large espresso. My addition to the barman's domain has caused more clients to notice me, as well as the manager from my floor.

"Are you auditioning for a job as a barman, sir?" She asks.

"No, but please place yourself on the stool here as I can tell from your demeanour that you have just finished as you have your handbag with you."

The manageress smiles and sits at the bar. The Barman looks as if to say he was here before I could stop him. I place two champagne clutes on the bar, some people call them saucers and I take the espresso and the boston shaker. I pack ice into the shaker and pour the hot espresso over the ice. I then add a large vodka and a shot of Kahlua and start to skake together with the glass fitted tight to the metal shaker. The barman smiles as if impressed. I tap the glass on the bar and separate the glass from the shaker and pour two espresso martinis.

"Ladies please," I say as I offer the glasses. There is a small part left that I ask the Barman to taste. He seems impressed, but to be honest it is an easy cocktail to make and the theatrics sell it.

"It seems you have gifts sir," says the Manageress and my new companion who by the way was not wearing knickers if case you are interested smiles as if she had finally had her Christmases all come at once.

I note two elderly ladies watching and ask them if I can make them a drink. Both notion to me the same as the others and before there was time to blink I was making espresso martinis for everyone. Forty in all so eight hundred euros. One of the gentlemen who had joined us then said how he played the piano and within seconds I was the other side of the bar and led him to the piano in the room. He looked a little concerned as if to say is it alright, and an hour later the bar is packed. People are singing at the bar and my female companion at the start of the night is singing at the piano. He was having the night of his life and loved the attention. I had found out he was often eating alone and was a solitary figure.

I start to make my excuses to leave and the manageress comes to me smiling.

"Can you charge the drinks to my room?" I ask.

"No," came her reply, "we have had the best night in the hotels history at this bar so may be this is our way to say thank you."

I smile and then ask the reception to give the manageress an envelope on her way out. I tipped the barman two hundred euros and told my female companion that I was off to bed and that she would be best to enjoy time with the man at the piano. She said that she really liked me and was willing to sleep with me all night for half her usual fee. I smiled and paid her three hundred euros to sleep with the pianist guy. Her reply was priceless.

" I will fuck him, but I will be thinking of you."

What a compliment.

15

Driving out of Berlin early the next morning I pass a huge billboard and on it is the face of the hooker from last night. My German is not at all good, non existent, but seeing her scantily clad, next to a pole, provocatively posed with the name of the club, in a private house in Kurfürstenstraße, a red light district of Berlin, I soon realised my earlier suspicions of her from the bar of her modelling was just one of her many talents that made me smile. Great believer in live and let live Readers. I drove off thinking that she caused no one any harm and in fact possibly made the businessman on the piano grin from ear to ear. He will never know she was a lady of the night as he was also leaving today.

With an hour gone and the city behind me I was enjoying the roads leading to Brussels. I was thinking of Megstar and thanks to Flo and the Polish adventure I was at peace with the loss. Now you never get over losing someone, but in time you learn to accept it.

Sat at the wheel of the Aston, it really is an incredible drive, I enjoyed the feeling of no attachments, no country ties and starting to realise that being a European was amazing. Sadly, after Brexit felt being British had been sullied as I was left with an over powering sadness as being British had left me feeling we were a nation of racists and even dumber than the rest of the countries we often looked down on. Our Empire had been strong, cruel in history, but that sense of stiff upper lip and doing the right thing prevailed and much of being British was wonderful. In many countries we had made a difference and from travels knew how much we were loved as a nation. Driving across the German border into the Netherlands I felt much of that had been lost. We were already great why did those self-effacing wannabe politicians' ruin and divide for their own gain; and why, as a people, a strong nation ever fall for their lies?

No apologies Reader if you were a Brexiter, but with the pound falling, no money for the NHS as promised, no trade deals outside European Community forthcoming, and sadly deals we are offered crippling, but being taken as all we have on offer, will see the pound not recover and will see our economy dip and never rise again. Many of the major nations with bases in the UK will opt to base themselves in Ireland or even Scotland when it leaves the United Kingdom.

But all is not lost as the Head of the New Order, our wicked witch the new PM is already using the parliamentary get out where the MP's can vote and the will of the people be ignored. It matters not to me as the damage has already been done. Thank heavens for the Americans and their leader horrendous racist rhetoric as at least they have taken the spotlight off us.

I stopped off and enjoyed a few breaks on the way and even the motorway, autobahn restaurants were way better than many of the local high street food outlets in the UK. I enjoyed seeing all the other drivers literally stop in their tracks and stare at the Aston. This is a great car, but hard to be Invisible in one would think. Actually not true. The people are spending so much time looking at the car and photographing themselves next to the car they never see or remember the driver.

I speed off into the heart of Belgium and soon I am parking under the hotel where the ex-PM is staying. I find my old House of Parliament badge for Sir John and walk in. He is on the twelfth floor, and has a selection of suites. Seems leaving office means no one really looks at what you spend as vigorously. As I exit the lift I see the Special Police Force guarding him and flash my badge. One stops me and reads then photos it on his phone and the door to the suite at the end opens and there stands Matthew.

Matthew smiles and beckons me to come in as the security stand to one side and I enter. Sat in the middle of the reception room is the ex-PM, his wife and, yes you guessed it, the leader of the opposition's wife. The ex-PM looks as if he is in hell, but smiling politely when looked at. He sees me and stands. The two ladies stop and look to me as I enter.

"Ladies, you can enjoy Sir John and my company a little later, but sadly we have urgent business to attend to."

The ex-PM grabs my arm and I nod acknowledging the ladies and we go into an adjoining room.

"My God man, you could not of come soon enough!"

I started to laugh as he sat in a chair laughing with me. "This women could talk for England, actually England, Ireland, Wales and Scotland."

"Nice to see you sir and Jimmy is on his way too I believe," I hear a toilet flush and see Jimmy appear, "So I see you got here before me?"

Jimmy and I embrace and we all sit as Matthew slides into the room and joins us with folders. Matthew hands both Jimmy and I a folder.

"Since Venice I have managed to find out quite a lot about my successor and she is truly not the lady I thought she was," he says.

"Not at all," says Matthew, " In fact she is here in Brussels for meetings and we notice she has not actually made one. Well she has entered rooms and said hello, but not had one solitary conversation on anything other than polite conversation."

I open the dossier to see a whole dossier on a Cancer Research programme. The ex-PM looks at me reading and then starts to say why he is in Brussels.

"I am being paid a fortune to start up a new campaign to help research alternative medicines to fight cancer."

I look as if what has this to do with us being there and look to Jimmy who seems to know something I do not.

Jimmy looks to me and starts to talk, "Well it seems the New Order have been using Cancer Charities to fund their activities. Did you know the research company in UK has over seven hundred million in the bank and raises a further two hundred million every year? The New Order syphon much of the money off to fund their projects and in Venice at Klutes found paperwork linking new PM and her New Order to this. Then did a search on other heads of state and all have links to special cancer research funds. So, against my wishes our friend here thought he would set up a committee into alternatives and rock her boat. In fact he has shaken up an international navy ready to go to war to literally blow him and his ideas off the face of this earth."

I look to my friend and see he is concerned, but thinks he is invincible. "You do realise that you have placed a lot of people, a lot of your family in danger, I mean Jimmy is right, you should of thought first."

"That cow was a good friend I thought and played us all for fools and I wanted to make her life a little more difficult. I did not support her openly in a debate and she was much criticised, and from therein it seems much of what I was looking to do with my life was being cut off. I knew it was her as now leaving politics, and thought there must be something I can do, found her sudden interest in Cancer Research and thought highlight she was placing everything in one basket etc etc etc then Matthew literally overheard a conversation with the ex-minister for health. I thought they had fallen out, but whilst everyone thinks he is no longer in the fold he can go off, as you say, invisible, doing her dirty work."

Matthew excitedly continues as he acts as if he is in a Bond movie, "Well I hid in the broom cupboard of the outer offices with my TransAm640 Dictaphone and recorded this."

Matthew plays the recorder, "Must buy Jacob those pretty ruby slippers..." Hurriedly he clicks it forward, "Sorry."

First voice, "So she now wants us to bump him off?!"

Second voice, easily recognisable as ex minister for health, "Well I would love to, but she's got me behind closed doors with the cancer research team."

"How do you want him gone?"

"As soon as he goes overseas, he'll have an accident and let no one look into the cancer research without scanning." Matthew stops the tape.

"So you know that as soon as you go overseas they are going to bump you off and here we all are in Brussels? Not exactly what I would of done my friend." I looked at a concerned ex-PM.

"Sir John, I have here passes for you and Jimmy to become Sir John again and work from Parliament seeing what you can find out. I need eyes nobody knows who can be seen and not seen themselves."

Jimmy stands and fetches a folder, much bigger than the one we were given each and hands it to the ex-PM.

"Well, I prompted you and did a little digging on the ex-minister for health's email account. Seems that the New Order is funding their new weapons sales and bases with the fund and seems Cancer Research is great business. A few breakthroughs where they produce a new miracle drug that makes ten times what the fund is worth and syphon that off to fund wars, drug running and all kinds of nefarious activities. You see each Head of the New Order, and there are twenty-three, all listed in that file, all farming the same amounts of cash through cancer research charities. It seems whilst the economy was floundering the new PM was amassing a fortune that could of paid off the national debt."

"You found all this out in four days?" exclaimed the ex-PM in disbelief.

"No of course not," smiled Jimmy, "two days as took me two days travelling."

I laughed and just loved the Invisible Man's natural ability to acquire what was visible to all, but never seen, until now. The ex-PM looked to me and I motioned as if to say, 'Don't look at me', and then got up and looked out the window,

"Have you the breakdown Jimmy?" I asked.

"What breakdown?" asked Matthew.

Jimmy leans forward with another smaller folder, "On the plane, here I put this together," and hands it to me.

"You see we have a list of all those involved, so we have a list of those not involved. What we do is have them join forces and make you such a visible target they cannot touch you, but family is another matter." I look at a confuse ex-PM.

Jimmy interrupts. "The PM is giving a speech today in three hours at the Haig on Britain's involvement in a world campaign on cancer development and global warming, I know the woman cannot see that she needs to discuss one at a time as she wants to use the global warming to deflect questions on the cancer research funds. She has no idea we know this is her key speech as lifted from ex minister for health email."

"So, and stop me if I am wrong Jimmy, we will be holding a press conference in two hours…."

"Sorry, ninety minutes," says Jimmy looking at his watch.

"And you will launch your initiative on alternative medicines to find a cure for cancer," I inform him.
Jimmy smiles and Matthew looks confused.

"Right Matthew, email everyone on that list, and call everyone on that list, I have their personal mobiles, that are here to join us as want them on board. How am I doing so far?"

'Not bad, sir, not bad," I reply and Jimmy has already left the room without anyone noticing. The ex-PM's mobile rings. "Hello? Oh hi…… sorry."

Jimmy returns and hands me another file, "Ok Matthew be quiet. Visit everyone in person? They will all be at the Thon Hotel with access from underground. Go with wives as they are all there waiting for me sir, tell him when he's off the phone, file and speech is in folder Sir John has? OK. See you there?"

I find the speech and smile. "I think we can make this in your voice en route sir and seems Matthew with thirty minutes notice call the press to announce that there is to be a major launch at the Thon Hotel. Just say it will be something no one will want to miss."

I open the doors to the adjoining room and the two wives are still heavily in conversation as if we never left. "Ladies at last I can say hello and wonder if you would like to join us as there is something very exciting about to happen and love it to be a surprise for you too."

"Oh, Sir John, your surprises are legendary," say the leader of the opposition's wife.

"Sir, if we all go out as if on an afternoon walk, the hotel is just 400 metres away."

"Come on ladies, let's walk, what do you say?"

Both laugh and putting on their coats agree as the ex-PM links arms with both and we all stride out of the building. Supported by secret services we nonchalantly walk into the Thon Hotel where the manager, as if he has been expecting us says that everything is ready.

We walk into a wonderful conference hall with a huge round table with thirty-five seats and name places all set up. A TV screen and projected on it the hunt for a world cure. The table is sat in the middle of the room and there are places set for TV and camera crews as well as an audience to sit.

"I think Jimmy knows me too well," says the ex-PM. "He knows I am a huge fan of the legends of King Arthur and feel this is how we should present the show." I look at the PM and giggle to myself. I was having fun and knew this would not only screw the UK Prime Minister over, she would be fuming in her surgical stockings, and unable to do anything to stop her adversary or have him taken out.

"Just one thing sir, I think this should be your seat looking at the entrance and do not mention me or Jimmy in anyway. Credit to Matthew and your wives, as well as yourself of course. We will be here, but invisible."

The doors start to open and security look to Matthew and the news crews and press start to tumble in jostling for a spot.

"My dear friends, no rush. We will wait for you to be ready and once you are all happy we can start?" He was in his element.

"Prime Minister, Prime Minister..." came a question from the press.

"Ex-Prime Minister I think you'll find Tony." He replied in jovial response, he knew the press and was flattered that the big names came out for him. He sat at his seat at the round table as the press and television cameras set up.

As if all at once a confused looking group of foreign politicians enter the room to see the ex-PM stand and greet them. The press and cameras are filming everything and it was going out live.

"Please, please my friends have a seat. I believe there is a space for all of you. It is a round table, there are no heads of the table here, and just like the knights of old we gather all equal."

There is a real buoyant mood in the room and I see Jimmy in a gallery ready to start proceedings. There is one place empty the Russian delegate. The ex-PM looks to Matthew who motions that he is in the toilet. With that moment the Russian Ambassador to Brussels enters and looks confused.

"Vladimir, my old friend, thank you for coming." The ex-PM greets him and shows him to his chair.

Vladimir whispers in his ear, "What's going on why the press? I heard you had strippers."

In true diplomat style the ex-PM slaps him on his back and says in a whisper back, "Don't worry later."

The lights dim and there is a moment of consternation as the projection starts. It shows how cancer still pillages the world's population, no cures to be found, billions spent, but may be it is time to find alternative cures? The world's suffering global warming and new biotechnologies can help lessen our exposure to cancerous elements man has created. Today is the first meeting called for a new project to be championed by the courageous and new society for Alternative Solutions.

The projection ends and the screen is focused on the ex-PM who addresses all in the room.

"Friends, and we are all friends. World leaders, the press and staff of the Thon Hotel, we are all the same. We sit here at a round table, no head, no one person in charge, but a united collective all helping each other find a solution to the world problems together. I am here declaring war on cancer, on global warning, on decreasing natural resources. Together we can collectively work together, share Intel and as I say together make a difference. In two weeks time I want to organise a mandate for all countries to sign to participate in the largest collective ever to combat world troubles. A global think tank and that is why I asked you, my friends and colleagues, who I know and trust to join me to start this initiative."

All the politicians around the table start nodding in agreement as they know they are being filmed and as if by magic the Russian minister stands and looks to all, "I say in English, I think this good idea."

All the room applauds as others stand and salute the idea. I see the ex-PM grinning like a little boy that has just got the cream.

I looked around as the TV crews all stayed and I flipped on the monitors all around the room showing live feeds of the meeting in the room. We see the ex-PM and his wife arm in arm talking about now he has left office wants to help make a difference and that his wife is always 50/50 with him on ideas (I actually gave him that one) and he even credited the leader of the oppositions wife as well. My biggest smile came as when this was said she actually enjoyed taking the credit.

I then flashed on the news from the main hall where there was a small audience for the British PM and as she announced her drive with the Cancer Research Campaign a reporter asked if this was in response to her predecessors campaign. Broadsided she was knocked off her feet and she had to say that she knew nothing about that, but welcomed any support.

Her big press announcement bought to a swift close and out she marched gritting through her teeth. She had called her predecessor to Brussels and on a tour where he would be taken out in a quiet way, but now if she went anywhere near him it would bring huge news to the front. Passing me he shook my hand and said, "Thank you I am no longer invisible, but will need you and friend in London for a few days to help formulate what to do next."

I nod in agreement and it is often at these moments when you see you have completely altered the future of the political scene and world for the better that makes the whole Invisible Network a joy to be part of. I look to the gallery to see Jimmy has gone and realise I should disappear also.
The British Prime Minister is just 400 metres away and was seen marching to the Thon Hotel. Every politician was there and it was obvious she was on her way and

desperately looking to make an appearance as if this is what she wanted.

I could see her entourage coming into the reception and had spent the last minute briefing a Dutch film crew to intercept and what to say. As she entered flash cameras went off and being the only reporter there my friend at the Dutch TV was easily heard and caught the British Prime Ministers' ear.

"Prime Minister, Prime Minister, would you say that your press conference has been eclipsed by these new Knights of the Round Table?"

"Sorry?" she replied. Bingo she was so angry so flustered she had totally forgotten to protocol and left open a door to the interview to happen. I was on the cameraman's headphones feeding questions, as many as I could get in before it all ended.

"Prime Minister, is it not true that your predecessor is now the most visible man in politics and his initiative, backed by all of your colleagues in Europe, really has made your small initiative redundant?"

"Redundant?!" it was as if she was on the ropes.

"Why yes. Did you not Prime Minister come in support of one multinational company to gain support for them alone, but your predecessor has a campaign embracing all companies and countries to work together to find cures for not just cancer, but other issues?"

"I think the bigger picture is how I look forward to discussing with my colleague how we can bring the British Government to assist in what we see as an truly great endeavour."

"I'm sorry Prime Minister?" said the reporter as I put words into her mouth, "but this is not a colleague as when you took power he resigned his position as an MP and has taken an independent stance you know nothing about? Is it not true that he has become a thorn in your side? As many of us see if he suddenly disappeared all eyes would be on you, would they not?"

"I am not sure what you are getting at, but we have been colleagues and close friends for many years and there is nothing but admiration and support from me and I can assure you he is a huge supporter of me and my leadership."

"But has he not shamed your policies and did not come to a meeting you asked for?"

"Where do you get these notions from young girl?" and the interview was over. I had moved position and with Matthew ushered the ex-PM and his fellow politicians, out of the hotel via a different exit, but lined up the press to greet the British Prime Minister as she entered the room.

I wish I had been there, but no one was. The doors opened and in she walked full of bravado to a line of cameras and reporters all smelling blood. Flash cameras went off and the doors closed behind her as the reporters started. The dreadful reality dawned on her face as she realised that she had entered an empty room, like an unwanted guest, and was easy pickings for the press to lampoon.

But I needn't of worried about not being there. For the next three days it was all the press showed and debated. I whisked the ex-PM and wife and entourage back to London and off to the countryside where I ensured he was seen playing golf, badly, at a fundraiser for a little girl needing cancer treatment overseas, to visiting cancer victims wherever he was enjoying a break from politics. Sometimes when we do this we can often create a monster, but I think our man got it, he got the bigger picture and saw that for once he truly could make a change.

The British Prime Minister of course stuck in the Haig for the whole time unable to get away. Not once did I feel sorry for her. This is an evil woman who is looking to be part of a New Order where people will be exterminated, abused and used to the New Order's will, creating a world of fear and her ruling without opposition the UK. She is such a despicable woman that in all truth I can see her eying up Buckingham Palace as her new residence.

We had released such anger we still have to be careful, but for the time being until she is seen as part of the movement her place in Parliament and the New Order is in jeopardy. Lives had been saved and the fact she had openly been seen to endorse just one Cancer Research Fund had meant that donations were at an all time low. Once described as a tigress I knew we were riding her back and there is a proverb is there not, Reader?

16

Back in London I walk into the Houses of Lords with my new ID badge for Sir John. I find that entering the Lords and then walk through into Parliament helps me be more invisible. The idiots in government are so blinded by their own importance that they look down on the Lords as if they are nobody, mainly because they are jealous and hate the fact they are given the role and never earn it.

A lot has changed and the political face of the globe is in greater threat than the man on the street truly comprehends. Remember Reader my mission in America, well the White House now has a white supremacist in the Oval Office. The American people are seen as the majority are, white racists, and even Hitler could not of planned such a coup. Dark days ahead and he is not part of the New Order that I found out in short time. Even the fascist's here feel he is too dumb to associate with.

The corridors of Parliament are even spookier. I mean to say that there are loads of junior juniors, whose job is to patrol the corridors listening to anything anyone says and report back to their masters. I was grateful as if I need to start anything to flush someone out it will be so easy.

I am in a corner table of the bar and see Henry come in. He looks a little down trodden. I smile and stand as if to say to join me and he does. Before he sits he looks around to see who is watching.

"It is OK Henry, you are with me, we are invisible, and anyway, all the spies are outside the Foreign Secretary's Office."

Henry looks at me and then looking round the room laughs as he sits, "So how did you achieve that Sir John?"

"Just the wrong word in the right ear and... listen enough of my fun, why the long face?"

Henry looked up and forced a smile. He looked out of the window and then back at the empty bar.

"I dreamt of this day, working at parliament, an important job doing something useful, and do not get me wrong, I am grateful, but Chastity and I never see each other. We had a row about....., well I have no idea what about and suddenly all this seems unimportant."

"So who are you working for Henry?"

"I am now a junior minister for the Minister for Internal Affairs. Sadly, after Brexit and the PM left I was then side-lined to worthless department as punishment and now the new PM knew of Chastity and my relationship thought it would be fun to promote her to the Foreign Office, yes back with the bumbling idiot. He does not try to molest her, but the other girls he does, and she tries to get them to accidently kick him in the balls like she did. Yes she actually kicked him in the balls disguised as a trip. He went down like a sack of spuds in the corner over there, and all confessed it was obviously an accident. In a need to show his power he makes her work late and on shit jobs, taking the bimbos he has hired on overseas meetings etc."

"Listen, thanks for confiding in me and you ready for a change?"

"Yes," said Henry tentatively and looked at me as he suddenly realised it was no coincidence we met.

"Good. Now here are two tickets to a box at the Opera for six. You will meet an old friend in the street who was hoping to catch the opera if there were spare tickets with friends. There will be four of them and you invite them to share your box. All will change from tonight and you'll find Chastity is free. Oh and one last thing tell her how beautiful she looks, that is all she needs to hear."

Henry takes the tickets and looks at them. Henry's phone rings and he looks to me.

"That'll be Chastity," I say.

Henry answers, "Hello Chastity? Yes yes I have tonight off and tickets to the opera..yes I know you love the opera. Listen how come you have tonight off?" Henry laughs. "seems a guardian angel looking over us again? See you at the flat at five then, oh and Chastity, I love you." Henry smiles and hangs up. "Well, saying you look beautiful didn't seem to be thing to say as could not see her and."

"I love you is all was needed. Now do as I say and have a great evening. Lovely meeting you Henry."

"You too Sir John."

With that Henry stood and left the bar. I look round and see that the bar is empty except for one SNP who spends all his time in the bar. He was elected I guess as the stereotypical Scotsman, drunk at the bar. Now Reader sadly this is not the case if you know the Scots, but this one was a politician representing his constituency, politicians are they bred in weird farms somewhere where they have their spines removed before entering into the affray?

I decide to have the rest of the day off. The bar and this place reminded me of Megstar. It was here we had one of my greatest triumphs. As I stand to leave the Leader of the Opposition walks in with his entourage. He stops to shake my hand.

"Sir John, isn't it? My wife tells me of a wonderful time in Venice where she saw you with the, well, the ex-PM. How are you?"

"I am fine sir and just helping this new global reach set up by our friend."

With this he nods his head and his entourage move to the bar and we stand alone.

"Sir John, I feel I can talk openly and safely. The corridors of power have changed sizematically of late. There are dark forces at work, I know I sound like a wizard novel, but things are being done without any form of constitutional reckoning. This new bitch in power has a bill to sell off the NHS and about to create a national fear of NHS a breeding ground for immigrants to sponge off the country and to be honest I am trying to find out what she has in mind to be able to thwart her plans before we are all swept aside like a nation of dumb ass Americans."

"To be honest sir, I have no idea, but hopefully by tonight I will have the file for you." With this I shook his hand and exited as the bar was starting to fill with the Prime Minister's henchmen and spies. She was such a dumb woman. She hired loyal people who were ruthless and pure evil above intelligence and reason. You could spot them a mile off.

Without one seeing me I exit the bar and walk to the offices used by the PM. I switch my badge. Sorry Reader forgot to say that I have a few badges and a few names so as with all my journals where I may seem confusing it is because I have trouble keeping up with myself also.

I walk up to two men stood outside making out they were having a meeting, but knew they were poorly disguised security, "Gentlemen, Quentin Pharrell. I have to collect a file for my man in Brussels."

With this they let me in and I enter a room with two pretty girls typing and the PM's own secretary, a six foot two brick shithouse of a man, who could not type a sentence let alone use a computer. I show him my badge and say that I have come for the file for my man in Brussels to which he says one moment and goes into the other adjoining room.

I smile at the secretaries and look at a file on the man mountains desk that says confidential. It literally is the file on the NHS plans. I sit on his desk and without detection open it and there is nothing inside. I stand and smile how easy all this was except sadly the file was empty. Thinking of making an excuse and leaving the adjoining room door opens and out comes the giant as I now call him. He hands me a file and I take it without looking. I turn and exit.

Just out of interest Reader are you wondering how it was so easy? Thought so. Well as well as spreading rumours I could collect information using the same system. In one rumour I spread that password was being changed and to make sure all knew it. Many looked as if to say 'what password?', but others nodded and a few said, "So do we still say come on behalf of my man in Brussels?" Of course I observed them as each nodded affirmative and tried it at the PM's office. Also with a name like Quentin Pharrell the men on the door see a pass that looks legit, but no one would invent a name like Quentin Pharrell so in I go. Confidence is the other trait.

I walk into the offices for Internal Affairs and see Henry.

"I have tonight's file to copy can I use your copier Henry?"

"Sure, of course." Henry points to a small room off the office and inside there is a copier, a fax machine even and I start to load the contents of the file to copy. Two copies.

As the copier does it's business I start to read what I am copying. On the pages are bank balances for off shore accounts in Guernsey, that is the UK Cayman Islands, as well as how funds, over £700,000,000 transferred a year from a Cancer Research Fund and a way that the research fund will buy hospitals on behalf of the New Order as a company called MayCo Investments and all funding for NHS will be trafficked through to New Order as well as they will own all hospitals and take over NHS to run like an American system. It truly is a ruthless approach and this new, unelected PM looks to say the losses in NHS due to immigrants abusing our generosity, but then I see the one page she stupidly highlights. Yes so confident no one would see, as she feels invincible, was a sheet on the real facts to hide.

I hear the door open and Henry enters.

"Henry, just the man. Can you do me a favour? I need you to make sure you hand this personally to the Leader of the Opposition immediately and tell him Sir John sends his best regards."

Henry looks slightly confused and nods OK. He never looks at the contents and just scurries away to deliver. I keep the second copy for me. I only gave the NHS stuff to the Opposition Leader, as he needs not to know about New Order just yet.

I exit the room and place the files to keep in my backpack I leave in the copy room and walk back to the PM office to return the file.

Outside the guys open the door without asking. Not great as this means they recognised me from before. I realise I am not invisible and inside the giant stands. I hand him back the file.

"My man in Brussels says thank you." And with this I turn and exit. As I am exiting I walk up to the two outside and hand them a photo of a picture of a tourist that I took doing the tour of Parliament.

"Guys, keep your eyes peeled for this man. Memorise his face and report back to the office if you ever see him."

They both take a long look and I take the picture and leave. You see the likelihood of them remembering me is decreased as they have another face imprinted on their minds. An old Invisible Man trick Reader and it actually works. Perfected by the legendary GJ Isaac when he was securing the release of political prisoners in Iraq in the seventies posing as an Arab who was acting on behalf of the UEA looking for the man in the picture. It worked and he managed to get all hostages out as if he was an envoy for the UEA and we all then knew that the Iraqis' were working covertly with all of the Arab states. This manages to save hundreds of lives and ensure the Invisible Men were all one-step ahead of the Middle East.

I am back in the copy room, collect my backpack and within forty-five minutes having a coffee in my beloved Notting Hill. Just round the corner from a friend who happened to have his man pass me by and invited me to another cup of tea in a house in Portobello Road.

Sat in a kitchen at the top of the house in walks my friend the ex-PM.

"Sorry Sir John, all a bit cloak and dagger, but PM wants to do a meeting and avoiding her until we speak. By the way, I was truly sorry to hear about Megstar, phenomenal young lady and a loss to us all."

"Yes, a true loss, but in the spirit of her name for life and fun I think we have uncovered something more than we expected." I hand him the file.
Whilst he is reading, I stand, "So I guess I'll make the tea then? Sugar?"

He looks up and smiles, "Where did you..? I mean how did you, actually never mind. This is incredible. Not sure what to do?"

"Nothing. Absolutely nothing. I have the Leader of the Opposition the NHS stuff and he will research the counter on that.."

"I have a confession," he says and I turn to see him looking pale and ashamed. "Sit and I'll make the tea. I was instrumental when in power at starting this NHS reform. Five major backers were looking to buy up the NHS and I let it happen. I saw with Brexit a rise in immigration haters and racists and saw that the public would buy it if we placed it on the back of immigrants in the country. I thought it was brilliant at the time, but realise how shallow I was now. The figures for the immigrants are exaggerated as we discuss them as if in a year and there are actually spaced out over twenty- five years. The electorate are mainly stupid, the believers, party faithful will follow and repeat as if true, social media etc and no matter how much a lie it is the people will be rounded up like cattle and onside before they see that the selling off to my business friends can be stopped. Huge funds for NHS would have been pumped into their hospitals and so they would be seen as successes and the NHS strongholds strangled of help and funds would highlight change was needed. The people would accept as only 500,000 strong labour supporters making a noise is nothing. Look at how successfully this tactic worked in America recently. They have a guy spouting Hitler gain power. Jesus Christ! Why does power make us all such idiots?

"Well, tonight you are going to the opera and handing this file to defeat PM in a social at the Opera with your wife tonight. Just the NHS stuff, not the New Order accounts, and just so you know, I knew about the initiative was started by you. Power often corrupts and we convince ourselves that in the bigger picture we are justified. I take two good sugars and I have another favour if I may be so bold?"

"Well let me make the tea and sit down as I feel I may need to."

Sat in silence we drank, well sipped our tea. Both forgetting how hot tea can be just poured. As we both reacted as if burnt our lips in synchronised movement we smiled and realised that there is a bigger picture to deal with. His confession had made me see that here was a man corrupted by power finding himself again now he was out of the office he needed to be in to make the changes needed.

"So now what am I doing?" he asked me with a wry smile.
I looked at my watch and saw it was four o'clock. "Firstly, call you wife about the opera and have her invite her friend the Leader of the Oppositions wife, tell her they both have to be there, he is a huge opera buff, but thinks cannot show as may loose his working class credentials, and then you need to start employing a team and I feel that the PM will fund you."

He started to laugh and smiled, "Why is it I think she actually might?"

17

Outside the Opera as planned stood Henry and Chastity. I was across the road in the doorway of the Bow Street Magistrate's Court. Standing on the second step I could see everyone milling around and saw the ex-PM and Leader of the Opposition with their wives pull up outside. There was a flash of photography from the press and I see Henry move forward and shake their hands with Chastity as the rain started and they all rushed inside.

As they entered their box with ladies on the front seats and gentlemen behind they did not even notice Jimmy was their usher. Each of them was given a program and soon the opera started. The women in tears, Henry and the ex-PM stoic and unmoved, in truth they had no idea what was going on, and the Leader for the Opposition holding back a tear. The curtain falls for the end of the first act. Lights come up and the six move back into a small room at the back of the box to enjoy champagne.

As the ladies chatted, the two men, with Henry, openly spoke of the material they had received. The ex-PM followed my instructions and the file with all the information to broadside the PM was given to him on a USB. As the conversation became more heated and involved the ladies looked to intervene.

"Gentlemen, business can wait. What I want to know is how this lovely couple managed to get us this box that we just happened to bump into them at the entrance and secure seats with them they were looking to possibly sell?"

Henry looked at the Leader of the Opposition's wife as if struggling and the ex-PM's wife stepped in.

"Well I think this may be something to do with Sir John and I think actually my darling husband has something to ask of these two lovebirds, do you not darling?"

"As always my wife sees through me totally. Henry and Chastity I would like you to accept offers to become my two senior fact finding junior ministers for my new special cause. I have spoken to your offices and they will let you go if you wish. It will be still employed as parliamentarians in the sense paid for by the government who will from tomorrow also be announcing the commitment from the PM. Also sir, I believe you have two young people working for you now, who defected from me once I stepped down that I would also like to ask to join the task and report back also to your good self."

"Delighted to, and really grateful to be asked to join as have to say, and not entirely sure why not said before, but your new global group on finding alternative cures for cancer etc., just outstanding. It may define you," replied the Leader for the Opposition.

"I hope it will define us both. Chastity can you call Quetty and Robert to join us tomorrow in the bar at two thirty?"

"Yes sir yes yes yes I can," replied Chastity.
"If I may sir, ladies," says Henry, "can I propose a toast?"

"Of course," say the ex-PM.

"To the ladies and how beautiful they look."

All chink glasses and the second act is about to commence.

Taking their seat all realise that tomorrow was going to be an exciting day.

As they left the room to their seats Jimmy cleared the glasses and removed the iCam I had watched and listened all on from the room on my mobile.

"Good lad Henry," I smiled and walked off to The Ivy for a well-deserved steak.

Entering I am met by the doorman and as I enter I realise I had not booked. It is a real haunt for celebs and seemed really busy.

I asked if there was a small table for one and the girl exited to see what she could do. A few seconds later she returns smiling and says that as long as I leave by nine thirty then they could squeeze me in. It was an hour and smiled back.

"If you can cook a fillet steak frites and have on the table in fifteen, be out of your hair in plenty of time."

We enter the restaurant and it is warm and has a real glow from the lights that make everything look like it is ready for a Christmas photo-shoot. In fact a man in the corner was wearing a dreadful jumper, yes he is in Eastenders. Soap stars often pay huge amounts of money for designer clothes looking at label not what they are buying.

I sit at my table and it is in a corner, I can see everyone in the room and across from me is American actress who I recognise, but the name escapes me. She is radiant and even more beautiful in the flesh than on the screen. I remember her name, but Reader will not divulge as realise she is with her girlfriend. It is a foursome, two girls and two boys and to the trained eye the boys are arm candy, walkers, and tomorrows press will be full of her with new man. Back home in America with the American people resorting back to being Neanderthal, being, black, gay, Muslim, different in any way is like a time bomb on not just your career, but your safety. I used to think it was great to be English, but even that is not something we can wear with pride as with the onslaught of Brexit the racists hide their evil outbursts of hatred and abuse as immigration fears.

I thought about moving to South of France, but the fascists are marching through there as well. I remember a very statement years ago after the great and late Nelson Mandela was released. As he walked free some commentator said that Africa was the future. I love the people and who knows possibly move there one day.

As I sit here in the restaurant writing this journal the waitress interrupts me with a perfect fish pie. The lady on the door suddenly sees my face and then looks in horror as we all realise she has got it wrong.

As she comes to the table I place my hand up and say, "Please I forgot about your fish pie and it is fate as I love it. Please let me enjoy and I am more than happy to find a seat."

Graciously she accepts and still full of remorse offers me more time if I need it and I smile and reply that I am more than happy.

As I tuck in to my delicious meal I notice an old adversary who is a reporter for one Britain's tackiest papers, The Sun. I can see that she had a secret camera and has been photographing the American Film Star. I can see her salivating over a really juicy piece of gossip set for her backside wiping paper.

As I finish I call my new friend to my table. She hurries over and asks if I wanted to take her up on offer for free desert. Now the Ivy takes great pride in the fact cameras and secrets are kept inside the restaurant and point out the activities of who the young lady opposite is, but would she mind if I helped out. Pie finished I told her this would be fun.

Before she could answer I asked if she would introduce me as the new manager for special events looking to offer free memberships. Then come to the table after five minutes and call me away. She agrees as I explain we will not be able to get the pictures without drawing attention to everyone and asked that she turn the Wi-Fi off to prevent anything being sent.

As I walk up to the table and am introduced I can see the panic in her face before the elation of a freebie and chance to enter the upper echelons of celeb partying. As I sit next to her I slide my hand in her bag and remove the camera and her mobile phone. We chat and ask her what she does? She decides to say she is an architect and I make out I know nothing about this and enjoy the conversation as I ask for her card. She cannot give me one. I ask for her telephone number, she cannot remember, but I say that no worries I can just send the membership card to her home address and this she readily hands over.

On time I am removed and walk into reception area outside the restaurant and look at her phone pictures as well as what was on the camera. Lots of incriminating shots of the star holding hands and even one where the arm candy holding hands. It seems like one big gay love in, then I realise the man in the picture is also a soap star in America. Seems the two acting stars support each other whenever they can.

Then the mother load falls into my lap. On her mobile and a few on the camera are photos to the young reporter naked and a video of her playing with herself with a dildo and using for anal sex. It was graphic and not pleasant. There was another of her with a man literally bringing an Alsatian dog off. I send all the files to my Internet and then delete the mail sent. I wipe the camera card and walk back into the restaurant where our reporter so full of herself was flirting with the handsome young waiter. I arrive back and manage to slip camera and phone back into the handbag without being noticed and say that the meal was on us as introduction to new card membership.

Feeling she should not ruin an amazing night she rises to leave and I had instructed all staff to be polite and the front of house to fetch her coat, wish her well and then make sure she never gets in again.
I walk to the two stars and their partners.

"Hello, my name is Alphonso and could not happen but notice lots of press outside that are looking to ensure that you are photographed and reported as couples, but as couples I think we all know you do not wish to be known. Please do not worry, but when you are ready to leave will have you exit via the kitchen and a car waiting. Have a lovely evening."

With that I left and paid my bill, as well as the reporters, and exited. I can imagine the Sun reporter rushing to her offices thinking she has the scoop of all scoops, and imagine her face in the taxi looking at the camera and phone to see no photos.

The following morning there are articles in rival papers about the Sun reporters on camera having sex with dogs. I had managed to give the videos to a nasty little porn site that hosted them and pictures were in the morning papers. The next few days the Sun was desperately back tracking trying to distance themselves after foolishly trying to insist the videos were not real and after a raid from the police it is found on her hard drive as well as more hideous videos of sex parties of Sun editors and staff. There was a major investigation as one boy being whipped by the editor kicked out for misuse of mobile phones recordings being under sixteen. I wished them no malice, but they wanted to create misery for people just trying to enjoy their lives with no harm being done to anyone else.

That Reader is the power of the press and when turned on themselves they use every favour and card they hold on people to make it go away. In America the people acted indignant and suddenly the new President tried to distance himself only to be drawn back into the debate as his friendship links them all at convicted paedophile Jeffrey Epstein parties. It seems our New President is in the pocket of the press magnet, no surprise there then. Crooks all round I guess.

Sadly as a rule of thumb we Invisible Men and Women do not always win as even though we show the people how bad our missions are they often carry on unchallenged, as the people are too dumb or too scared to stand up. Evil men rule when good men are too weak to speak up, but history will always catch up with the deeds.

18

Now with how we left things after the Ivy it is ironic that I am called by Marco. When I say called there is only one way to contact me, well Philippe, via an advert in a dating site. Yes I use dating sites and a certain young lady called Jessica Rabbit will be asked to contact Mr. Fox. Stupid I know, but it works and no trace to me ever as written in her profile. Jessica Rabbit email and identity if followed up leads to a woman in Texas who died over 300 years ago of syphilis. It seems there is more going on in Europe that may need Philippe's attention.

I decide to give it a day to sort out how the girls are getting on and of course it was first day for office set up in Parliament for ex-PM and his new team. I assume that when he meets the Prime Minister today she will offer offices and assistance and keep it all close where she can spy on what they are doing. Of course, this megalomaniac would, exactly as we expect. She has power and position, but brains very little. Her skills are Machiavellian and not intellectual. She thinks power is what you need, whereas most of the most powerful people in the world have always been the advisors and private assistants. In truth Invisible Men and Women have often been this person until it became impossible to work without endangering their own lives, and then they often were replaced by another Invisible. So how to tell if an Invisible is not present. The idiot they work for self-destructs and is soon having to resign or loses all power. Often Invisibles keep all together until they see the real danger is unavoidable then leave for the power mad to feel impregnable and watch their decline.

Now the newly unelected Prime Minister is one such woman, but we, the Invisibles, realise that she may have her ten seconds of fame, but when she poses national threat we will expose. There are Invisibles as we speak exiting the White House for the next incumbent is an imbecile and extremely dangerous, but there are hopefully good men to come through. Plus often when the Invisibles encounter such a vile creature as the new President of the United States they often find impossible to stay invisible. Watching daily a paedophile in office, molesting the staff as if his ordained right, they will break cover and in that moment place all at risk. Before Megstar's death Jimmy called the recent election and asked whether I was going to America. My reply was that I am sure that at some point I will have to, but for now we have other missions.

At the new offices the party is in full swing as Henry, Chastity, Quetty and Robert all sort out their desks and arrange so they are all equal. They even have a spare desk set up and you can see the room has been designed circular and the ex-PM has his desk in with the others. All are equal. Off this room is a computer hub and printing room and another room that is beautifully decorated and designed in the round with a boardroom and place private meetings can be held.

As I enter I see Jimmy, the maintenance man, invisible to all helping set up the room. In walks the ex-PM and notices Jimmy, then me and my eye action notes that he should not acknowledge Jimmy. Jimmy goes into the printer room. As the four new knights of the committee, as we will call them, actually I thought this up as watched them excitedly, and with passion, greet the ex-PM and shake his hand. Once all settled he turns to me.

"Sir John, this is an exciting moment is it not?"

"It is sir, and let me show you around. Your desk is opposite the main door and in here if you'll follow me is the boardroom."

"My word this is stunning, it must of cost a fortune to decorate," he beamed.

"It was, ex-minister of health spent three hundred thousand on it, seriously we have spent nothing, but if we go to the printer room I can show you a few modifications we have made."

I walk the ex-PM into the printer room and notion to the others that we will just be a minute. As we enter I shut the door behind us.

"Sir," says Jimmy holding out his hand. The ex-PM shakes it and looks mischievous in his smile. "Sorry to say we will have to loose that smile when you meet the Prime Minister in an hour."

He looks at Jimmy then me.

"OK Jimmy what have we got?"

Jimmy opens a box of cameras and bugging devices and sensors, "Latest technology espionage."

"Are we using this?" asked the ex-PM.

"No, this is what the Prime Minister was looking to use," says Jimmy.

"Let us never forget sir that the Prime Minister is the Head of the New Order in the UK. Like when we found the enigma machine and broke the code it was not until many years later we let anyone know. She must never know that we know. No matter how delectable it may be to suddenly reveal yourself, do not." The ex-PM gave me a serious look as if he understood. "So what do we have Jimmy?"

"Well, we have two printers, both print beautifully and both have little millage on the clock," Jimmy smiles. "This one is the surveillance system that feeds back to the Prime Minister and this one is the telephone and email router to ensure messages are so encrypted they cannot be deciphered unless on the receivers personal laptop, so sir, if anyone gives away secrets we will know who they are."

"What do you suspect one of those in there?" he asks in a whisper.

"No of course not, they are your knights of the round table. The people we will be monitoring will be the heads of state on committees and working with. In the box I gather Jimmy was all the surveillance equipment fitted last night by the Prime Minister's goons. And there is a little incoming line on your telephones that will indicate a new bug has been added, but from this printer we will see everything as recording with the cameras we replaced them with. Also for the next few days we will record footage and then play on a loop to the PM's monitors we connected up to."

Jimmy looking at his watch interrupts me, "So sir, everything recorded in this room we record and transmit either what we want transmitted, interference as well as every conversation on the bugged phones we can detect when being recorded and transmit what we want heard. You just go about your business looking for new ways to fight cancer, do press, give the PM a little credit, but make her work for it, and know we have your back as long as you stick to the plan."

"Of course, but what about my 'knights' outside?"

"Well let's brief them now." With this I open the door and invite all into the boardroom as a hearty breakfast is served. Jimmy exits with the bugs and cameras and has them all destroyed in a compactor at the rear of parliament.

There were a few shocked faces when told about surveillance and bugging devices to be aware of, but not of the monitoring system or New Order, just a careless talk costs lives type of speech, to which all responded well to. Henry tapped his watch and stood to give a toast with teacups.

"I am proud to be given this wonderful opportunity to become a knight of the round table. I thank you sir, and you Sir John on behalf of us four, and like to say from this day forth will serve, so please everyone stand, equals, well if that is right sir?"

The ex-PM nods, "Proud to stand as equals Henry."

"Then let us toast to the Knights, and finding ways to benefit the people."

All stand and raise their teacups and toast and drink to the Knights.

"Now sir, I know we are all equal, but in George Orwellian manner, you are still more equal than others and believe you have a meeting with the PM?"

Suddenly aware of the time the ex-PM reacts, "Oh blimey, thanks Henry. Actually who wants to come? With me that is to the meeting, that'll give me advantage of her not being able to try to pull rank, ask questions not ready to answer etc."

"I would love to sir, I think seeing me would be a little more than disconcerting as she once called me to a meeting during your premiership sir and threatened me not to bring my ideas forward unless she asked for them, she was more than a little bit racist in her overtones always, well just saying it'll make her really uncomfortable and I have no fear to sit there, even if she tries to motion me to leave," says Quetty.
"Of course Quetty and call me..."

"Arthur," says Robert, "well as we are all the Knights I feel in referring to you as numbers grow you should always be referred to as Arthur."

The ex-PM looks to me and I smile, "Excellent Robert, I love it. That'll put the wind up her and in time we only respond to her requests when discussing you if she refers to you as Arthur. So Quetty, 'Arthur', I think you both have a wonderful meeting to attend."

Chastity hugs Quetty and the boys all shake hands and then shake hands with the girls and as they do Quetty comes to me.

"I have no idea how you do all this," she says, "but I will always be your servant," and kisses me on the cheek.

"Come on Quetty, let's be having you," says the ex-PM. And with that the two exit on a wave of enthusiasm not often seen in politicians.

As I exit the offices I see it is being watched and manage to loose my followers and meet up with Jimmy.

"I have all the surveillance locked into my mobile and it is on detection mode. Movement sensors triggered once all leave office. No movement for thirty seconds and on it goes. But of course we can see now by clicking here."

Jimmy clicks the button on screen and we see Robert, Chastity and Henry sat at their desks all wondering what to do next. I decide to call to test the new system. I start to laugh.

"What's funny?" asks Jimmy.

"I suddenly realise that we are the Invisible Men, who can see without being seen, move in circles undetected and yet observe all, yet I do not actually know the office number."

Both Jimmy and I start to laugh. Jimmy even more than me.

"Me neither," he confesses, "I forgot to write it down."

I ring the main Parliament switchboard.

"Can you put me through to the offices of the Knights? Yes the Knights, the Knights of the Round Table, and the ex-PM's new initiative. Yes that's it….thank you. From now on anyone calling asks for the Knights..oh hello Chastity," watching her answer, "yes I recognised your voice. Now I reckon you are all sat there wondering what to do, well lets start by finding all known alternative cures for cancer, wacky or not, in fact wackier the better as they can be fun, and put together in file for all to discuss with Arthur when he and Quetty return. Yes that'll be great and tell Robert to stop fretting, Quetty can more than handle herself…. " I see Chastity replay the message and Chastity forwards the call to Robert's phone and he answers, "Robert, ask yourself whenever have you felt you were ever in control of a conversation with Quetty? You see she will be fine."

"Well here's hoping she doesn't let the Prime Minister take charge as I know in one sentence she can put her down." Robert replies.

"Robert as I have said before, Mark Twain once said words to the effect that life is full of problems that do not exist. Now research your first trip to discover a cure, I hear that there is a guy in South Africa that has a cure, may be you and Quetty could go there first? That's it smile Robert life is fun, now talk to you all later, oh and one thing, whoever answers the phone answers it 'the Knights' can I help you? Talk later."

I hang up and on Jimmy's phone we listen to Robert convey the way all should answer the phone and they all laugh. We hear Robert discuss South Africa and then see it is not far from where Cape Town where they both wanted to go on a romantic holiday. Robert then straightens up and feels he is abusing power and it would not be appropriate. I call them again. Henry answers.

"Hello..I mean The Knights, can I help you?" The others laugh.

"Henry, it is me Sir John. Tell Robert that through his passion of sharing with Quetty they will achieve more together than worrying about having a good time etc. And want you and Chastity to look into fact-finding trip to Florida. A woman called Erin Elizabeth and Health Nut News, something Megstar told me about ages ago, and time you too had a paid vacation to the sun. You are only good to the Knights if you enjoy what you do and you were chosen as you are trusted and working together on a project I am sure you will both love as will Quetty and Robert is why we need you to stop feeling guilty. Embrace this moment and ensure you are ready to travel the globe finding cures. Sorry got to go." I hang up watch a second as Henry trying to intake everything and then see him smile and a rush of excitement come across his face. Message received and switch off monitor.

"What do you need me to do?" asks Jimmy.

"Jimmy you see what I see, you are even better than me on so many things invisible, so follow your heart. Gather Intel from Venice and why not host the first major meeting at the hotel there. I hear that the hotel bought the building next door so expansion can handle numbers. You can handle security and I know all will be safe. By the way Marco seems to need to talk, any ideas?"

"Talk later, I will see what is happening? Seems seeing a racist pervert become President the Italians feel out done."

And with that Jimmy and I depart.

I realise we have no intel on the inside of the PM's office so decide to join the others back at the Knight's offices. One thing I know that Jimmy told me was that there is a secret entrance from the broom cupboard on the wall that joins the printer room. I thought I would use it to enter.

In the broom cupboard all looks solid, but push a certain roof tile the back wall slides back and you walk between rooms. There is another door that is behind a two-way mirror so you can see no one is in the room. There are also two switches on the mirror you can switch to see into the room behind.

I am in the printer room and enter the room when all three are looking elsewhere. They have no idea I did not enter via the main door and also avoided the goons the PM so poorly posted.

"Knights, I am back, how is it going?"

"Well the woman in Florida is really pro vitamin C and seems that there has been huge success unreported. Like lots of cures we have found they are left online as the old style websites make them seem unhinged conspiracy theorists."

"Yes, I know what you mean Chastity, but in Poland they stop giving Vitamin C in hospitals with cancer patients and it had been successful when given with Vitamin B. There is no evidence or reason why. No email or memo given direct order, but the pharmaceutical giant in the area threw a party for all to attend and it seems many prominent doctors got a new Mercedes."

"Henry, leave that one till later. Let's be seen to be researching in earnest and in a positive way. Place it on file so when the time comes we will be able to use to our advantage."

And as I talk the jubilant Quetty returns to the room. She is punching the air and loving the whole moment. After a few seconds of us all staring at her she calms and looks at us all as if to say 'What?'

"Ok, it was amazing and I just couldn't stop laughing as every time I said a reply used Arthur, and she kept saying who is Arthur? And then 'Arthur' says something that she misses and just as she catches back onto the conversation I would say something like 'I can organise that if you want Arthur' or 'I'll make a note of that Arthur' and she just got more confused then asked me to leave at which point I stated that we were all equal and any meeting held with one can be heard by all and as her blood boiled said 'is that not right Arthur?' to which she looked at him as to say what is going on?"

"And?" says Chastity.

"Well, 'Arthur' then says, that now that the Prime Minister has agreed to the fifty million pound government backing for research could he have a moment with her alone. So I stood and offered to shake her hand and slowly she shook it and could see she had no idea what was going on, then 'Arthur', oh Sir John I love calling him 'Arthur', well 'Arthur says that I should take the signed agreement back to the office and we can work on a press release with the Prime Minister for tomorrow. Then 'Arthur' hands a contract for the money to the Prime Minister to sign and here it flipping is!"

In walks the ex-PM, "And yes Arthur wants it photocopied ten times so all have a copy and too many copies so it cannot be destroyed. By the way Quetty, you're winding the Prime Minister up?" Quetty looks worried as if she went too far, "was just brilliant. Never seen the old hag so beaten up. Now photocopy or shall I do it as we are a democracy?"

"No, we'll do it, 'Arthur'," says Robert and both go into the copy room laughing.

"Now what have you three been up to since I have been with that hideous woman, she has the worst breath I have ever known."

"Well 'Arthur', we have found in South Africa a guy who has been working on a cure and also researching a woman in Florida about her work and research," says Chastity.

"Florida and South Africa sound like fun excursions I am sure the wife would be happy to assist." He sees the faces of Henry and Chastity deflate and starts to laugh. "So who is going where? Chastity you and Henry..?"

"Florida.." says Henry.

"And the others to South Africa. Good that's settled then. I think I want to host a meeting here in Exeter. Wife has relatives to visit and too far from London from the dragon with bad breath and you Sir John?"

"Off to Poland again to check on hospital there from research already done and feel this is where much of business is starting." Ex-PM knew I was talking about New Order and nodded.

"Well I will get the summit sorted....yes a bloody summit, boy it feels good to be back." Sitting in central desk, "This me here then?"

"Yes sir, I mean yes Arthur."

Quetty and Robert return from the copy room and seem ready to burst.

"Right everyone, no secrets so into the boardroom and let me tell you what my conversation with the PM was about. I want her to know that everything we talk about I discuss with all of you."

We all move into the boardroom and sit round the table. I sit slightly to one side so that if anyone walked into the front room I would not be seen.

"Basically, just as you predicted Sir John, our new adventure pissed on her bonfire. No one turned up for the announcement and walking into a room of journalists after we had left was the most embarrassing moment of her life. She was furious. I just hope is not the most embarrassing moment of her life and look forward to many more. She then said that we should work solely with her charity for cancer research to which I replied that would mean all of the other countries involved looking into her charity as they may not be happy, in fact they will also all be raising fifty million to the fund to look at resources they have and share. Realising this she backed down and at present we have a free remit. One thing though is met Charlie Porter in the corridor and he has a constituent that has survived cancer, but needs to find help for others to receive treating they paid for, wants an introduction so if all good with everyone hear like to invite her tomorrow to say hello. Her name is Roseanna something."

"Quetty, you were talking about her were you not? Something the PM did not want made a fuss of her as it was a one off and Shorty went off very upset. We call Porter Shorty as he is..."

"Short," says Quetty. "Can I suggest we do not tell anyone about her and is the PM coming to launch or summit? I know let's have a summit dinner here in London before all travel to Exeter and have Roseanna come as our special guest. Sit her next to PM and then force the PM in front of cameras to endorse that research. Sorry folks but if you had been in that room …. Arthur what do you think?"

We all look at ex-PM, now referred to as Arthur Reader. In fact I never knew he had such a great sense of humour.

Arthur walked to the window and then back at the five of us, "Guys, I have been in politics all my life, I have seen the way it works, played the game and yet today is the first day I actually felt like I was leading not following. You know in just a week on this and with you 'Knights' I wonder why the hell I wasn't more irreverent from the beginning. Too bloody right Quetty, and Robert can you make me a memo?"

"Certainly, sir, I mean Arthur"

"Got pen and paper, I think you should all write this down, under no circumstances whatsoever should I, Arthur, be ever allowed to piss off Quetty, full stop. Did you get that, good. Now we will need a couple of secretaries and want to hire from outside."

"Can I suggest two people to assist on events and also would be excellent confidents?" I enquired, "Yes, well then I suggest your wife Arthur and The Leader of the Oppositions wife."

Chastity screams with delight, "Oh sorry was that too loud. Oh please Arthur I love your wife, we all do and we can call her Guinevere."

"What about the Leader of the Oppositions wife? What do we call her?" asked Arthur.

"Elaine of Corbenic," said Arthur, "The round table is one of my favourite stories, always will be and know more about the story than most. Elaine was the lover of Lancelot. I think she would like to be the lover of Lancelot and let us make her husband Lancelot."

"This is so exciting, who can I be?" asked Chastity.

"You four can be anyone you want, for your four brilliant bright young minds have shown me that I should have been open to collective intelligence a long time ago." Then Arthur looked at me. "I think Sir John you should remain as Sir John."

"I had rather thought I might have been Merlin." I replied.

"No, too visible," quipped Arthur, "Jimmy will be Merlin, he is a magician after all."

"He'll like that." I replied and the others looked as if to say 'Who is Jimmy?' "Do not worry you'll all meet Jimmy soon enough, now let's get straight to work and have the rest of the day off. Well I will you have a launch to plan, bye."

And with that I left via the print room exit and out of Parliament into the streets of London where I was invisible. Off to BAFTA for a cold drink and decide what to do about Marco.

19

Been a few days now since last entry and thought I would bring you up to date Reader. I am now in Ghana and staying with my gorgeous new friend and model here in Accra called Stephanie. I have taken the persona of photographer Mr Reportage and taking shots of beautiful women in Ghana in beauty spots all over the country. This is my mission for Marco as Philippe. Yes, it seems that the family have a new problem down here in Africa.

The family have interests all over the world and as stated before at present the New Order is mainly gaining momentum in Europe and the old Eastern Block.

Chastity and Henry are researching in Florida as Quetty and Robert visit South America. Arthur and Guinevere, hope you are keeping up Reader, are in Brussels after a victorious meeting with thirty-five countries all joining his new find a cure campaign. Even the Royals have come on board to help as Ambassadors. I think Arthur is starting to feel like King Arthur.

At the meeting Arthur thanked the PM for her incredible help in setting up the initiative, which of course has given her huge problems with the New Order as this initiative will be taking millions of pounds, dollars, yen, yes the Japanese on board, and reducing the New Order's cancer research funds. As she stood there happily taking the platform to announce the wonderful initiative Jimmy was in the crowd as a journalist from Bulgaria and it was hysterical as he asked her to explain where the concept came from and Arthur holding back the tears from laughing as she stumbled left her out to dry as they say long enough to make sure she looked stupid. In fact the YouTube hit has surpassed the eleven million hit mark. Not that eleven million have watched the clip, just like all marketing companies we hired an Indian firm to click through the clip that many times.

Arthur stood up, took the stage and was glorious in his speech on what he hoped the fund would achieve and had wonderful praise for all his compatriots that have joined the Round Table as Knights in a bid to join forces for the good of the world. The PM, well she tried to exit soon after all done and the Bulgarian pressman had one last question as to whether she intended to champion the Round Table herself as well and scrap her cancer research plans in favour of a bigger effort and on camera the witch agreed.

So all in all Reader, things going well: Arthur and team safe and all in order and I am here in Ghana photographing beautiful women whilst trying to sort out a mission for Marco.

Oh the mission, well seems that there is a man on the run for killing his wife that needs to be apprehended. He is facing the death penalty and I have suspicions that there is of course more to this than meets the eye.

I am sat on the banks of the River at Ada Foah, just west of Accra, with Stephanie the sun beats down. We sit drinking lemonade and eating sandwiches as we take a break from the shoot. Stephanie is one of the most beautiful women I have ever met. Only five foot five tall, with rich dark skin, and slim figure and a DD cup chest, there is just no angle to shoot her from that looks unflattering.

At first we did evening dresses in the sun with big hats. The bikinis with big hats, then in the river naked with big hats and now leaning against an old Palm Tree and then as she lay in an old canoe on the river naked I took my last photos as the sun set.

It has now been two months since Megstar passed away and I still feel her presence in the wind as it cools over my body. I think of her and as I close my eyes and smile see her face. It was at this moment sat on the riverbank after having packed up all the cameras that I closed my eyes and truly relaxed that Stephanie leaned in and kissed me. Her lips were so soft and her mouth parted slightly as she kissed me and I felt myself lean into her mouth and kiss her back.
For a second I lingered and neither of us pressed further just gently still kissing each other delicately and then slowly parted. I looked into her big brown eyes and smiled. I was relaxed, felt no guilt and realised Megstar was there with me always.

"I always wanted to kiss you, and surprised I did," said Stephanie. "It was nice. You are gentle and good man, I think we would be good lovers too."

"Why were you surprised you did kiss me?"

"Well surprised I could find you as have really bad eyesight and need glasses for most things," she laughed and I laughed too placing my arm around her and kissing her gently on the cheek.

"Come on, let's get in the car and drive back." As I said this I was confused as to what to do when we returned. I had an incredible urge to take Stephanie to bed and yet still I held back, still I was not sure because of Megstar.

The drive in the car as the sun setting was one of calm and tranquillity. Breath-taking views, Notting Hill Sound Machine on the iPad and Stephanie cuddled up under my right arm sleepily resting as I drive my automatic four-wheeled beast homeward.

I drop Stephanie off at her apartment where her friend meets us at the door. She smiles and a wave as Stephanie gets out. Stephanie turns and looks at me as if to say something, but seems to feel the moment has passed for anything more than the kiss we shared.

"Call me at the hotel if you fancy coming for something to eat tonight. If too tired I fully understand, but should have some of the pictures for us to look through."

Stephanie smiled and asked if she could call me in an hour as would have to deal with domestic duties first. I smiled and gave her my Ghanaian mobile number.

"I had a great time," she said.

"Me too," I replied and like a scene from a low budget American RomCom I drove off saying no more.

About an hour later my mobile signifies a text received. It was from unknown user. Well let's face it user, no one has the number so everyone is an unknown user. I open to see it is from Stephanie. Quite a long message saying in brief that she would meet me at the hotel in an hour. I say in brief that is what it said, but it was a long explicit message of how she would like to have rough sex with me and would knock on my room door in sixty minutes.

I text her back, room, cabana 16; a small bungalow on the edge of the hotel. As I pressed send I smiled then realised I had agreed to a night of passion and like some daft sixteen year old schoolboy fretted over what to wear. I saw my photo of Megstar by the bed and smiled. Stephanie had made me feel alive again and as I looked at Megstar mixed feelings awoke. I lay on the bed and closed my eyes and felt as if I heard Megstar say, 'live your life'. I smiled and her face came into my mind and next thing I know I heard a knock on the door of the cabana. It was Stephanie. I must of blacked out and rise to answer the door.

Stephanie looks at me standing there in my shorts and smiles. She looked amazing in a long black evening dress and with long sleeved silk gloves.

"May I come in?" she asked and of course as she entered I saw her smile at me and squeeze past me in the entrance that led into the main reception room.

As I closed the door I turned and could see Stephanie unzip her dress and it fell to the floor. She looked back at me as she stepped out of where it fell and placed it carefully on the armchair. As she walked to me she turned her back to me and I undid her bra and kissed her neck. She reached back to touch me and softly said, "You read my text."

Sat on the patio to the cabana that evening both Stephanie and I were ravenous. We had dressed and as I had a coca cola and she a glass of prosecco we called the hotel for a table for dinner.

Walking across the hotel gardens to the main reception it felt good to have Stephanie holding my arm, hugging tight affectionately. Making love had made me alive again and I was truly starting to feel more in tune to all around me.

Our table was perfect, sat across from the main pool area and the best spot for an amazing glow of the moon in the waters. We ate and laughed and finally Stephanie asked me, "Who is the beautiful woman in your picture?"

"Megstar, you would have loved her, and I think she would have loved you too."

"Would of," Stephanie asked, "I am sorry she has passed, yes?"

"Yes, she is now here." As I said this I touched my heart and a tear welled in Stephanie's eye.

Stephanie takes my hand and places it on her heart, "And now you are in my heart."

I kiss her gently on the lips and smile, "You will always be in mine," I said and the walk back to my cabana was so peaceful as we just strolled without saying another word.

20

As I woke this morning lying next to Stephanie I saw it was five am and slowly rise as not to disturb my beautiful companion. As I walk to the French windows I look at the skyline ahead and as if on cue the sun begins to rise. As I feel the warmth of the sun's rays I sense the presence of my perfect friend standing naked next to me. We both just stood there holding hands like Adam and Eve.

I felt the softness of her ebony skin against mine and felt moved to have shared such a beautiful moment. I know the sun rises everyday, but often Reader we never stop to see the marvel in its full glory. And I remember enjoying the sun rise elsewhere, in London or Devon or some phenomenal sun rises in the West Coast of Scotland. I believe Reader if we all just take a second to do nothing but watch the sun as it rises in all its glory. Forget everything about to happen, forget everything that has passed and experience the moment, the now and just realise how lucky we are because today we woke up.

Stephanie places her hand in mine and walks me back to bed where we lay entwined just feeling the touching of our skin and the beat of our hearts.

I look to see the clock by the bed show it is 7am and Stephanie rises to get dressed.

"I have a boxing show promotion I am doing for my Little Feets Charity. Call me if free tonight and thanks for wonderful time."

She kisses my cheek and exits.

I look around the room and open a file I have kept under the mattress. In it is my mission and of course I am sure Reader you are wondering what I am doing here.

Well a young lawyer is wanted for murder, he shot his wife and has been on the run ever since. It seems he is hiding here in Ghana. I have been sent to find him and bring him to justice, but also know that until he is bought to justice land he owns cannot be sold. A billion pound deal is in limbo until he is either produced dead or alive.

I have my usual Invisible Man radar saying that this is not as straight forward as all would of wanted. My mission is a forty-eight year old man, married for twenty years, no children, yet no sign of unrest. His business was in buying land to protect the tribes and people of Africa and acted as solicitor to protect their rights. One case he won for a group of local inhabitants of an area in Botswana made sure that those trying to mine the land had to pay fees to the people; so the people profit from companies having to respectfully and responsibly mine lands.

Something did not make sense and it seems the man's business partner after a short space of time suddenly tried to sell the land to a Chinese Businessman that was being organised via the family running Africa. The Mafia needed to find the body, and I say body, dead or alive in order for the land to be able to be sold. A legal loophole is that my hit had all the paperwork placed into his man before he disappeared. Why, and what did he know I have to discover.

Last seen in Kumasi I decide to travel posing as a geologist looking to find untapped minerals to help local farmers mine responsibly and looking at Land that I already own. Yes I bought a piece of land from a crooked official and know this will flag up the deal and my appearance to interest those in the area. From my research this guy I am looking for would not be able to not help the people. He is a man I feel who would risk his life to help another; so why did he kill his wife?

Driving northwest towards Konongo en-route to Kumasi I am expected to appear on behalf of Philippe to see the land I have acquired. It is an area rich in minerals to mine with possibly a huge Gold Mine sat right in the centre of the plot. A few hours pass and I realise I am here in the middle of nowhere. There is nothing here, except poverty and emptiness. I pass two tall young men struggling with large barrels of water. I stop, now I do not recommend you can just stop and trust everyone, but often a chance encounter can lead to a wonderful moment.

Both men look at me and they seem more nervous than I do. I get out of the car and ask if I can give them a lift. Both look and realise not everybody speaks English. So I decide to try charades and act out them placing water in the car boot and getting in the car and me driving them.

Then one starts to laugh, "You white people are so funny." Then both laugh and I laugh and in a moment we are driving to a small village about six miles away. Their names are Isaac and Abraham. They are brothers and their mother had seven children all named from the bible. I said that it was lucky they were not called Cain and Abel as brothers they may not of been so close. We laughed I learnt a lot and they told me of their fears for the village they come from as a new land owner may devastate the village from mining.

They knew of the rich deposits and were trying to find a loophole for the people to retain ownership, as it was state owned. They had to walk miles to a water pump the government installed so that although they were seen to be doing wonderful work, sadly it bought great hardship to the village. The brothers had returned as both had left to seek better jobs in the city and came back to try to protect their family and friends.

You see Reader I feel that the biggest problem in Africa is not the tribal warfare and fallouts, not the influence of foreign countries, but the fact that the greatest resource, the men and women that are educated leave their villages and there is no one to stay and help the village survive.

I was not in a hurry as Isaac took me around the village whilst Abraham filled the village homes with the water they had fetched.

Isaac told me of how the village was always a great source of farming and previous mining had left land barren. His mother was old and a few weeks ago men had appeared and sabotaged a well a few hundred miles outside the village. Then other problems arose and a fire in the school burnt out the clinic built in the nineties and soon things became difficult. His sister, Mary, managed to message

Abraham, he called Isaac and so here they are trying to find out what is going on.

It turns out the piece of land I bought is the land in question, but the piece of land that the Mafia wants surrounds the village and town nearby. Villagers have been made unwelcome by the local police in Konongo. No one knows why, but the brothers hoped to find out. I was on my way into town and offered them a lift.

As the boys said goodbye to their aging mother I saw the look in her eyes of fear that she may never see them again. I shook her hand and told her I would be back with her sons and that we would bring good news.

The town of Konongo is a strange town where the people are very colourful and whatever they have they share and it is another great example of a people who have little material wealth, yet are richer in community than the whole of the vacuous Chelsea set in their million pound homes back in the UK.

The brothers tried to see a friend who is a local magistrate and he agreed to meet us all on the edge of town in a disused lorry driver's café. It had been closed for years as no mining meant never any custom in the area.

Cautiously the Magistrate met the boys and hugged them. I stayed in the car out of sight. There was a feeling of real fear from this man and he was agitated and kept looking round as if he was being followed. He shook their hands and palmed off into their palms some money before rushing to his car crying. It was a weird experience to watch and off he drove.

The brothers returned and seemed perplexed, as they had no idea what was going on. I decided that possibly a trip to Kumasi was on the cards and I would reveal more to them in a place away from the village and prying eyes.

My mobile beeped as a text message from Stephanie came in. I open and it is a picture. Well the imagination was not needed to convey the message sent. I think I may need some vitamins if back before sunset. I text to say rushed to Kumasi and back very late, but would call.

In the car to Kumasi Abraham and Isaac seemed really worried.

"Listen lads, I think fate has bought us together. I need to check one thing then lunch on me, and a revelation where we might be able to help each other. Just sit tight and let's enjoy the scenery."

Both look quizzically at each other and then at me.

"So tell me, what line of work where you both in before returning?"

"I was a lawyer for a corporation and Abraham was a solicitor for a body protecting villages in areas of risk."
"Areas of risk?" I asked.

"Yes, many villages like ours sit on prime mining lands. The land is sold and the villagers either work like slaves in the mines or they are ejected from their homes. Isaac would often hear where corporations and his were looking and tip me off," said Abraham, "it was risky at times, but nobody knew we were brothers."

"So who could help you?" I asked.

"There was a lawyer in Accra who is on the run for murder," says Abraham who is interrupted by Isaac, "But he was innocent."

"Really?" I say, intrigued as I feel that again the life of coincidence is about to fall into my lap. "What was the man's name?"

"It was Ben Timbury. He was from Cambridge who settled in Ghana with his wife after setting up practice after winning major court battle for a group of villages in South Africa. We went to him and he moved up with his wife." Said Isaac.

"She was beautiful," said Abraham, "and there were many cases he was working on making sure illegally done deals were not passed unnoticed and then legitimised by paying off officials. Ours was one and we worked closely with his business partner who flew in from London."

"So what was the murder?" I enquired.

"His wife, but we think it was a set up. He is on the run."

I looked at Isaac and realised I had been sent to find their man.

"So what makes you think he was innocent?"

"After the trial where he was convicted of the murder of his wife the partner started to organise the selling of the land he was protecting to a corporation owned by a Chinese Mining Company called The Chenguang Foundation. It is named after the owner's only daughter and translated means..."

"Morning Glory." I reply.

"You speak Chinese?" asks Isaac.

"No," I say as I pull up in the car to a post-box mail centre, "I think our paths crossed for different reasons." I get out of the car, put on a peak cap covering my face, and enter the offices. I take out a key in my pocket and open the box number 16. My favourite number as well as had it years and in it is mail I have forwarded on by a friend in Pakistan. You see mail is sent to post boxes and people are paid lots of money to them send on the mail to another box as in the back of the box it can be opened so nobody knows mail has been taken. There is a package and in it a credit card with £250,000 credit on it. I exit and walk across the road to a government building and walk in. All the while my two new friends sit in the car and watch, a little confused, but they know the building I entered.
At the front desk I ask for a file, number PQR2D23CPU. A clerk fetches the file and I am given an account number. I take the file to the bank across the street. The file is empty. I enter the bank and with peak cap covering my face enter the manager's room. I deposit £150,000 into the account I was given and once exchanged the file is

filed with the deeds to the land I have bribed the corrupt official to sell to me. I then place the card in the machine and draw out the remaining £100,000 and another case is given to me with £95,000 in it. I look at the manager who smugly smiles and says, "Five thousand for the case."

"Not a problem, I am sure Philippe will be happy to visit you to return."

At this point I see the manager's face change and panic sets in. You see I know this routine so well as a few years back I, well Philippe, managed to wipe out a whole family, all killed and disappeared without any trace. In fact I just moved them all to South Africa, set up new identities and one runs a post-box office for me there. Suddenly from a drawer the manager produces the five thousand pounds he had taken. I take the money and look at him in the eye. Taking £1,000 from the cash I hand it to him.

"Philippe is a fair man and it is a nice case. I guess this is more than generous."

I exit leaving the manager frightened, but happy and exit to get in the car and drive off with the boys back to the village.

"What is going on?" asked Isaac.

"Who are you?" asked Abraham.

About a mile out of Kumasi I pulled over and stated that I work for a man coming to fix a situation. That this man would find a way to sort without violence the problems he has been sent to clean up. Both look at me a little scared as if they were in the car with a devil.

"My name is irrelevant. I saw that the partner of the man you think has been framed of his wife's murder trying to sell land, mining land, your village is sat in the middle of, to some very unsavoury customers. They would think nothing of wiping out your village if it were not for the fact that the deal came under the scrutiny of the United Nations as Partner trying to sell thought he was protecting himself. Now he did not realise that in doing so laws surfaced to show that the wanted man, your lawyer guy, owned the land. It cannot be sold or anything done with it until he is found to be dead or captured and hung for his crime. Sadly the partner had already done deal with Mafia who had sold on to Chinese company and suddenly this is a major embarrassment. So my guy sent to clean up and make sure all can happen legally in full view of anyone wanting to watch."

"Are you about to threaten us?" asked Isaac.

"Not at all, I feel fate has thrown us together. I am going to use you to secure the deal our wanted man wanted, but need to find out what he was planning."

"We can help," says Isaac.

"Shut up you stupid boy!" replied Abraham.

"Lads it is OK. I work for a man by the name of Philippe."

"Oh My God! We are all going to die!" says Isaac.

"Oh, I don't think so," I smiled, "Gentlemen this is going to be the start of a beautiful friendship."

"Casablanca," says Abraham.

"Casablanca," I reply, "Casablanca indeed." And with that we all drive off.

Now I still have told the boys hardly anything, but the fear of Philippe is enough to make them help without asking too much. I know they have contact with the lawyer and soon they would be the way to put into place my plan.

Now Reader I love the idea that I say I have a plan as this particular plan is just formulating in my head as I write. I know often my writing is not grammatically correct or set out in a normal manner, but this is a journal, my ramblings and recordings of events as they happen.

I made the transaction the card has been used and Marco knows Philippe is in Ghana. He now knows Kumasi so happy to be driving back to Accra, but the Mafia are everywhere and the family have more friends then even they can count. In no time we are back in Konongo and as the boys exit the car I get out and let them see the file.

"Lads, I am more involved than you realise. I need to know the lawyers plan, meet if possible, but also want to look into his case in Accra. That is where I will be for the next week. In this file are the deeds to your village, your town and homes sold via a dodgy politician and all legal. This means that at present the town is safe and the people. I want you to be seen to be helping the village and overseeing a new water well for the village as well as new generators for the town."

"But that will cost £20,000 and we have.."

"Sixty." I say as I interrupt Abraham and hand him the money. "We need prying eyes to see that you are here helping the village and that is all. Do not worry when this is over will find way to have you safe and protected even if the mine areas are sold. Tell anyone asking you are working for Leo Bloom."

"Who are you?" asked Isaac.

"His name is irrelevant, but we will call you Rick. Casablanca. We know where to get pumps and generators and will start to have people think this is all we do. I will also talk to a man that may be able to help." Abraham shook my hand, "If anyone asks, we are working for Mr. Bloom."

I looked at Abraham, "Tell that man you knew, that I will try to clear his name, but he may need to help."
I get in the car and drive off. It is a good four-hour drive back to the hotel on the outskirts of Accra and it was already late.

As I drive back I message Stephanie and tell her that I am sorry will not be back until very late and within seconds a message comes back saying she will go to a club with her friend promoting the fight and it ends at 2am so call when you get back and she will give me a bath.

There was a lot more description in the text about the bath and what amazed me is how she got my message and managed to text a small novel as a reply in no time at all. Do women go to speed texting classes and why is it my texting is so crap? I do not know about you reader, but it takes me ages to send one line text and even then spell correct changes what I am saying.

As I drive back I listen to David Bowie on the radio. Seems that man was a God everywhere. I love Bowie.

21

Back in Accra I drive into my hotel and park. I see the light on in my cabana and look to see if restaurant still open. I go to the restaurant and call the room. There is no answer. I call Stephanie who answers and is still partying and wonders if I can pick her up, she wants me to join the party, but in all honesty I am too tired. I tell her I will eat first and hang up.

Looking across the way I see that all seems quiet at the cabana, but feel a little food may bring the answers required. My mobile bleeps and as I walk to my table with the waitress I open it up. A picture from Stephanie taken in the ladies toilets I guess and was taken to entice me to go to her. If ever you need a convincing argument to win a case then this picture would solve most deliberations. I text back a picture of my food on table, a beautiful steak frites. Yes I waited before answering. Message below I wrote, 'Just let me eat this as it will help build up my stamina and be over for you, text address.'

Address text straight back and I fear I may need two steak frites for Stephanie.

Still pondering why my lights are on the manager comes to my table to ask if everything is going well with my stay. We chat and he is just signing off so ask him to join me. I ask about the light and he says that the maid went in each night to change towels and light left on, as you were not back. Seems nothing sinister so enjoyed the meal.

He was a local man and asked him about the mission I am on as to what he knew of the fugitive on the run. At first he was coy and then realised that I was curious and not police. Seems my mission was well liked and his 'friend' was also. Yes the plot thickens Reader.

Gist of the story is thus: man I am searching for was gay and was in love with another man whom his wife knew about as she was having an affair with a young man from a village not far away called Abraham. Stay with this Reader; do not get ahead of yourself, as although you have started right conclusion there is more. My hit was clever lawyer who bought a huge piece of land to protect the people where his wife's lover lived and his boyfriend was working on a highly sensitive program to help cure cancer. The wife liked black men and so did the husband.

Theory is that the partner of the hit was trying to expose them all and thus the hit was already in fear for his life, as homosexuality is not greatly received in Ghana or Nigeria where boyfriend came from, as you can be hanged for this as a crime. The partner fearing exposure would force the hit to sell, but he would not place the whole area, the villages at risk just to save him or his boyfriend. Realising that he was not going to secure the sale the partner, my hotel manager thought, framed the murder of his wife on the hit. Following as I got confused and still confused trying to write this all down for you now Reader.

Apparently this story came from a local prostitute that the partner frequently hired and whilst drunk told her in anger what he had done. She told the manager, who often helped her find clients at the hotel, and she has not been seen since. It seems the partner is also a gambler and needs money for debts to local mob.

Remember Reader how often coincidence comes about? Well my mission now is to tell Abraham I know who he is, find the hit and boyfriend, get them to safety, have the partner in the frame as murderer and get the gay boyfriend's friend to Arthur and have him work on his cancer theory.

I finished my steak and the manager walked me back to the cabana as I offered him the contents of the package picked up from post box earlier with credit card. It was a box of Cuban cigars. It seems Philippe was a huge cigar smoker, but often I used them to get information in exchange. Weird, but true. In the cabana all was as left and I set up my iCam and wondered why I had not earlier. As I left I decided to leave the light on in the bedroom window behind the curtain.

I get in the car and drive to Stephanie. Well the party was in full swing and so was Stephanie's best friend Ntombi. Actually from South Africa she was visiting friends and working on promotions with Stephanie. I could not of arrived at a more opportune moment. Stephanie was trying to get Ntombi safe from club promoter who wanted to show her his offices. As I entered Stephanie pulled Ntombi over to meet me. To which Ntombi, who was really drunk, looked me up and down and exclaimed, "You right bitch, I'd shag him."

As compliments go this is not a bad one. Stephanie looked at me and I motioned we should all leave. There was a moment when the club promoter came over with his heavies as if to say the girls stay until I say they can leave, but before they could say a word I jumped straight in.

"Hi, thanks for keeping the girls safe. Sadly both are in the last tests for Hepatitis B and really they should not be drinking. Highly contagious through sexual contact and a killer if not caught soon enough."

The heavies and the promoter jumped back away from the girls and looked at each other as if to say that they never touched them and soon we were asked to leave.

Stephanie laughed her head off and asked if Ntombi could stay as well as she lived miles away. Of course I agreed and all I remember, yes folks another blackout, is waking up with both girls naked in my bed with me.

Sadly to report, after Stephanie and I had got Ntombi undressed, well she stripped when she walked into the room, Stephanie kissed me, got naked, got into bed and both fell asleep. I got in and seems I passed out too. Stephanie remembered everything and Ntombi remembered nothing.

I took both girls to breakfast and then organised a taxi for Ntombi and Stephanie and I enjoyed lazing by the pool. I had to buy her a costume and for me too as cannot remember the last time I lazed by the pool. All was restful and serene until the manager from the night before greeted me. He seemed flustered and wanted a quiet word. Stephanie was recovering from her previous night so we wondered to the bar area.

It appeared that his friend the hooker's body has turned up in a field outside of town. He wanted to know if I was anything to do with government and could help get the police to look into her death. It seems the death of a local, especially a prostitute was no big deal or ever investigated by police. Only investigation they do is when paid to investigate. It was at this moment we were distracted by the sound of a group of men cheering loudly from the sports bar on the other side of the pool. England playing Moldavia and England had scored.

"It is him," said the manager, "he is killer."

I looked to see a sunburnt Englishman entertaining local officials and other British banker types and Americans.

"He the partner of good man," he continued and there it was in my lap the man I now feel is at the bottom of all this misery. I had seen him somewhere before and then it hit me. He was at the Houses of Parliament talking to Prime Minister, new Head of New Order that is, and met via a partner in Jeremy the painter's wife's firm. There were more connections than anyone could of believed, but I decided to say hello nevertheless. I told my new friend the manager to sit tight and I will see what I can do.

I walk over to the men and start to laugh with them and make fun of seventy minutes of play England have only just managed to score one goal against Moldavia. I introduce myself as Leo Bloom a tax accountant. I was interested to see who would Google me when I left and in fact after five minutes the American piped up, "Aren't you the accountant in the Producers played by Gene Wilder?"

I laughed and said that the fact people all think that makes me laugh. My new hit looked at him giving away I knew they were in some joint venture and laughed to say that was the funniest thing ever. I walked away and back to Stephanie. I knew they were watching so I made a hash of passing a waiter and spilt drinks all over myself and could hear them saying things like 'what a klutz' and 'accountants so boring'. I saw as I helped the waiter collect the bottle I knocked over and could see them return to their game.

What the hit and American did not realise was as I shook their hands I was wearing a really nice bit of kit given to me, once again at the financial expense of a Russian Agent, albeit unknowingly to him, a watch from Dimitri that can detect a phone at ten feet and Bluetooth a link so all calls are monitored and transferred to place wished. I had both men's mobile numbers and was able to click from this innocuous watch data to my monitoring system in the cabana.

As I lay on my stomach next to Stephanie she rose and asked if I would like some lotion on my back. I smiled and enjoyed her rubbing it into my neck and shoulders and then realised that all the men at the bar opposite would be able to see. She was stunning and this would only draw attention to me that may make me more visible than intended. At this point the manager comes by to ask how it went?

"What went?" asked Stephanie.

"Discretion, how did my discretion go," I replied looking at a very nervous manager. "My friend the gentleman is here with the American and I am sorry to say did not get his name for you as asked, but may be we can get the barman to find it."

The Manager looks at me confused then at the sports bar.

"Certainly, I will, thank you."

And with that the Manager rang the bar from the bar on our side of the pool. The barman answered and looked across confused. It appears that the Manager just said find out the American's name. The barman was far savvier and I enjoyed as he held his hand to the mouthpiece of the phone and called the American over. Having years of lip reading skills he handed the American a pen and piece of paper saying please write down the names of all the party that do not want to be disturbed. Seems a London and American office trying to find people. The American wrote both his name and that of my hit. I saw the barman mouth no worries make sure you have all calls screened at which moment the American showed his appreciation and gave the barman a hundred dollar bill. England score and again attention is all given to the game.

The barman then folds the note and hands it to a waitress who brings it to the Manager, who then in turn gives it to me. I look at the note and read the names, Sylvester Willis and my hit, Paul Rudd. I was now ready to work out how Philippe was to sort out this conundrum before it got any more complicated.

I decide time to become Invisible and ask Stephanie to excuse me and when she is finished at the pool to join me. She is still a little hung-over and orders a pineapple juice. I motion to the manager that everything was to be on my account. He smiles back in acknowledgement as I see Abraham at my Cabana Door. I note he looks vexed and as I walk up he sees me, and smiles.

As we enter the Cabana Abraham looks nervously around and I offer him a drink. We share a cold coke and I can see Abraham is uncomfortable.

"So you spoke to your friend then?" I say.

Abraham looks at me as if to say how did I know and then a look as if he thinks I was watching.

"No need to worry, I guessed that is why you are here."

"Yes, I managed to talk to Ben," this is the man on the runs name by the way Reader, and Abraham still seems nervous as he continues, "He is concerned that me has been tracked. He never killed his wife, he loved her, but he cannot use his alibi as that would only place others at risk."

Now I am intrigued and often reader it is best to never second-guess a situation. And for what was to proceed proved this better than ever before.

Abraham took a mouthful of coke and gathered himself to explain, "Ben is gay."

"What? How does that matter?"

"How does it matter? We are sat in Ghana where for being gay you can be imprisoned for three years without any defence. When I met Ben he was guarded, but happy and had a wife he loved. It was at an event and working late I saw that they were really close and over a drink too many his wife revealed that their marriage was a marriage of convenience. Nervously they wanted me to know as did not want any secrets, as we became colleagues. It was a few weeks later that I met Earl, the man who was helping Ben with local knowledge. They were more than work friends and in the months to come I realise that Earl was an accepted lover with Ben's wife and trying not to pry realised his wife was gay too; a real marriage of convenience. I was even thought of as her lover. We were working on the lands surrounding my family village when we found a loop hole to buy the land and scupper an aggressive land buy from Chinese. Suddenly his partner, Rudd, flew in and they argued over the deal and how we had to let this one deal go through, as there were other options to make on the deal. Ben was confused and after a massive stand up the partner would benefit millions if the land were sold. It seems an American in London had recruited him. They knew that if the land went to the Chinaman then other deals would come through in South Africa. Ben of course refused and for about a month it was pure hell here. Then one day when Ben was away with Earl he came home to find the police all over the house. Earl recognised one of the police inspectors, a nasty piece of work called Telcom. He was notorious for heading up gay enquiries and beating anyone suspected of being gay. They turned and ran. I got a call and found that the partner had found the wife murdered and no sign of Ben. Telcom is not an intelligent man and soon posted Ben wanted for murder. Knowing his alibi was he was gay meant he would have been convicted by case Telcom would of fabricated and fled to Ghana. Earl had friends there."

"So who killed the wife?" I asked and Abraham held his head in his hands.

"I have no idea and feel the partner was involved, but when investigated he had a strong alibi as at dinner with local magistrate. All Ben remembers is that there seemed to be an American guy orchestrating investigation with Telcom."

My mind went back to Willis met early enjoying the game at the bar with Rudd. I wondered if they were still there.

"Did you meet the partner?" I asked.

"Yes once, but Ben and him were in a heated argument and that was the only time, so I left them to it and had a drink with the wife in the kitchen who filled me in on the partner trying to get Ben to sell the land. I then found out Ben had used their own money to pose as an overseas buyer with the ministers selling land and managed to buy it. The partner realised that they would make even more money if they sold to the Chinese and was furious all owned by Ben and his wife and not their company."

"So he needed Ben and wife to sign over the land?"

"Yes." Abraham looked up to me as if it was his entire fault, I could see he felt as if he had let his friend down and how he is completely felt useless. I walked over to where Abraham sat and placed my hand on his shoulder.

"Would you recognise the American if you saw him again?" I asked.
Abraham looked at me and in a quizzical manner stated that he would so I asked him to come for a drink at the pool and would introduce him to Stephanie.

We crossed the gardens back to the pool and Stephanie was happily sunning herself and England still winning the football so everyone was still in place. I asked Abraham to sit with Stephanie and they chatted making their acquaintance as I went back to the bar across from the pool.

I watched Abraham watch me chatting to Stephanie as well as not letting on whom he was, just a friend of mine as introduced who met me on a photo-shoot. Stephanie was dazzling him with her beauty and I reached the sports bar I managed to tap Sylvester Willis on the shoulder to get to the bar. As he stepped back and smiled as I ordered drinks. Abraham knew immediately this was the American and I knew he recognised him and therefore there was more to this than Rudd was telling.

Walking back we enjoyed the drinks and we all walked back to the cabana. Stephanie walked in to have a shower and I walked Abraham to my car and handed him the keys.

"Take the car to your friend and tell him in a few days I will have more information. Best to use different car in case anyone is watching. Then return with the car tomorrow and we will talk. Also tell your friend I now own the land that your village sits on in the middle of the land he owns. Say no more and see you tomorrow. I must return and look after Stephanie as I am sure she is hungry." I turn and walk away as I hear Abraham drive off in my car.

In the cabana Stephanie is on her mobile to Ntombi and she seems to be comforting her. I pass by to say taking a shower and casually ask Stephanie to invite Ntombi to join us for something to eat. Stephanie smiles and giggles down the phone as I felt that this was something she was hoping to do.

Standing in the shower with the warm water crashing down over my body I try to encapsulate all going on around me. Ben was innocent, and gay. Rudd did a deal with American and he is possibly killer, but I still have to placate Marco and sorting out the sale, but what will they get if sold to the Chinese? All still confusing. As I stand with head under shower I hear the shower door open and feel the soft hand of Stephanie touch my back.

"Ntombi will be a couple of hours."

22

Sat at the table enjoying a wonderful meal with Ntombi and Stephanie I look to see the locals and guests watching me with envy. Now this will make you realise Reader I am now not invisible. The thought has occurred to me too. I smile at the manager who offers me a table by the pool for after dinner drinks. I happily accept and we exit to the wonderful warm night by the pool.

The pool is lit and the bars have twinkling fairy lights draped all over the rooftops. We were alone, but again this means we were more visible and I was happy to see a group of models from a TV fashion show join the bar to party quite loudly. All focus was on them.

Ntombi squeals with delight as she recognises a friend and she and Stephanie join them before Stephanie returns and falls into her chair next to me exhausted. She has done nothing all day, but the conversation and excitement the girls exude would wear out the fittest of partygoers.

All the girls are going to an event in a club owned by a friend of theirs called Nelson. Stephanie describes Nelson as a real character who helps lots of people in the community. I can see a twinkle in her eye as she recalls a madcap evening they had together at a fundraising fete where she was the girl that was dunked into the pool every time you hit the target next to her. It seemed not only was Nelson a great shot and dunked Stephanie more times than she cared to remember he donated five thousand pound for the privilege to make it up to her in his club later. Nelson was a complete gentleman, all the ladies chase him yet it seems no one seems to succeed. I think to myself in light of recent revelations that may be Nelson is gay too.

Ntombi returns and is more than a little excited. Unable to contain her excitement she bursts out a little scream, and then waves back at the girls by the bar.

"Sebe has introduced me to the director and I am in the show!"

"Ntombi that is amazing," says Stephanie as I see the cabana door a few down from mine open and out steps Willis. He shakes a Chinese Businessman's hand and then goes back inside.

At this moment I see my car return and driven by Abraham. I realise that Harvey is obviously closer to home than thought. As he gets out of the car I motion to him to join us. It is only now that I realise that Abraham is a really tall handsome young man and see Ntombi see him approach and look awkwardly at me and then lose her balance just as Abraham arrives and he catches her from falling.

"Abraham, welcome. In your arms is Ntombi who is now part of a televised fashion show, congratulations, and Stephanie you already know." I smile as Ntombi takes a double take as she learns Stephanie already met Abraham.

"Is that not the show at Nelson's club?" asks Abraham.

"You know Nelson?" asks Ntombi.

"I am a good friend of his brother," says Abraham.

"Oh," says Ntombi as if disappointed.

"Well we are all off to Nelson's, do you want to join us?" says Stephanie.

"We are?" I say to Stephanie. "Well are you in a rush as my cabana is two bedroom so you are more than welcome to stay and we can have a catch up chat?"

"Great sorted, Nelson will love to see you all since his brother disappeared." And with that Stephanie grabs Ntombi's hand and drags her off to the bar to the other girls. "You boys chat than at the club, no business, no men's talk, just dancing, laughing and enjoying life, OK?"

For some inexplicable reason both Abraham and I both simultaneously salute and say 'yes ma'am' and then look to each other and laugh.

"Your car keys and my friend would be happy to meet," and then notices the American leave the cabana. "Is he staying here?"

"Just seen that myself and yes, but he has no idea who either of us are. I am Leo Bloom and he thinks I am an accountant. It seems your Mr. Rudd used a local prostitute who then disappeared and washed up a few days ago dead. In the next few days you are going to have to trust me and I feel that by tomorrow I will have a plan to start sorting out this mess."

"You know Earl is Nelson's brother?"

"Sorry?" I said.

"Earl, who was Ben's boyfriend and also Nelson's brother. Ben who is on the run from his wife's murder, I thought you might of known."

"I am now going to need pen and paper as it seems this is a small world down here. We will talk tomorrow, but tonight we take a break and tomorrow I have another man to meet in Accra."

At the club we are having a ball, I am completely visible and all the models and actresses are having a great time as local press are there to take photos and yes you have it, I am in none of them. As soon as I saw one girl with long lens I managed to get him into VIP area and then helped him have set ups photographing the girls. The promoters were grateful too as I managed to get all the press in photographing the girls and not me.

Sat in a corner alone watching the party in full swing I am joined by Nelson. He is smiling, but as he has seen me with Abraham and is curious as he does not know who I am. I moved over on the settee sat at and he joins me. I watch Stephanie pose with Ntombi.

"She is a wonderful girl," he says.

"They both are," I reply and then see how he looks at Stephanie. This is a man in love.

"What are you doing in Accra?"

I looked at him and explained that I was a photographer and did a shoot with Stephanie and then met everyone, but Nelson is much wiser than his age.

"And Abraham? Have you been photographing him too?" he smiled and laughed.

"No, but he is a handsome man. I met him and his brother on the road and we found a mutual interest."

"You both like women?" he asked.

"Yes we both like women, but both interested in righting a wrong. Nelson I know your brother has disappeared, I know he went away with a man on the run and that man is more than his friend, he is also convicted in his absence of a crime I do not think he committed."

"Who are you, really?" he asked.

"Leo Bloom, and work for important people who sent me here to uncover what they thought was a problem to realise that the problem may be the cure to their ailments."

"So you are a friend? For the moment I guess you are, well nice to meet you Leo Bloom, but I warn you, I do not care who your important friends are as if they ever move against my brother I will not stop to make war on them. He is a great man, a wonderful heart and I miss him. I knew that his being... different was always going to bring about situations, but it was all contained, now I have no idea what to do next."

I looked at Nelson and smiled as Abraham joined us a little tipsy with Ntombi.

"Leo, you not joining the party?" he asked.

I smiled and Nelson answered, "No he has been getting to know me."

I raise my glass and look to Nelson, "A toast, to Earl."

Abraham and Nelson clink glasses and repeat 'To Earl' as Ntombi looks confused and drinks down the last of her champagne. Abraham looks at Ntombi and laughs and I see Stephanie looking at Nelson and me. Nelson is recharging Ntombi's glass.

Now Reader, especially women Reader's, let it be known men also have good intuition and can see that I have entered a situation that has been on-going for many years. I can see Stephanie realising if I tell Nelson that we have been sleeping together will ruin her relationship with Nelson and I also sense she looks a little disappointed and can see she is in love, or has been for a long time, with Nelson. Nelson and she I find have played out their friendship like Shakespearian lovers always battling wits afraid to relax and give in to the other. I see my photographer coming to the table to get a photo and of course move out the way as I take Stephanie's arm leading us to the table.

I feel a slight hesitation as she pulls a little back and I whisper in her ear, "Nelson knows nothing of our friendship and he never will, I know you are in love with him. Just you need to admit it to yourself." And with that sat Stephanie next to Nelson and confused she looks to me and then as Nelson puts his arm around her shoulder I wink at her and walk to the boys room. Later looking at the photographs with the photographer on his camera, ensuring I am not in any without him realising, but I see the one's later of Stephanie and Nelson and as they banter and verbally duel like Petruchio and Kate, I can see in their eyes a fire that means I happened along at the wrong moment. This is going to need diplomatic skills long left the British Government.

Ntombi and Abraham have moved onto a corner of the club and are in full chat up mode. They seem to of hit it off, and Ntombi seeing this handsome man was not gay as first thought as he did say he was a friend of Earl, is bowled over by Abraham who is a complete gentleman.

I see it is now 2am and everyone is worse for wear and Stephanie has not left Nelson's side. I am not annoyed, unhappy, pissed off, as I realise that she is with a man she truly loves. I am happy to stand back as however much I have feelings for her I realise that he loves her more.
Now Reader, many years ago I attended the marriage of a girl I would of married in a shot. We were together for a while and she met someone else and then left him for me and still was conflicted as to the other guy. I have always

stated I will never be second fiddle to anyone, never date someone who is seeing another and recognise that everyone has the right to say no; just as much I they should respect my right to say no also.

I was at the bar when Stephanie came up to me. A little tipsy, but stunning. She looked confused and unsure of herself. I smile and gave her a hug, more of a fatherly hug and she seemed upset.
"Listen, you were single as was I, I really have fallen for you, but you have had this unfinished business, this love for Nelson, who is a great man and feel he is also right for you if you'd let it develop. I feel that tonight, until you sort out how you feel about Nelson, we should remain great friends. Of course stay at mine tonight and have the bedroom and the fact others staying will see us not together and make the transition for you easier."

"Please, I feel awful," she says and I feel her trembling.

"You love him don't you, you always have so why the games?"

"I was scared as relationships never last in this environment."

"Well take it from me, this environment is only a small part of the world you live in. I will always be here for you and let's collect Abraham and Ntombi, work out who is coming back to the cabana and make our leave."

I see Nelson come over to me and sees Stephanie in my arms. He seems knocked back and forces a smile. Stephanie looks and notices and then looks at me.

"Nelson, we are all making a move shortly and promised to get this lot home. Seems you have been a true gent and made this young ladies night. Thank you and for your hospitality. Are you free tomorrow to meet?"

"Leo, it was nice meeting you, but tomorrow is the fashion TV show event so going to be busy. But we could meet late the day after."

"Great, then let me come by about three in the afternoon. I think I will have a plan to discuss I will need your assistance with. Got to find Earl."

"Give him my love."

"Oh before I go any chance the club can accommodate Little Feets Charity banners that may subliminally get on screen?"

Stephanie looks at me, and Nelson smiles and says, "I could do that."

"Well Stephanie can you get materials here and be free to work with this tomorrow?"

"I am sure, that would be amazing," Stephanie beamed.

"Great so that sorted and I will see you soon. Nelson, believe me I understand your brother's plight more than you realise. Lovely meeting you."

I shake Nelson's hand and Stephanie gives Nelson a big hug and kiss on the cheek then rushes off to the cloakroom to get her coat.

For a second Nelson and I stand alone and he looks to me and starts to say, "Are you...?"

"She is in love with you and if you don't act soon you'll kick yourself. I am happy yes." As I replied I turned and walked off.

You see Reader at the woman of my dream's wedding I was discussing before I saw the bride and groom dance their first dance. I took a photo and whenever I think of that photo I remember how looking through the lens at how she looked at him I realised that was what true love looked like. Later in the evening friends of the bride were all in amazement that I was there and the groom was becoming curious. His new wife had always talked of me throughout their courtship as her best friend and how she loved the things we did together.

Halfway through the evening a slightly drunk groom decided to come over to me to see how his wife and I met. I watched as all of the bride's friends gathered and giggled, some friends were jealous always and looked for a moment in this perfect wedding to be spoilt. I saw in the other corner of my eye the bride see what was going to happen rooted to the spot as her father-in-law boring her senseless could not move.

Confronted by a slightly troubled groom he asked me direct, which I respected and realised he was a good man, how I met his wife, what is the connection? As he was asking his beautiful bride comes and holds his arm.

In my stride, as any Invisible Man would, smiled and looked him straight in the eye, "Through Harvey." The groom looks to his stunning bride who also looks confused. "Well your wife was good friends with my boyfriend Harvey first and that is how we met."

His face suddenly dropped and he hugged me to say how great it was I was able to come and then did she. I whispered in her ear that his thinking I am gay will mean she never has a problem for your future happiness and I still love you and realise this is where you are meant to be. We hugged and I let her go. I suppose having to break my own heart and let her go was something I would always live to be proud of.

If you love someone let them go, if they come back they are yours forever; if they do not, then they were never yours at all.

I saw Stephanie rush off giggling and realised we had a moment I will always treasure, but her happiness is here with Nelson. Well for the moment, they just have to admit how much they like each other and remove the fear. Remember I always say 'Life is full of problems that do not exist'?

Back at the cabana Abraham offers his bed to Ntombi and says he will sleep on the couch. Stephanie looks to me and I laugh.

"Yes Stephanie you can have my bed as always, see you in the morning. Just need to grab the bathroom for two secs if OK?"

"So you two not doing it?" asked Ntombi.

"No we are not doing it, Ntombi. Stephanie was my muse and we have become very good friends, that is all."

"Boy did I get that wrong." Ntombi then looks at Abraham, "you're not gay are you?"

Shocked and almost falling over the settee Abraham looks as if to say 'What?' and I laugh.

"Come on Abraham are you gay?" I say playfully.

Abraham says, "No!" He then grabs Ntombi by the wrist and marches her into the bedroom.

"Night guys," says Ntombi grinning and the door shuts.

I turn to see a forlorn Stephanie and lift her face in my hands and kiss her gently, "We will always have the last few days and it is time you admitted to Nelson how much you really love him. Also I am off early tomorrow, but leave you a car to take you to club to help run the event for the club with Nelson."

The next morning I was up and gone before the rest woke and left a note for Stephanie. It read: 'Organised you to go to printer pick up banners for Little Feets and all paid for. Left you car to use and see you in few days as going away on business.'

23

It was noon as I looked from a hilltop at a farm in the distance below. You see Reader when I lent Abraham the car it had a tracker on board and therefore had the tracker take me to where he went and then suddenly below I saw him in broad daylight, Ben Timbury. An elegant man, smart, handsome, all you would expect from stereotypical gay man, but I watch from a far to see him greet another tall black young man who pulled up in an old American jeep. They embrace and I can make out smiles. Is this Earl? Then another strong athletic black man comes from the farmhouse. Is this Earl? Blimey Reader it seems Ben is a really popular guy. I see the man from the house look around and motion for the two others to go into the house quickly.

I have a plan hatching, but I need to know how best to implement and at this moment I have no idea what is going on, on any level. So Reader time to go say hello. I know these are the good guys, well I hope they are the good guys, but often as an Invisible you have to turn up and announce you are here. I slip back from my hilltop vantage point and jump into my car. I decide to drive down and meet my new friends.

What I did not expect to happen was what I write to you now Reader. Often we prejudge and assess a situation and nine times out of ten we get it wrong; well this was no exception.

As I pull up to the front door and stop the car the first handsome black man from before appears and stands on the porch.

"Can I help you mister?" he says.

"Yes I think you can, you're not earl are you?"

I watch as the young man twitches and tightens his fist. "No, not Earl, no Earl here."

"I know no Earl here," I reply calmly. "Earl is inside with Ben. Tell him a friend of Abraham and Isaac is here to share a cup of tea and sort out this mess."

A moment as we stand in a Mexican standoff then Ben appears. "You're from Philippe aren't you?"

I smile and look at Ben, "Yes I am, but trust me Philippe is on your side. Can I come in? Can I?"

Ben smiles and tells his friend to step aside. "Yes, please do. I am fed up with hiding."

Suddenly the other man arrives with a kitchen knife in his hand as I approach. Calmly I keep walking and look to the man, "You must be Earl, I met your brother, really great guy, misses you a lot. Hope the knife is for cooking as I am starving." I walk past them and into a modest little house. There is an array of computers on one table and an office set up in a room off the main room. I see that the conservatory area has been developed into some kind of lab.

"So, who's the chemistry set?" I ask.

"Please have a seat," says Ben. "Can I get you a drink?"

I look to see Earl and friend poised to pounce if I make one false move. I look at Earl and he still has the knife clenched in his hand.

"Earl, are you looking to cut some cheese to have with biscuits with the knife or what? I suggest you come inside, close the door and fetch a couple of cold soft drinks. We have a lot to talk about and there is much to do; sorry," I look to the second man, "and you are?"

The young man looks to Earl and then Ben. It seems no one can talk. Ben lets out a nervous gasp, "This is Joseph, he is, sorry, he has found a cure for cancer."

"Wow! Impressive. Have you been working on natural fruits as reading up on vitamin C has properties.."

"Yes," he replied curiously. "I have found that with the right dosage fused with vitamin B you can take as part of your normal intake and they seem to fight the cancer cells, not only that take the mixture on a daily basis, whether you have cancer or not, it will prevent cancer."

"Awesome work," I exclaim. "So what's the next step and how come you hiding out here with the boys on the run?" Joseph looks to Ben and then all to me.

"OK guys please have a seat. I will tell you who I am and what I propose and then you can tell me what you think and we can either go from there or not at all."

Ben sits on the sofa and motions for Earl to join him. Earl sits all manly and away from Ben as Joseph sits next to me on a rickety stool. For a few seconds we all wait as he balances as we all think the stool will break. I laugh and they all look at me and I move up the sofa I am sat on and pat the seat next to me for Joseph to sit on.

"Please sit, I won't bite, and by the way Earl I know you are gay and I know that you and Ben have more than a friendship. Basically I care not one jot your sexuality, but from what I hear I think I would like you both a lot, and I am sure once you hear my plan you may find I am not a bad guy either."

Joseph sits next to me, and Earl hands me the knife. I look and wonder for a second the meaning and then Ben laughs as Earl actually offers me some cheese. Well that was how we broke the ice, it seems we are all fans of cheese.

In the conversation I learn how Ben bought the land that he had found was to be used to mine by huge Chinese corporation.

Now Reader I am not going into detail of every word that was said but for your guidance thought just write in the gist of the situation. Actually also do as with so much going on need to paraphrase for journal as I cannot take it all in.

Well here goes, Chinese hear of mining lands up for grabs via grubby local interior minister. They send a man to meet, but Ben and Earl have a friend, Isaac, who heard of the meeting and realised it was the lands surrounding their village. Wanting to save the village Isaac had his brother, Abraham; persuade Ben to buy the land. In a very clever move He manages to go over the Interior Minister's head and buy direct from another corrupt minister by not only buying the land, but buying a house in Bruges where the Minister can house his prostitute over there when he is on diplomatic business.

So Ben owns the Land. But I inform them that I now own their village, so we own all the land. The joke is the Ministers would not give Abraham and Isaac or locals mining rights and there was a major shit storm at the President's house as he too was looking to make a profitable sale to the Chinese himself and now the Chinaman had arrived with nothing to sell him.

Suddenly. Ben's business partner, Paul Rudd, appears. He then with the subtly of a knee to the groin, brings up that he has an American friend working for a very important man in America who wants to buy land over Chinese and then sell on to another foreign body.

Now Reader, you remember my first mission in first journal where I exposed a corrupt American Businessman running for President? Well it seems even though he was exposed as the worst possible choice the people in the poorest parts of the country and the wealthy looking to get back to slave labour voted the racist in. I know hard to believe, but now he is the President of America. You really could not make this stuff up sometimes Reader, but the scary part is it is all true! So this new player in the mix is using American secret service now under his command and hence the introduction of Sylvester Willis.

Willis was sent to London, to meet Rudd, as misconception that his company with Ben owned land. Willis finds that Rudd knew nothing and both fly out to meet Ben. Ben knows nothing of Willis, as he does not go to meeting as at meeting posing, as servants were Isaac and Abraham. In the meeting Rudd got very heated, as he had promised the sale would go through and learnt that Ben and his wife owned the land jointly. Rudd stormed out furious and that was the last that was heard from him until the murder.

Ben told me that he loved his wife dearly and that she married him knowing he was gay as secretly she was too. They made a pact and it worked wonderfully for them. They even fell in love and thought of adopting, they were the strangest of life partners and if ever a child had the fortune to of been adopted by them then that child would have been the happiest kid alive.

On the night of the murder, Ben and Earl were in Nigeria. They had gone on a business trip, romantic break, as Ben was annoyed by Rudd. Rudd had then made himself highly visible at a casino and in town as they felt Willis went to the house to kill both Ben and his wife. Sadly Ben's wife was in and strangled. There were signs of someone running from the scene and it was thought to have been Ben. It was in fact a local prostitute who was found dead recently. Ben's wife was taking the time alone to indulge in a night with…. Well she was gay too. Ben knew the girl and in fact she was also friend of Earl's. I said that the manager at the hotel knew her and Ben said that she was in fact using her activities to hide her sexuality. In fact the clients she stayed with were gay friends of Ben's and thus hiding the fact that they were there with their boyfriends. It was a huge operation and that the girl actually never worked as a prostitute at all.

With Willis having only killed the wife this caused a major screw up. Ben was alive and had an alibi. But an alibi he could not use. You see Reader being gay carries a death penalty if not in the court then you will be murdered and no one cares in Africa in many parts of the country. Ben could not return until murder was found so went into hiding.

Willis, with a phone call from the new President to the then Ghanaian President had a swift trial and Ben was tried in his absence and found guilty of his wife's murder. But then that was a cock-up for our greedy Americans. You see the law states that the land cannot be relinquished until the person or persons that own the land have been quantified as dead or a period of ten years pass. The deal was dead for ten years event though the President tried to change the law it was seen as being coerced by outside forces and defeated in the parliament. What had happened was Ben had managed to pay enough corrupt officials believing that they would seriously benefit from the sale in the future. Corruption is a great thing Reader if used correctly.

So now Willis and team have to find Ben, produce a body, Rudd claim land as owned by their company as the company would after the passing of Ben and his wife, and then do, as they wanted in the first place, rip off the Chinaman.

This Reader is our ace in the hole.

I then outline that I will intervene in a sale to the Chinese company somehow and see if there can be more gained and possibly use clout to influence investigation that can clear Ben's name, safely. I actually had a plan and smiled as I could see another daft operation, so simple in it's complexity that it defied belief. You see when the answer is so far fetched Reader, often no one has a thought to challenge. They cannot comprehend it is true, but would feel stupid questioning something that means they do not have to work to bother dealing with again. Yes, laziness of the people in charge is key to many Invisible plans working.

To conclude Reader there is another elephant in the room that will be my key to access without anyone seeing what I am up to.

"Joseph, I think you should meet Sir John and he will introduce you to Arthur and we can start to make everything right in no time at all."

All three looked at each other and then quizzically at me.

"I am not sure we follow, but I feel that you are my only help. What can we do?" asked Ben.

"Well firstly, I want the keys to your house and you to sell it to me via Isaac. It can be sold to me via your wife's family, as I am sure we can find some legal precedence. I will have Arthur and his team stay there and will meet Joseph there. This can happen quickly and also I feel I would like you be ready to come out of a coma in a hospital in a village not too far away. Abraham will see that you are registered there the day before you left with Earl. The rest is down to me. Gentlemen, I think this is going to be another beautiful friendship and don't worry will see myself out."

With this Reader I stood and left. Inside I heard nothing come from the house, not a sound. The guys were speechless and then I saw Joseph exit and walk to me at the car as I started the engine.

"Here is a number to call me. We wait for your call. We trust you, but please note these are good men. I believe you too good man, so I wish you God's speed and all this nightmare end soon."

"Joseph, I want you to gather all your work for a presentation and have ready for next week. I am off to buy a house, and tell Ben he can buy it back for same price once all sorted."

I drove off back to the hotel feeling positive, charged and excited as a plan starts to come together.
Mind you meeting Abraham and enlightening him that I had used him was going to be a moment that may go south.

I am at my hotel, Abraham and Ntombi are by the pool like lovebirds and I wave. Abraham rises to greet me, but I gesture to stay put and walk into the hotel main reception.

There I see the smiling face of the manager and then see he is troubled.

"I am sorry my friend," I say, "I must apologise as I do not remember your name?"

"I am Mr. Shibambo, from South Africa originally."

"Your first name Mr. Shibambo?"

"Tony, you would never be able to say my tribal name, no disrespect, but everyone calls me Tony."

"Tony, wonderful to meet you and from now on I am Sir John, when I scratch my nose and Leo when I do not. Do you think we can chat in your office a second?"

Tony leads me into his office and when the door close I inform him of a plan I have to be two different people to two different groups at the same time and that I will use guises to bring down his friend, the prostitutes killers. He looks at me awkwardly as I told him I knew that she was gay and that her clients were also gay and that I knew he must have been in on the situation. I felt that he was scared of being found out as Tony, yes reader, Tony was also gay. In my travels most of the most intelligent, beautiful people in the world are actually gay.

In Istanbul I met a ruthless killer. He was sent by Marco to do the jobs Philippe would not touch, mainly as I knew as Philippe the people that they wanted killed were not worthy of saving. Fate had it one night in the old quarter of town that our paths crossed. There was a hit on him taken out by another family fraction to Marco and Marco needed information. I found Rudy, the killer in his room with one of the 'Lady-boys' from travelling show. Without a way to defend himself if you get my drift Reader I sat at the end of the bed and gave him the dossier on the people that had placed a contract out on him before giving Marco the heads up. When needed Rudy helps me out and is a true friend. Rudy managed in one night to clear the whole contents of the folder, those that ordered the hit and all bar one member of the family concerned so that they could tell Marco what had been done. Also the youngest member of that family spared was also gay and Rudy implemented a plan where I suggested that that young man be the head of the organisation and under Marco's wing be reinstated and work jointly together. Marco knew Philippe had done the hit with Rudy and all was a huge success.

I digress, but Reader never mistake being gay as a sign of weakness. On the contrary we are all born equal, except on the funny side being gay often means marrying someone you love, two incomes, one mortgage, fantastic sex and no children. Mind you cost of dogs and cats often exceed the costs of a child.

Tony was still incredibly uncomfortable with his newfound knowledge and scared he would get it wrong. I remember the look on his face as I turned to him and said as I left, "What is the worst that can happen if you fuck up? Eh? You fuck up, it happens and we adapt and I feel that no matter what happens you'll be fine. In the words of the great John Belushi, 'What can I say, you fucked up you trusted me!' Seriously, whatever happens it will be down to me and smile for we are going to get those bastards."

Tony stands and punches his clenched fist in the air with a big 'Yeah' and then composes himself as I exit and close the door.

As I stand in the reception chatting to another guest Tony comes out of his office and I scratch my nose.

"Morning Sir John," he says as he smiles passing me into the pool area outside.

I smile and follow him to greet Abraham and Ntombi. Ntombi looks outstanding. She is in an olive green bikini and looks every inch the super model she wants to be. Abraham stands and we walk to the cabana.

Inside I sit Abraham down and he smiles as Isaac appears from the bathroom.

"I saw the tracker on the back seat and felt you wanted me to see it so when you left yesterday Isaac followed, well he was at the house on the trees nearby. We know everything and to be honest you have inspired us to be more cunning than we thought possible."

I laughed at Abraham and sat with a cold coke.

"No ice?" asked Isaac.

"No, it is the water frozen and use bottled water to clean teeth. Been here a month and not had the shits." All three of us laugh and Isaac gets up to go to the bathroom again.

"May be I should lay off the ice," says Isaac and Abraham and I are in fits of laughter. "So Leo, what do we do next as Isaac almost bumped into the American at the bar?"

"Be seen, you have nothing to fear, he feels he has escaped and whilst feeling above the law as most American Secret Service operatives do, will make many mistakes. You two will draw him out for his final mistake."

"At last!" shouts Isaac as he emerges from the bathroom. "Gentlemen we have solid landings once again."

We all laugh and the door knocks it is Tony. Tony enters and tells me that the American has new friends arrived and taken another cabana, he then nods, and exits. More CIA.

"Boys to the poolside and feel you should play in the pool with Ntombi. That girl is seriously sexy and will draw loads of attention. Time that you are seen. Oh and next to that girl everyone's heads will turn, just make sure you are seen too."

"What you doing Leo?" asked Isaac.

"Two things, buying a house and inviting the ex-PM to come meet Joseph. Actually three things, Isaac, you need a young lady to come to dinner with."

"Actually Ntombi has a friend that is looking to join us later. Seems this hotel and cabana is the highlight of the models weeks so far."

"Well Abraham, let us throw a huge party and ask Ntombi to help arrange with Stephanie and get Nelson involved too. I am off to see Tony to invite all guests staying here and make Ntombi feel you guys are throwing not me, I'll pay boys no worries, just need you to be seen happy, living life and let the Americans see you as no future threat. You are going to meet face to face with Willis and make him feel you do not even remember meeting him before. Sorry, Isaac need you with me with Tony as need you to sell me house. Come on we have a party to throw this weekend and have top-level guests there as well who will add to your safety. Come on Isaac, hurry up, There is a toilet in reception by Tony's office, you'll be safe with me."

Abraham laughs and Isaac grimaces at being the butt of the joke. Abraham jumps up and looks like the cat that just got the cream. He even rushes past Isaac and me to the pool to Ntombi.

Isaac looks at me, and laughs, "He has been without a woman for too long. I am so happy to see him like this. Leo, we are going to be able to save Ben and Earl aren't we?"
"I bloody hope so, this is costing me a fortune so far."

I place my arm around Isaac's shoulder and laugh as we enter the hotel and there in the foyer is Willis with his new guests. Willis does a double take and Isaac looks straight at him.

"Hello, sorry you look like we've met before?" says Isaac.

"No, no not at all, but you look familiar," says Willis.

"Don't worry my friend, you are in Ghana, we all look the same to you guys." Isaac laughs as do I and then the other CIA guys laugh and finally Willis does and shakes Isaac's Hand.

"Hey guys, you here for the weekend?" asks Isaac, "Just my brother and I are looking to throw a huge party here and you must all come. Lots of models and drinks and dancing and... well you can sort your own entertainment out from there on." Isaac gives out a huge laugh and Tony exits his office.

"Ah, Tony," I call to Tony, "can we have a moment of your time?"

"Certainly, step into my office Leo, and gentlemen my receptionist has one of the conference offices set up for your use during your stay. This way gentlemen," and Tony guides us into his office.

"How was that?" asks Isaac, "Always wanted to be an actor, played a mean Stanley Kowalski last year in our amateur dramatics society, got great reviews."

'I can believe it," I replied and we sit down to arrange the party with Tony and also I call Dimitri from Tony's office to see if he can get me intel on the American guests and possibly have him transfer fund from their accounts to the Russian's account and then to the hotel to pay for an elaborate party. Tony sits listening totally enthralled, but truly no idea it seems half of what is going on.

Ten minutes later we are at the pool with Abraham and Isaac whispers in his ear and he laughs as he calls Ntombi from the bar with the drinks in hand.

"Ntombi, listen call everyone, money no object, as you and Stephany have a limitless pot to throw the party of the century. Also we will need top security, as top people will be attending. Actually we will sort security, but we will need guest list."

Ntombi is hugging Abraham and squealing with delight as Isaac looks to me and says, "I think she is happy."

24

Party preparations are in hand, well in full swing. Ntombi and Stephany have amassed two hundred and forty guests and Nelson has been helping fit a stage and sound systems. All the guests, including our friends in CIA have gratefully accepted the invitation, and Tony is happy, as the newly elected President has accepted an offer to attend. When the official reply came Tony had to sit in his office for an hour staring at the wall as he was so overwhelmed. There is also another major player coming tonight. Have you guessed it Reader? I hear you shouting 'of course you said earlier', but just checking.

Two days have passed and amazing what can be achieved in Africa. I have managed to exchange deeds of Ben's house and getting it ready as tomorrow Arthur and crew arrive. The house is truly a palatial home. Lavish and with so many truly tasteful items; I bought the house and all contents. Ben and his wife had exquisite taste. While sat in the impressive sixty foot by forty-foot reception room I felt a bit like the Godfather sat in a room defining the trappings that go with his world. Then it struck me I needed to deal with Marco. Marco, Marco, Marco, I thought, you are constant in my mind. I also thought about calling Rudy and seeing if he wanted to work security. I wanted the CIA watched and in searching the house for bugs I found only a staff toilet by the pool house did not have one. The CIA and Willis had this place seriously monitored. I had all bugs left active and at the click of a switch all they would hear was static, break up of signal and then a sudden burst of audible voice saying 'so that's agreed then?' Just to wind them up. Of course on the night stage a fake power cut and let all-important guests know. All was being to take shape and then Isaac appears looking distressed.

"What's up?"

"It's the Chinese, they are here. Meeting Willis in an hour; Tony intercepted a call."

The game was a foot Reader and I was suddenly getting really excited. I smiled at Isaac. He looked around the house nervously and then sat on the sofa by the fire.

"Tonight I want Ben and Earl to come and stay in the top room. I have made it all up myself, enjoy a bit of domesticity as it keeps me relaxed. I have fitted it so that they will be totally self-sufficient and can relax as if on holiday. I feel we need to meet the Chinese and I have just the man to introduce us. It is good to be scared Isaac, keeps you alert. The night before the party we will have a drinks event here for Joseph and I have a little bit of fun that will spice up the party Saturday. Nothing to worry about, seriously, how is Abraham?"

"Working closely with Ntombi. Seems Nelson and Stephany are an item too. What did happen as Nelson seems to think you are gay?"

I laughed and grabbed my car keys, "Come on Isaac, let's go to the hotel and see how everyone is doing. Stephany and I were just model and photographer, nothing more, but it does not hurt for Nelson to think I am gay to avert his thoughts from me to her and it seems to be working. They are happy together. You got a woman for the weekend?"

"No, er, no I am..."

"Gay?"

"CHRIST NO!," exclaimed Isaac and then suddenly did the knee jerk reaction most men go through, "but I have nothing against gay people, I have many gay friends.."

"Of course you have," I replied laughing and exited. Isaac followed and then caught him laughing behind my back as he realised the joke and we headed off to the hotel.

Driving passed the main hotel on the high street I saw the Chinese entourage, and a very pretty young girl with her father opening the door for her. This was the mission, well part of it, the girl was the daughter, her name was Chenguang, yes this was a day full of Morning Glory, as I saw how we can win by having her join our cause. They were off to the President, but stopped to shop first. This gave me time to sort, well Reader you'll find out later as loving this.

As we reach the hotel Isaac says he will take the car and get the others. I hand him the house keys and walk into the cabana. Music is playing and I hear a laugh come from the spare room. The door opens and a naked Abraham appears.

"Oh Jesus Christ, you're back, I mean Hi, sorry one second...."

I grab the towel robe, my towel robe from the sofa and hand it to Abraham. And just as he covers himself up a stunning Ntombi appears, "You coming back to bed?..." Oh hi Leo? You back then?"

"Yes just to make sure CIA do not know I am at house bought, I mean, yes back. WOW! Sorry run out of robes so may be..."

Ntombi is totally at ease naked, "Oh sorry I will get dressed."

"No, I just wanted my laptop under my bed and I'll be off to the pool. Anyway you two have lots of things to sort I do not need to be present for."

Ntombi goes back to the room, "OK, see you later by the pool."

Abraham is still at a loss not knowing what to do.

"For God sake Abraham, you should be enjoying life and the next hour you should be in that room enjoying it, so go, before I take your place if you're not interested. Go on see you at the pool whenever you are free...or able to stand," I laugh as I exit to my room and retrieve laptop and then exit to the pool.

But before I go I see Abraham still standing frozen. "What's up? Listen you have done so much for so many people I find out and yet you have never had something for yourself. Ntombi is not a player, she really likes you, and you like her. So why look so guilty. We spend half our lives running from adventure and often lovers as we feel we are not good enough to get better than which we opt for. You two fit like a glove and as the next Ghanaian Ambassador for Overseas Development you need a beautiful wife to escort you on business and woo the diplomats into coming to all your events."

Abraham suddenly looks up and says, "Ghanaian Ambassador? Really Leo?"

"Yes, really, all part of new plan. I like the fact that you never questioned that was your future wife waiting for you in the bed." I laugh as I go to the door. "And by the way at the meeting I am Sir John, OK?"

"I have no idea who you are, I can't keep up, but I do know you are my guardian angel of sorts. I believe in you Sir John and have gratitude you believe in me."

"Abraham, I am just the invisible stranger that gets forgotten once all settles."

And with that I left the room. I did not see Abraham again for about three hours, and when he did emerge he looked like he needed to go back to bed. Ntombi was perfect wife material; beautiful, intelligent, funny and unafraid to show her true feelings. Reader, it is so much better to be hurt than to live in uncertainty.

25

It was Thursday and the weekend party was drawing attention as Arthur and his wife flew into Accra. The locals felt that the house had been bought by a company that houses top officials and of course with Arthur was Guinevere. She was an older version of Ntombi I said to Abraham as he and Isaac greeted them with Nelson and Stephanie and Ntombi of course. They all looked amazing.

Behind Arthur I could see the team. Arm in arm like powerhouses strode Quetty and Robert, Chastity and Henry, but before I could relax and smile there was the Leader for the Oppositions wife, Elaine of Corbenic. She was on her own and without prompting Ntombi rushes to greet her. I smile as does 'Elaine' and then looks to me. I walk to her and smile.

"Welcome, I see you have met Ntombi, and can I say how radiant you look?"

"Sir John, ever the charmer and my husband did some research on you and found nothing. I think he likes you even more." And with this she laughs uncontrollably.

"Well I am Ntombi, and will be assisting you in the event planned for Saturday."

"I think you are too gracious young lady, I am here to assist you and call me.."

"Elaine," I say. "We all use our Round Table Names. "Is Sir Lancelot joining us later?"

"Yes, and he loved that as well. I have never seen him smile as much as he has since you appeared. Will I ever find out who you really are?"

"I will always be Sir John for you and I am unimportant, I am just one of the Invisible Men and Women that watch over and look out for the folks that are worth watching."

"The Invisible Man. Sir Lancelot calls you that." And with that Ntombi takes Elaine's arm and they walk through a stream of photographers to meet cars after customs ignored. There to my amazement was the new President and it seems Isaac is better equipped than I thought. I exit via the baggage area claiming to be security watching over delegates' bags and see a co-pilot exit in front of me using the same route. He stops takes off his hat turns, removes his glasses and standing there, smiling, and holding a bunch of flowers is Jimmy.

"Flowers? You shouldn't of."

"I didn't," says Jimmy as he hands them to one of the luggage girls, "used to hide face coming off plane. So let's have a drink you and me and catch up as I actually have sneaked in to report to you."

And with this Jimmy picks up his luggage and we both exit watching the paparazzi getting all the shots of Arthur and Knights with New President. Just the sort of moment an Invisible Man can use to disappear, although one person saw us and gave me a smile as she stood at the end of the group photo, Elaine.

Sat at the back of a café close to the airport Jimmy returns to our table with two teas. "Saw the coffee given to guy in front and felt we'd be safer with the tea. You've got green tea, last bag, and I have honey and ginger with fresh squeezed lemon as have a cold trying to avoid."

"So how is Venice?"

"Girls are doing really well and Marco came and stayed for a week and hired whole hotel with all his friends. He was incredibly generous and gave the girls a big hug and then introduced his wife to them. Mind you he was a little pissed on the third night and introduced another woman as his wife and then threw caution to the wind and attempted to introduce another woman as his wife. Each flew in for a days shopping and one night stay. I feel Marco may be a polygamous soul and has wives in every port. Any way he was interested also in Ghana as a minister came to sell him some land that had already been sold. I guess you knew about this, but seems the wrong piece of land had been bought and the land he wanted not available. Minister he met ended up leaving and seemed truly worried. Then a call from States as someone from new White House on Marco's back. I get the impression Marco is being blackmailed. Then I intercept a call to the Knights, as the PM wants to meet Arthur and sounds really pissed. Arthur was brilliant by the way and even though I briefed him a little he knew what to know nothing about. Then you call with this new plan and it is in Ghana, so, I thought may be I better come cover your arse as there may be things happening you are not aware of."

"Well I always love seeing you Jimmy and yes a few things for you. CIA operative killed landowner's wife then pinned murder on husband who was one they were meant to kill. Husband has alibi that cannot be used as gay; we are in Africa and still backward about whole gay rights. Then the business partner of the hit finds out that their joint company does not own land as thought to sell to American as deeds still with husband and cannot be sold until he is dead or convicted and ten years pass, law or something, but the detail is in who was acquiring land for American and which American? Seems Marco was being blackmailed to buy land and sell at loss to a company in States, secretly owned by corrupt new President, the bozo we hoped we had bought down a year ago, and so Philippe hired to sort and so there we have situation."

Jimmy looks at me, and smiles, "Without being too presumptive, has Philippe a plan then?"

"Oh yes, and it is a doozie."

"A doozie, who says a doozie?" laughs Jimmy.

"Well Philippe does and no one wants to piss Philippe off do they? Listen Marco will also be at party and at meeting tomorrow night but got to get Chinese daughter to meet Joseph."

"Who is Joseph?"

"I will tell you on the way to the house, best we all meet in person and have car waiting for us."

"For us? You knew I was coming?" says Jimmy grinning.

"The spare seat in cockpit given to pilot called Casey Jones, come on Jimmy even I laughed at that one."
Jimmy smiles.

"Come on Jones more in the car," I said as Jimmy follows and we pass a crowd listening to new President still thanking Arthur for visiting. The Royals are not even use to this kind of welcome.

As we get in the car Jimmy looks in at me, "We also have more trouble with the New Order as it seems they also are part of this American cock up."

"Let's get to the house, get settled, get the team together and then deal with plan," I say as Jimmy looks to me, and smiles.

"So you have a plan? A real plan or is it more of an idea we are playing out?"

"Let's enjoy the drive, the sun is getting up and Sir John is not a fan of the heat. Come on Casey Jones we need to get steaming and a rolling," I say and Jimmy gets in car and we speed off.

In the car I see arriving also and getting into their limo Chenguang, she is beautiful and has a lovely olive skin, flawless style and perfect bone structure. I say this as realise that she is part Chinese I feel. Then I see looking annoyed ordering the luggage man and driver around her father. I recognised his face.

I noted to Jimmy who they were and he like me nodded and then in a whispered voice said it, "Seoul."

Yes we had crossed paths before and Jimmy in Seoul and me in Budapest. Both incidents were trying to prevent atrocities, and both we failed. You see Reader not all missions go to plan.

Chenguang Foundation was set up his company in his daughter's name and reportedly is involved in lots of good causes. Often the good causes are in areas or countries he is about to create huge devastation and unrest.

In Seoul he had a whole family, he was trying at first unsuccessfully to buy out their company, disappearing and signing contracts to sell from a base in North Korea. The family were staunch adversaries of North Korea and feared for their lives so would sign anything to escape. They were never seen again. In Budapest he tortured a Romanian family and a Cypriot Family in a barn outside the city. His goal was to buy the land on the sea front of Paphos that they had done a deal on. I was in Budapest getting them out to safety, but somehow he managed to get the land, part of it for his hotels, and the families disappeared. This is a man who was trying to buy the land to mine for the copper and if you know anything about China at the moment they are buying all the world copper reserves.

I discussed how the deal to buy the land Ben and I owed had slipped out of his grasp and then he is in town as he is meeting new President to get it no matter what. Jimmy looked even more concerned, but I smiled and laughed,

"Don't be so glum buddy, you know this never is easy and we will be fine….. I am sure of it…. Not buying it?" Jimmy sat motionless.

I took one last look at the beautiful daughter Chenguang and wound my window down so she could see me smile. She had loads of shopping and father looking at his watch then smiling.

"You know you can be a real dick sometimes? Chenguang! Christ I can hardly pronounce it let alone spell it! Mind you she is gorgeous." And with that Jimmy smiled and we laughed. "I think I have an idea," concluded Jimmy and he started playing on his mobile.

"Is it a good plan?" I asked.

"Who knows, can't get bloody internet signal. I am not going to like this mission."

We pulled up to the house and jumped out. There was Caitlyn my new PA from Knights of the Round Table who was in charge of Arthur and gang. She flew on ahead and looked concerned.

"Hi, Caitlyn this is my friend."

Caitlyn held out her hand and smiled. "If you are Jimmy then Arthur is going to be happy to see you. He talks of you and Sir John in stories of how the Knights were set up."

"He does, does he?" said Jimmy and raised an eyebrow at me.

We walk into the house and Caitlyn stops and then attempts to say something, then stops.

"Come on Caitlyn, what's up?" I ask.

"Well I am not sure, but I think there is someone else in the house."

"There is and soon it is going to be packed. Tonight we have a fun high level drinks do here and you are going to be the hostess with the mostess." Caitlyn looked at me even more confused as I said this and I don't know why Reader, But I gave her a hug. She looked kind of awkward as a parliamentary bod soon part of be seen and not heard brigade. Jimmy walks over and smiles, as there is an awkward silence. Jimmy hugs Caitlyn still frozen to the spot and kisses her on the lips.

"It is a pleasure to meet you Caitlyn and now we have all met have you a room Sir John and I can have?"

Caitlyn blushes and smiles at Jimmy. She is smitten, seems he is Prince Charming and she was Aurora, Sleeping Beauty for those not huge Disney fans like me.

Again a moment of silence and I grab Jimmy's case. "This way Prince Charming I have a room for you. He's in the East wing."

Jimmy and I walk off and Caitlyn waves. It was surreal then she shouts, "I'll make you some tea Jimmy."

Grinning Jimmy looks at me, "Hear that, she is making me tea, you're getting sod all."

I laugh and look to Jimmy, "The start of a beautiful friendship and just as well as gave her the room adjoining yours..... in case you need to make an exit of course."

"I fear if I enter her room it'll be a month before I return. I think I like this mission after all, but have a lady back in Venice now."

"Intrigue," I say and we walk smiling.

As we settle, I have Ben and Earl in the East Wing secret apartment. Jimmy, Caitlyn, and me in the East Wing next to the secret apartment. When Arthur arrives he and his wife have the master suite, Lady Elaine the main guest suite, when I say suite Reader I mean this house is huge, a real mansion. I have two suites in the West Wing for Chastity, Robert, Quetty and Henry to share, not necessarily in that order, and then I have rooms for the Chenguang family, two floors as their booking at the hotel is about to go tits up and I need to make a move on to get there to save the day. Joseph will be in the rooms next to theirs.

As I leave Arthur arrives. As does Isaac, Abraham, Ntombi, Stephanie with Nelson and all descend together. Caitlyn looks overwhelmed. As we all stand in the grand front entrance I hand Caitlyn her list and Jimmy appears.

"OK everyone, lots still to do for tomorrow, but tonight Caitlyn here is throwing a drinks party." Of course Caitlyn looks to me in shock and then at Arthur as if to say she is innocent of whatever I am suggesting.

"Don't worry Caitlyn, we will all help you. Ah, Jimmy how are you?" says Arthur.

"Ntombi and Stephanie please introduce yourselves and I will be back in an hour maximum as got to collect last guests, Arthur we will be entertaining the Chenguang Foundation as well." Jimmy's face as he hears this is priceless. "Oh and Arthur can you and your wife invite the President to join us?" With this I exit as Chastity, Henry, Robert and Quetty arrive. I see Quetty look to Jimmy and hug him as they watch me drive off.

"What's Sir John up to?" she asks.

"No flipping idea," replies Jimmy, "Caitlyn shall we get everyone settled?"

"Great idea," says Guinevere and all enter the house.

I am driving fast to the hotel where my cock up for the Chenguang Foundation is about to happen. I pull up to see the family enter and with all their security. The old man himself is already flustered and hates the heat. His daughter reprimands him and he smiles, he is putty in her hands. She has no idea of the kind of businessman he is, or how ruthless and murderous his past and present are. I thought he was the main suspect to the murder of Ben and his wife, but it seems it was Willis, the American.

I pull up in my car and a valet parks it for me. Entering in the reception I can see it has all just kicked off. The old man is incandescent. If he could pull out a gun and shoot the receptionist and manager there and then he would of. I managed to switch part of the Saudi Royal Family into his rooms, as they will be coming to the party. The opportunity to have his goons go to his pre-arranged suite, kill the occupants or just throw them out is now not an option. I make my move.

I see Chenguang, who smiles embarrassed at me, and then does a double take as she remembers me from the airport. Deliberate Reader.

"Hello Miss how strange to see such beauty twice in one day."

The Old Man turns furious and looks at me then his daughter, "Who are you?"

"Oh hello sir, my name is Sir John. I am here to see my friends in the Presidential Suite."

"That is my suite!" he shouts.

"I am sorry sir I don't follow?"

"I book and now they loose booking."

"Well let me and the Knights come to your rescue," I say and the old man looks at me even angrier than before, "I am hosting the ex-Prime Minister of Great Britain as well as holding a drinks party for the President tonight and have a whole floor we would happily give to you for your disposal. Come join us we are all family and be more fun as tomorrow night we have a huge party as well."

"Knights, who bloody Knights?" He asks still unable to calm.

"Why the Knights of the Round Table, finding a cure for cancer."

At this moment Chenguang steps forward and places her hand on her father's arm, "Daddy, please be calm. This has been a dreadful error and no one is to blame. Is there room for all of us we have five security as well? Well their rooms are gone too it seems."

"Yes there are eight rooms available so a suite for you sir, a suite for you young lady, and gentlemen rooms for you too. And a lot of people your age also miss to enjoy meeting. Listen let me have the manager arrange to bring the limo out front, load up the luggage, you can come see the house and rooms and if no good for you then no harm done, but as an Englishman I could not see you in distress."

"Thank you sir, that is very kind of you. We would be extremely grateful. Daddy, as Mummy would say, another adventure."

The old man mellows and a tear is in his eye, "My late wife was the same, I loose it, she grabbed my arm, calmed me down and whatever trouble befell us would say that this was nothing more than a great adventure. I should be honoured sir and like to know more as think saw press on your Knights. We lost my wife to cancer three years ago."

"Without another word shall I take two of your security team to come with me and we will give the driver of the limo the address to follow on. They can then check out security and that you will be safe?"

"You are indeed a Knight Sir John, it was Sir John was it not?"

I shook the old man's hand, "Yes sir."

"My name is Aiguo and this is my daughter Chenguang."

"Morning Glory and Patriotic, love country, am I close?"

"You are a truly interesting man Sir John indeed you are more than close."

"Well I shall see you at the house sir, Aiguo. And I will have the ladies of the house ready to greet you as well Chenguang."

With this turn and exit with two security guards. They are huge and laugh to myself as one of them takes up the whole backseat and the other fills the passenger seat. The journey to the house is made in complete silence. They do not say a word. As I drive into the forecourt Caitlyn arrives.

"Sir John you are back, and is this…?"

"Hello Caitlyn these gentlemen will be looking at the rooms marked free on your list if you would be so good to show them around. Gentlemen please follow Caitlyn." The two follow Caitlyn and I realise they speak excellent English as they listen to Caitlyn gibber on about lovely to meet them. Quetty appears in a bathing costume and waves as she passes then rushes to hug me. One guard almost trips over the other and they straighten themselves and disappear.

Almost jumping on me squealing with delight, "This place is amazing and we met Joseph, Jimmy introduced us and his work is outstanding."

Quetty looked amazing and it was one of those Woody Allen moments where I wasn't sure whether to sing to her, write her a poem or jump on her. She really is stunning and a body to die for. I see Robert appear in the entrance.

"Oh hello Sir John, we were just going for a swim, have you seen the pool it is amazing. Sorry just trying to get over the jetlag, you know swim to freshen up and..."

"I will see you all out there in a moment go enjoy life."

I watch Quetty run back to Robert and watch her phenomenal figure then wave at Robert, oh Robert you lucky bastard. Right, I thought, time to chat to Jimmy.

In the kitchen Jimmy and I discuss my ever evolving plan and he has some info he has found and together we formulate the next two days events as we would like them to unfold. In true Sherlock mode we laugh and Jimmy says out loud 'The Games Afoot'. At this moment Arthur arrives with Caitlyn.

"Guys, this place is amazing and Caitlyn said you were back Sir John, so thought I would catch up on what exactly is going on."

"Caitlyn, How are our Chinese guests?"

"Oh they have just called their boss and they are all on their way, Sir John."

"Now Caitlyn, you are newest member of the team so want you to be visible throughout all events. You are to make sure that Guinevere and Elaine are always looked after, make sure that main players outlined in file will give you later are bought together and please, please, please, relax and enjoy yourself. Jimmy did you..?"

"Yes I did and did surveillance while you were gone. Caitlyn you have not packed a swimming costume or any party dresses apart from one use for all occasions' dresses. Now Guinevere and Elaine.."

"That's my wife and the leader of the oppo... sorry just Caitlyn is not used to you two yet, don't worry Caitlyn I haven't a clue either. Sorry carry on Jimmy."

"Thank you Arthur." In walk Guinevere and Elaine.

"Ah, Ladies right on cue. Now Ladies Sir John and I were thinking that until you have spent a few hours here it normally does not take that long for ladies, to realise you may need different clothing for the heat. So would you both please join me and helping me find dresses, a swimming costume and other essentials for you both as well as Caitlyn, so that she can be the bell of the ball as well as our top negotiator?"

I hand Jimmy an envelope. He looks in it and laughs, "Well ladies I think we are about to buy more than three wardrobes each. Ladies what do you say?"

"Can we go to the Art Museum the President mentioned?" asked Elaine.

"Top of the agenda," said Jimmy.

"Come on Caitlyn, do not look worried, we three girls are about to have a fun afternoon away from these stuffy old men and their conversations," say Guinevere.

"Well that'll be you Sir John, I cannot image my wife would think me a stuffy old man."

All laugh and I see Caitlyn still rooted to the spot like a rabbit in headlights. I walk over to her and whisper in her ear, "Welcome to the Knights and please note we are all equal except today you have more spending rights."

Caitlyn gives me a huge hug and Guinevere walks over and places her arm in Caitlyn's, "Come on Caitlyn let's shop"

With this we hear the Chinese limo pull up. "Ah our other new guests."

"Let's all go meet them," says Arthur.

With this I laugh at Jimmy as our old adversary, an evil tyrant as we knew him is greeted by the ex-Prime Minister of Great Britain and his wife, the Leader of the Oppositions wife and his security guards looking as if not knowing what to do.

Aiguo is dumbstruck.

"My old fellow, I believe we had a spat together three years ago. Seems we finally meet and this time I am sure we will get on famously." Arthur shakes Aiguo's hand.

"Prime Minister.."

"No they all call me Arthur now."

"I am Aiguo and this is my daughter Chenguang."

"My word, I had heard she was beautiful, Morning Glory is translation is it not? But you are all welcome to what is our family and extended family."

"It is an honour to meet you sir and thank you for coming to our rescue," say Chenguang.

"I think you will find that is Sir John," said Guinevere who then introduces herself and Elaine.

"And this is Caitlyn, our hostess at the house," says Jimmy. "Listen Chenguang, I hope you do not mind me being forward, but I am taking the ladies into town to shop for outfits for the weather here and swimming costumes for Caitlyn who did not pack hers. Would you like to join us?"

"I would love to, father?"

"Then may I suggest that we wait fifteen minutes and you can see your rooms and if all OK with you sir may be one of your men would be so kind to come along too. They look like they would be better equipped to carry all the shopping than me?" Jimmy was on fire and suddenly enjoying the situation.

"I insist you take the limo, but can we get our luggage out first?" laughs Aiguo. I have a feeling this is the first time he has laughed in years.

At this point Chastity walks past in her swimming costume and waves on her way to the kitchen, "Anyone else want an orange juice, the bar by the pool has run out."

Aiguo looks to me and then we hear the limo driver pop the trunk of the limo. Arthur strides to the rear of the limo, "Come on guys many hands make light work, Caitlyn as hostess with the mostess where we going?"

So there we are all taking the Chinese luggage into their suites. The security team look worried and Aiguo laughs.

"Here I will take that small one, can't have an ex Prime Minister carry all my luggage," and he laughs, "better let my men carry Chenguang's luggage that girl does not know how to travel light.

The smile on Jimmy's face is just a picture I will never forget and he relaxes and sees that we have managed to diffuse one obstacle only to see another fuse lit.

As we all enter Joseph is there with Robert helping fetch ice and drinks also needed at the bar by the pool. Chenguang stops in her tracks and is unable to complete a sentence saying hello. Joseph takes her luggage she is carrying and asks her to walk ahead. Like a true gentleman he walks her to her room and with her father watching takes it into the room and exit.

As Joseph exits both Arthur and Aiguo both watch Chenguang look on like a love struck girl.

"I knew it would happen one day, I had same look when first saw her mother, who is he?" asked Aiguo.

"Oh Joseph, he has the cure for cancer," replied Arthur.

Jimmy looked at me and I him, Reader this may be something that could jeopardise everything.

26

Well I manage to get a moment alone with Arthur as there are some parts to this plan only he, Jimmy and I should know until ready to off load.

I decide to take Arthur to the East Wing and introduce him to Ben and Earl. At first Arthur looks cautiously at me then walks into the room. Both Ben and Earl look terrified.

"We saw Chenguang here. We thought they wanted us dead?" said Ben.

Arthur looks at me confused.

"No it was the New Order."

Arthur then looks towards them and me.

"OK, Sir John shall I sit down?" Arthur sits and then Ben and Earl sit on sofa opposite. They hold hands and Arthur looks to me, and then smiles, "Hi I am Arthur for all intense purposes and if it makes you more comfortable I have no idea what's going on either."

There is a knock on the door and all look startled. I open it and it is Joseph who enters, sees Arthur, looks to me and then looks startled back to Ben and Earl.

"What's up Joseph?" I ask.

"Jimmy asked me to give you this and said you'd be here." Joseph hands me a file.

"Cheers, that Jimmy, always one step ahead."

"Come in Joseph, you probably know as much as the rest of us, we are now officially the one step behind gang," all laugh at Arthur's joke and Joseph sits in the armchair and I join Arthur on the sofa facing Ben and Earl.

"Right, so firstly introductions and Arthur is sat to my right. I know you all know who he is, but at this moment he heads up one of the biggest global task forces to find cures for cancer and other major illnesses. Arthur opposite are Ben and his boyfriend Earl, Ben is on the run and wanted for the killing of his wife."

"Which he did not do, I assume, he didn't did you?" asked Arthur.

"No he did not. Ben bought a huge piece of land when Isaac and Abraham heard it had huge mining deposits under it and engulfed their home village and towns. He did not buy it to make money, he bought it to protect the people from being abused by ruthless buyers that also wanted the land. Ben found a loophole to buy, but forgot to buy the actual land the villages and towns sit on in the centre."
"But no one can buy those." Ben said looking at me as if he had made a huge error.

"Sadly they were bought…. by me, using money I was paid to find Ben and kill him and have his body found by police.

Paid by my friend Marco who is high up in the family based in Italy. Stay with this. Once the land was found not to be for sale Chenguang Foundation was furious as they were set to buy from their dodgy politician from the old administration. It appears the CIA heard of the purchase and new President Elect used his powers to get to one Paul Rudd, a business partner of Ben, who flew Paul to see Ben to say sell the land to a new tax haven company owned by one of the new President Elects children. This is his way of making sure the deals that are now illegal to him are possible as farmed out through different companies he sets up for his moronic children. You must have noticed they are say behind him in all business deals as President? Anyway, he saw an opportunity to screw the Chinese, as he hates the Chinese. Ben, you refused to sell and then Paul Rudd introduced friend Sylvester Willis. Willis is an assassin for the CIA and for the new President Elect as a sideline. They thought, as they would be stupid and not looking into the legal side of things properly, that if they killed Ben and his wife then the company, Paul Rudd had a stake in, could sell the land to the President's dumb ass kid. But Willis killed Ben's wife and Ben was away. Ben was with Earl. Ben is gay and so was Ben's wife. It was a marriage of convenience and sadly Ben's alibi is that he was with his gay lover in a country where you are hung for being a homosexual by mobs who would then go unchallenged as if they had committed no crime; I hope you are keeping up Arthur. Now Jimmy has found in this file a link to the new President and Willis. I intend to have a meeting with Chenguang Corporation main man, a nasty piece of work we know, but never the less this is Aiguo, who now also happens to be staying here. This is Joseph who is close to a cure for cancer using vitamins and some other revolutionary cures, but he can tell you all that in due course as this is why you are here Arthur."

"I gather I am not fully up to speed, Sir John? But happy to catch up."

"Well my apologies, but this all fell into our laps last minute and with new President we also have here communications with new British PM and crooked President of United States delivered by your old friend the idiot that is now Foreign Minister. I actually think he didn't even know what he was carrying. Seems that their New Order are keen to get the Americans on side as part of their global take over. And here is what we propose to do."

I pull a copy of the email for Arthur to see and then hand a piece of paper from a doctor in Kumasi, who is a friend of Isaac and Abraham.

"The paper you have there Ben is back dated to before your wife was killed. You had an accident in Kumasi and have been in a coma for, well you have just returned. Tonight we introduce you to the new President of Ghana and have him verify the papers and we have other papers on Willis showing he sent this email to Rudd. It explains how to enter the house unseen and a plan of how to get to your bedroom where sadly your wife was murdered."

"What about the Chinaman?" asked Arthur.

"Well in front of his daughter we are going to sell him part of the land to mine in cooperation with the people of the area with all profiting. His daughter has no idea what a dreadful tyrant her father is and at this moment we have no need to tell her or have her be any the wiser."

"What about the Mafia? How do they factor in all this?" asked Earl.

"Well until earlier my friend and I had a chat with them and they too are coming to the party. It seems the new President has six main bosses in America ready to take a wrap on crimes that they are not all guilty of. For their freedom they need to assist in the reclaiming of the land at any cost to themselves for his kids quango so that he can loose all the paperwork. Marco hired a team and that team is me, but as you will be happy to note we always find a way, well in most cases to not kill anyone and help people escape."

"So what is in it for them?" asked Arthur.

"Well no doubt whilst shopping with the ladies my friend has managed to get all the papers we need to have them join us to alert the new President we know what they are up to, that we have links to his children as the ones ordering the executions and that it can all go away if he allows the six bosses to walk free."

"Well I have got most of that, but what do you need me to do, and also sorry meant to say to you guys, hello, nice to meet you, sorry about your wife, and cannot wait to stick it to my corrupt party as well as help however I can. You said that the PM has sent the Foreign Secretary here for the party tomorrow. She could not come so sending him and expected a ticket. We had no choice, he arrives here tomorrow." Arthur looked at me to see if I had an answer, I did not.

"Let me work that one out later, but tonight at the party going to get you from the rooms here to a car and then arrive not knowing what went on Ben OK?"

"And me?" asked Joseph.

"Just be you and tell everyone about your discoveries." I said to be interrupted by Arthur, "And by the way, the china man's daughter likes you. May be good to have her in on your project."

"She is beautiful, but I am black and.." started Joseph.

"And Aiguo's wife was black, so just be you. You may end up being financed for your research as well as marrying one of the wealthiest young women in the world." I laughed and so did Arthur.

"She is pretty," laughed Joseph and my mobile rang. It was Jimmy who told me Chastity rang Caitlyn to get me to tell you that the Chinese man wants to know where we are.

"Right we are all up to speed, Arthur, Joseph, you come with me, be good to have Aiguo listen in to you telling Arthur about your cure, and Ben and Earl, you two sit tight and Jimmy will come for you at seven and whisk you out as everyone will be watching who comes in not who leaves."

I stand and hand folder to Ben, "It's all going to be fine, hopefully."

Ben smiles and Earl stands. "Sir John, I know not who you are or where you come from, are you British Agent like that Bond fellow, but I thank you for all you do and no matter if works or not know I am grateful for you giving us hope."

"Oh we are all in that boat Earl, I still have no real idea who he works for or who he is, but the wife likes him so that is good enough for me," says Arthur and we all laugh. I smile embarrassed, but proud to be an Invisible Man, and named after the greatest Invisible Man ever, Sir John Isaac.

27

Walking into the impressive study full of pictures of Ben I just realised we had not changed a thing and Aiguo holds a picture in his hand, "Who this I know him."

"He made the papers, he has gone missing apparently, previous owner of the house. Sad story, but guess we will never know truth." I replied. "How are your rooms?"

"They are amazing," said one of the guards and Aiguo looked in amazement as his man has talked out of turn.

Arthur chips in, "Yes I am in the house too and so secure and the air conditioning works a treat, you know mad dogs and Englishmen go out in the midday sun, but not me."

"Yes the suites are better than the hotel and I must thank you, what do I owe you?" asked Aiguo.

"Nothing and truly grateful to have you hear as our guests. There is an office next door and a boardroom adjoining that if you need to do business please feel free."

"Round table?" joked Arthur.

"Oval I believe," and we laughed.

"I have no idea what they are on about with their English humour also sir, my name is Joseph and I am here to present my cures I have found for cancer."

"I am interested to know more young man. Sadly my beloved wife passed away from cancer. I had all the money in the world, seriously I have all the money in the world, yet I could not save her."

"I am sorry to hear sir, but with the world cancer research banks making so much money I fear cures for cancer will be halted or side-lined. This is why I am honoured to meet the Knights of the Round Table."

"The Round Table, I get it," laughs Aiguo, "that is why you ask round table? No?"

"Yes," replies Arthur.

"So what is Round Table?" asks Aiguo.

"Well with a round table there is no head we are all equal and therefore all as important as the next. We work together as one, I remember a young filmmaker said to me who shot a commercial for me, that his motto filmmaking was Collective Intelligence, without one person on the crew pulling together nothing would happen. I thought what a smart lad, and then he told me he was not voting for me. I remember smiling and laughing in the car home as my next speech I used that very phrase, which was a pivotal point in my campaign, to win the general election. Anyway I digress, please join us Aiguo your input would be greatly received and I apologise to both you and Joseph if you do not understand all I say, but speaking foreign languages was never my forte."

Aiguo sits and he has his men sit also and relax. "I like this collective intelligence, so you got the Americans with you?" Aiguo asks.

"Actually no, well their medical sales account for too much of their income at present, but we have all the European and Russia and Japan, and may be you can influence China to join. I cannot offer profits, but the good will to save a life…. I am sorry I am being insensitive Aiguo." Arthur stops in his tracks.

"You know Arthur, my wife she would like you. So what's to be done?"

"Well Joseph, why don't you start us off by telling us a little about your research?" and I sit as I invite Joseph to stand and talk.

"I apologise as I am a doctor not a speaker politician.."

"Well we do not need any more politicians," joked Arthur.

Joseph starts to tell us how he started out on his quest. And what he said was fascinating with his look at America being the hook that got Aiguo interested. It seems Aiguo hates the Americans as much as he dislikes having to do business properly.

"The reason I got into finding a cure was selfish, I lost my mother," Joseph started, "often until something effects you our interest is a momentary glance at a headline. My mother went through Chemotherapy and after a long battle, suffering greatly from the side effects of the drugs, she lost her battle. I wanted to know what alternatives could she of had and then after a ten minute research online found there was nothing. Nothing sanctioned to be researched and wondered why?"

"My wife was beautiful even as she passed she was the most beautiful human this planet had ever known, and yet I could not save her," I watched as Aiguo cried as he said this. Joseph walked up to him and offered him his handkerchief, which he took and smiled then apologised for interrupting. I sat in awe of how simple it can be to bring worlds together when the cause is right.

"In my study on cancer I found for adults researched over twelve years in the United States of America undergoing chemotherapy 97% of the time it does not work. I was angry. Why put my mother through such suffering if the chance it would work so little, OK it gave us hope, but they knew it would probably not work. I then thought if we know this why do we still use and then obviously the answer hits me, follow the money."

Joseph is now emotional and looks to me. I stand and offer him a box of tissues and he smiles. Arthur is moved, we all are and I see the security men present also heads hung low.

Aiguo looks at them and they pull themselves together and one who is also teary bows respectfully to Aiguo and then looks up and says, "Sir, your wife was the most amazing lady to me and my family, I am sorry."

There was a short silence as Arthur looked at me and it was his diplomatic skills that turned this whole situation into not just helping the Knights, the fight against cancer, but halting the New Order, halting the American Presidential machine and tyranny, saving Ben, sorry Reader but these are moments we witness very rarely.

"Tell me Joseph, how can we help you help others, what is it you have learnt?"

Aiguo looks up, "Yes young man, tell us."

Joseph looks to me and I nod.

Joseph looks at Arthur and Aiguo and begins again, "Follow the money. If a doctor in America gives a patient antibiotic he gets no remuneration, if he give five thousand people the same that Drug Company may give him a free holiday in Hawaii. With chemotherapy drugs the doctor gets from the pharmaceutical company the drugs for five thousand dollars, which he sells to the patient for twelve thousand dollars. Insurance pay out often nine thousand dollars so the least the doctor makes is four thousand dollars per treatment. If a car company had made a car that failed 97% of the time would they still sell it? No. And therein lies the problem. The drugs companies have all the control on all of us in every department. America has to admit it has lost the war on cancer."

"I have to concur, the Knight's findings have been similar. We have people running marathons for cancer research charities and all that sponsorship raised goes to fund more drugs and surgery that does not work. I had no idea it was 97% with chemo, which has been a major shock to me. I wondered what was being developed by cancer charities that were alternatives to streams already being proven futile so we will happily support you Joseph and you have my word. Also with our global network, with your permission, we will share your findings so other countries will share and help with your research their data they find as well. I am sad to say as an ex-leader of my country I did nothing until now, but today I am hoping to make amends. What facilities have you been using for your research?"

Joseph looks to me and I realise that he is funded, in small set-ups by Ben, and answer for him.
"Well Arthur that is another dilemma. You see local entrepreneur had been helping Joseph privately, as anyone looking to find a cure outside the pharmaceutical companies faced corporate business closing them down. Follow the money a phrase I first heard from a clever man and good friend of mine, Tony Berger, and I wondered if all those amazing people raising money for charity whether any of it went to alternatives. There is a new drug that can prevent breast cancer and money into that is nil I found and why I Joseph will help you to be fully funded to carry on your work here in Ghana if you wish. Arthur and I are meeting the new President tonight and like to announce with him if that is OK with you? Arthur?"

"In total agreement and from the notes I have read you use vitamin C and other herbal remedies I believe?"

"Yes sir, and also in India great advances have been made with tamarind. Each vitamin and herb battles different cancers and tamarind has been highly successful in pancreatic cancer for example."

"I own a pharmaceutical company, why do I not know this?" asks Aiguo.

"I ruled a country," said Arthur, "and had no idea so please do not blame yourself Aiguo. We know now and I would like to honour your late wife and name the research after her and Joseph's mother."

"Arthur, this whirlwind of a day has been a lot for me to take in. I was here to conclude business on a land deal and must take a few moments if I may to deal with that, but please note tonight I will also have some news I feel I would like to impart."

And with this Aiguo stands and shakes Joseph's hand and ours before exiting with his men.

"Well done Joseph, so what do you need tonight to show off your findings?" I ask.

"The opportunity to talk."

"And talk you shall," says Arthur, "now to sort out the couple in the belfry eh Sir John?"

"I think this may be a platform to help them too. It was Ben and Earl supporting Joseph and think as we get ready for tonight I need to find the boys some old dusty clothes to wear. Just going to make a call." With this I exit on the phone as Arthur and Joseph chat.

I am by the pool and manage to get Ntombi's phone that is answered by Stephanie as trying to reach Abraham. This is why Reader we Invisibles often work alone.

"Hi, Stephanie...yes it is me," I say. Then after a conversation of how she and Nelson are so in love and Isaac is about I manage to get the phone passed to Isaac. "Isaac, Hi. Listen I need you to come to the house now and collect a package and meet Doctor at the old house and get the packages dressed in outfits that look as if been worn for months. Yes that is right so see you in an hour, half an hour even better call the house and park by the rear gates."

As I hang up I see Aiguo and his men approach me. In other circumstances they look ominous, but he is smiling. I go behind the bar and stand as if barman.

"Gentlemen can I fix you a drink?"

"I would love a gin and tonic."

Looking at Aiguo's two men in suits dying in the heat, "And you gentlemen, please join us."

Aiguo looks as if to say 'why not?'

"Orange juice please would be good." The other nods in agreement and I see them trying to survive the heat.

"May I make one more suggestion?" I venture, "can I suggest you allow me to have my friend pick up linen suits for all your men in town as they will return soon and the last thing you want is your men passing out."

Aiguo looks at his men and smiles, "I can ask my daughter also."

"Great idea and please can you write down your sizes here on this pad and get it to them ASAP?"

Aiguo laughs, his mood is completely chilled and he is totally relaxed, "No let me impress my daughter, modern technology I 'facetime' her," and with this he laughs and takes out his mobile, "She is always on to me to get more with it." Aiguo dials and looks at his screen and the phone rings and goes to answer machine. Aiguo looks annoyed, he has a quick temper.

Arthur and Joseph join us at the pool and Arthur is quick to see Aiguo looking frustrated at his phone, "Please Aiguo, don't tell me mobile phone not working or trying to talk to a woman on it?"

Arthur laughs and I say, "I have an idea, I will call Jimmy, Jimmy will make sure the women have their phones on and then we can try again."

After a quick call to Jimmy he texts me back. "Gentlemen the following message arrived: all women have phones now on, I managed to turn off silence button so call and I will prompt whoever has phone ringing. And by the way shopping has been a great success, women all bonded and I am grateful for help carrying bags."

Aiguo rings and his daughter answers, "Daddy, you face time me!" we hear her screaming and laughing with joy. Aiguo looks at us then laughs, as he was a little embarrassed.

"Yes, daughter, your father not too stupid as to not know how to use phone."

"Daddy, dad I cannot hear you, you have mute on again."

Aiguo looks at phone and his security man touches screen from over his shoulder and Aiguo nervously says, "Hello" and Chenguang continues, "Daddy, I am having a wonderful time. We went to the gallery, small but what beautiful pieces, and the ladies are wonderful and Chastity and Quetty now face book friends, and I have bought you a beautiful handkerchief made locally from the finest silks."

"Yes yes, darling that is wonderful, but I need you to do some more shopping. Can you buy five, no ten linen suits for my men. It is too hot for them in the suits they are in. I have a list of sizes I will email to you and get a nice dark blue and a camel colour as well."

"This is the best trip ever Daddy and please thank Chao for turning the mute off. Will be back in an hour and a half, by menswear shop now, oh and Daddy they have lovely hats, Caitlyn suggested for you in sun, I get you hat, bye.." And with that Chenguang hangs up.

Aiguo looks to Chao and smiles then to Arthur, "Chao means excellent. Seems there is much I need to learn."

"Well firstly I wish Chao would give me help on my mobile and you Aiguo can teach me how you have such powers to make an excited woman shopping too busy to talk to you. I swear my wife will return with a ten second anecdote that will last an hour," laughs Arthur and we all laugh even Chao.

It is full height of the sun and I suggest may be a move indoors would be advisable. All agree and we decide to rest before the big night. Aiguo asks as if we would need him to be scarce when meeting President tonight and I was truly blown away.

"Good grief man, of course not, you are an extra guest of honour. Just one favour to ask, the Saudi's who are staying in your rooms will be coming, and not bragging but the hotel is nowhere near as nice as the house. Please do not say I offered you a stranger over them to stay, they may just shoot me."

Aiguo laughs, "You know I had already forgotten hotel cock-up. We have secret yes?"

"Yes we have secret," I say in return.
As we walk in Arthur goes to his room and Joseph stands in the hallway. Aiguo grabs him by the arm, "Please can you tell me more about yourself?" Joseph smiles and both walk off, with guards in tow to the living room.

I am on my way to get Ben and Earl.

28

I enter the room to see Ben pacing up and down. He looks worried and then turns to see me.

"That Chinaman, you know who he is? I mean we just looked online, well nothing else to do, and he is reputably a monster. I know three cases where he had humans mine climbing hills with rocks rather than donkeys as donkeys were more expensive."

"Well he is turning over a new leaf, in a manner of speaking and slowly, slowly. His daughter is the future she will be the one we will look to work with when he is gone, but for now ignore all that, know he is a man who can buy a country, make people disappear, but he is also a man that can make many more safe. You just need to follow my lead. Now let's get to the back gates to meet Isaac and start to get you two reinstated. What you wearing?"

"We thought the light blue linen suit and….." says Earl before I interrupt him.

"Earl he has just come out of a coma, the fact he is beautifully shaved I can sort of explain, but at the old house where we met put on the old suits, roll in the dust and mess up your hair. Chipped fingernails wouldn't go amiss. I have to sell this on the world stage, so no blue linen suits. I will have them ready for you to change into after we sell your coma story!"

"I think Sir John is right," says Ben and then laughs, "Sorry Sir John two silly queens desperate to dress up in our peacock suits."

"Come on lets be having you and walk normally and do not stop whatever happens until you are in the car and both of you need to wear a hat. You are still fugitives."

There is a text on my phone and it is Jimmy. 'Five minutes be ready. Got Isaac by back gate and I will arrive at front causing commotion so you should easily be able to get out without being seen. Give the guys my best and see them tonight.'

As I read out the message both men hold hands.

"Ok gentlemen this is it. See you tonight and here is a script that you and doctor need to stick to."

We walk to the top of the stairs and Ben taps me on the shoulder, "Why not take secret exit to back door through the priest hole. Had it fixed in case of storming house by gay bashers."

Ben clicks a switch on the mirror at the top of the hall landing and behind it we disappear and into a room and from there downstairs and underground to the rear gate coming up in what looks like an electrical junction box outside the gate. We even surprise Isaac in his car.

Ben hands me a piece of paper, "This is a list of all the secret passages and entrances etc. Thought we could trust you with it, anyway you own the house now."

And with that they are in the car and drive off into the distance. I re-enter the secret passageway and look to see if I can get to the library via the map, and I could. Sorry Reader if you have ever played Cluedo as a kid you will totally understand how much fun this is. As I tuck the paper into my pocket I see Jimmy laden with store bags and see Chenguang in the centre with Caitlyn like old school friends. Arthur appears and I smile as he stands next to me he asks, "Did the boys get out OK?"

"Yes fine thanks, and by the way Caitlyn is a great selection for the Knights."

"It seems you and Jimmy have a way of making all my appointments great. Listen I never would run for power again as this is far much more fun. Foreign Secretary just about to land and got a text from PM to meet him."

"Did you reply?"

"Not yet."

"Well don't, bad mobile reception, I have someone picking him up and taking him to his hotel six miles out of town. It'll be gone eleven by the time he gets there and then he is getting taxi to meet us, but sadly he will be in a strip club surrounded by naked women."

"He'll love that."

"Not when all the males in the room are paparazzi he won't," I laugh, "have that one on me." I walk and greet the ladies and Jimmy and hand him the secret labyrinth of tunnels to the house, which he pockets and looking exhausted looks to me to mouth 'you owe me'.

"Let me help you Jimmy, Caitlyn looks radiant. I hope you got her all she needs." I smile and Jimmy nods in disapproval.

As we start to trudge off carrying eight bags each we hear Caitlyn scream out, "Ladies, Ladies one second. Jimmy?" we stop and turn. "Jimmy, on behalf of us all we would like to thank you for the best day out."

"The best day ever!" exclaims Chenguang and Aiguo looks at us both as we nod laughing and Jimmy subserviently replies, "Yes my lady and if I may I will drop off your bags and collapse in my room."

All the ladies cheer, and laugh. Robert and Henry join us, and they carry Guinevere and Elaine's bags and taking bags from his men is Aiguo to carry for his daughter. Arthur laughs and announces, "Well as there are no bags left for me to carry, may be I can meet you all at the poolside bar and be your barman?"

"You people are wonderful," cries Chenguang and Aiguo turns and looks at how happy she is. Joseph takes her bag she is carrying and they smile. It is truly love at first sight stuff Reader and even Aiguo has mellowed. In fact watching Chenguang flanked by Joseph and her father carrying her bags, followed by security men was a sight I had not envisaged at any stage of this mission.

Jimmy looks to me, "We are not there yet my friend, but there is still too much to sort before tonight. We have a quick briefing with Ntombi and Stephanie in the library about tomorrow and also Nelson should be over, BUT and I mean this nicely, can I get ten minutes for a shower?"

I laugh and together we drop off bags and I watch him limp off to his room and disappear.

I hear Caitlyn calling my name and Stephanie giggling loudly as she so infectiously does. With her is Nelson and she too shouts, "Sir John, Sir John, come out wherever you are we have a wonderful surprise for you."

I walk into the hall to be hugged by Stephanie and then Nelson shakes my hand.

"You mentioned in a conversation in the club about a DJ you liked so we hired her for the party," Nelson says beaming a huge smile.

I look beyond him and see Caitlyn helping the DJ in. A huge smile comes across my face and I cannot believe the amount of joy that surges through my body. It is Flo, Little Mayo.

Looking as if this must be some kind of mistake she has been chosen to play suddenly sees me. The relief on her face as she has had the Royal treatment. I embrace my beautiful young friend and tell her that she has rooms here with us as Chenguang appears.

"Sir John, oh I am sorry, is this your daughter?"

Flo looks at me and looks confused, as I belly laugh, "No. This is our special guest DJ Nelson procured for us."

"Oh my apologies, silly me," says Chenguang, "are you two just business or is there pleasure too?"

Flo raises an eyebrow and looks at me giggling, "No," I say, "This young lady is just starting out and I feel another great friend for us all to have for the party. Well done Stephanie and Nelson, you have surprised me, and what a wonderful surprise. Here Caitlyn let me have Flo's bags and let's get you settled in."

I take Flo's bags and Chenguang hugs Flo as Joseph appears in his swimming trunks. All turn and look as he suddenly stands there feeling awkward, he was not expecting to see anyone but Chenguang.

"Listen Joseph, why do you not get some drinks sorted, Flo, what would you like? Actually, Joseph surprise us, he makes cocktails apparently, and if I may Flo you must join us for a swim."

"Sure Chenguang," says Joseph and retreats to the pool.

Flo looks to me then Chenguang, "I would love to but have not packed a costume."

"No worries you are same size as me and just bought three new so you can come to my room and chose one of your choice," says Caitlyn.

I take Flo to the only available room now and deposit her bags. Flo still looks slightly worried.

"Flo, this is going fun. Now Nelson has all the records and I have sorted you out two iPods with more dance music than humanly possible. They plug into the consul and also there are some fifteen-minute mixes done just to get you going. I am so happy to see you. And listen there is no pressure at all, just playing for the new President of Ghana, The ex-PM of the UK and half the Royal Saudi family as well as other prominent guests. Walk in the park." And with this spun on my heel and walked out of the roof laughing.

I could hear Flo shout after me 'Thanks' and then hear her say to Caitlyn and Chenguang, "I think I need that drink, Joseph better be bloody good."

All the girls giggled then ran out the room past me to Caitlyn's and off to find swimwear. I was suddenly fully aware that I still had much to do. I needed to call Marco. I had booked two cabanas at the hotel for Marco and guests. This was my master plan as told him to fly into Accra this afternoon and he agreed. Marco would need to know what was happening and how he fitted in, plus Jimmy and I had a cunning plan to screw the Americans and get his colleagues in States off the hook.

Of course getting out of the house was not easy. I had to see Nelson and of course Ntombi and Abraham had arrived. We went into the meeting room by the office.

"Everything is all sorted, the drinks, the staffing, security, liaising with five security teams, guest lists, sound systems, stages, five different cuisines as you asked for, a VIP area that is not segregated, but easily made accessible to who you decide, and we managed to get John Barr in to perform on the main stage at the beginning of the evening. He came in yesterday and what a set of pipes is the phrase I think," said Nelson.

"Blimey, you lot have been busy," I remark.

"I should have had these two work for me years ago. Ntombi and Stephanie seem to have the hardest of my contacts agree to whatever we need without any aggravation whatsoever. Mind you, I have to say I realise I am working for them," laughed Nelson.

"Are you settled in the cabana?" I asked.

"We did stay there to be on site yesterday, but will be out for you tomorrow," says Abraham sheepishly as if they had taken too many liberties.

"Don't be daft, you two couples have it for the next three days I have left and enjoy. The room is paid for as is all the room service you can request. I also need you to make sure you all take credit for the event management, well you have basically, and not me. You will find that there will be endless work coming your way after this and I look forward to having Arthur support Little Feet Charity. And is Isaac still coming tonight? He will be staying in cabana next to you guys with your sister Mary if she is free?"

"Shit! I forgot to invite Mary?" exclaims Abraham.

"Who's Mary?" asks Ntombi.

"Your future sister-in-law," I reply and all laugh as Abraham blushes. "Listen kindly note all paid for and Abraham can you collate everyone's bank details so services paid for as well. You will all be paid and thank you all." I exit. And Nelson stops me leaving.

"No we all you a debt of thanks and to be honest I do not expect payment."

Nelson hugs me and I whisper in his ear, "Be ready to see Earl tonight."

Nelson looks at me then hugs me even harder crying and I exit.

"What did he say? What did he say?" asks Stephanie.

Nelson just turns to her with a tear in his eye and hugs her tight.

29

I drive up to the hotel and have to wave to the manager beyond a stream of security and military barricades as word is out of the event. He shouts and I am ushered through. I pull up at the cabana and park the car. Walking back to the hotel and the manager I smile and am greeted warmly by him and his assistant.

"I have news," he says as he greets me. "Telcom has been here with American. They have been asking questions about Leo Bloom?"

"Thanks and listen has the money all been deposited to the hotel account to pay for the party etc?"

"Yes, and my bosses are over the moon. They have offered a discount of 7%. I know cheap bastards, but it amounts to just over £50,000. You deposited £750,000 and we have about £100,000 on hold, what would you like me to do with it?"

"I have a plan and will give you a request later for you to carry out," I say.

"All our bosses are coming to the event," says the assistant.

"I hope this is OK, I could not stop them," sighed the manager.
"Of course, when do they arrive?"

"They are in the hotel now," says the assistant.

"Well let's go say hello and I must have your names, I apologies as never known your first names. I am Sir John and you are?" I point to the Assistant.

"Femi, Sir John."

"And I am still Tony, Sir John, but why?"

"Gentlemen let us go have a moment together. Lead on, let's find these bosses."

And with that I am in the main reception area and greeting all the top brass of the hotel, their wives and in some cases extended family. After a few pleasantries and jovial bowing and hand shaking I decide to enjoy the moment.

"Now ladies and gentlemen, let me say the reason I have chosen this hotel is very much down to the staff and the incredible service of and Tony here, whom I think of now as extended family. I was talking to your new President praising them as well as all your staff. Tomorrow night is a big occasion and we want not only all of you and your family to be here, but I am going to ask Femi to invite all employees of yours here at the hotel to come and bring their families. The extra cost on wages I will cover and we have a few barmen and waiters from our crews coming so no one will be working more than a couple of hours. We want them all to enjoy the party with us."

"This is very generous and we too are very proud of our staff and we will not charge you for staff, that will be our gift as you have already been so generous." As the obvious Chairman of the group spoke the rest nodded in agreement.

"Wonderful," I said, "If you will all excuse me I must look after a few last minute details and Femi and Tony have asked if you would all be able to join us for the cocktail party tonight at our house to meet the President and guests, to which Femi I think was a great idea of yours. I look forward to seeing you all tonight and Tony and Femi would it be possible for you to give me your staff numbers and names etc., for tomorrow for security?"

"Of course Sir John, and your party arrived from Rome are settled into the two cabanas you asked for as well."

"Great then let's adjourn to your office and ladies and gentlemen I look forward to seeing you with Femi and Tony tonight at the house."

As I stride off I can sense Femi and Ade laughing, as they loved every second of that. We walk into the office close the door and the two burst out laughing.

"OK Femi, I would like every member of staff, no exceptions enjoying the party tomorrow. And both of you are plus one or two if you like tonight, just get me names. Lastly, I will need the account payroll for all your staff."

"Payroll? This is unusual Sir John?" said Tony.

Well I want to make sure that me not paying for staff means that they do not, not get paid, and make sure the tip I leave is with the people it should be with. Listen, I once worked as a barman come waiter, well I was the worst waiter in Devon, at a golf club. A two star run operation that had delusions of grandeur. The two top bosses would collect all cash tips and I remember taking over £1,800 myself to only be paid in an envelope my share, which they said amounted to £10. I am used to seeing bosses spread the wealth so my tips will be direct and if the employee has no bank account then they will receive cash. In fact have my excess and bill done now and transfer the cash over payment. I will sort it all for tomorrow. I want this to be the best party Ghana has ever seen. Right off to see my Italian friends, are they in the cabana now?"

"Yes, Sir John."

"Thanks gentlemen and smile for this is going to be a weekend to remember. Be back in thirty and need all names of employees OK as well as positions." With this I exited and shut the door behind me.

As I walked back out in the baking heat I texted Jimmy and walked to meet Marco. The next part of this ridiculously, elaborate plan was now about to unfold. Readers, another tip, if you do anything, do it with confidence.

I saw Willis sat outside his cabana with what must be Telcom. They watched me and suddenly felt less invisible and not good, as I was about to meet Marco. I noticed two goons outside Marco's cabana and saw Willis tip a nod to him that I was the one they had been talking about.

Reader, I had found out that Marco was hiring Philippe to kill Ben to get the land for his American after Willis cocked up. Pressure on Marco from America as his bosses about to be imprisoned if things did not go American Businessman's way. Of course I have a plan, but as always we truly never know how things will go and this actually was the first time I had ever met Marco.

As I walk up to the cabana I can see the goon on the door flex his muscles and look at me as if to say out of bounds.

"Calm down son, I am here to see Marco. Tell him Philippe sent me."

The guard's demeanour changes and he goes into the cabana as his friend smiles at me. Marco appears and walks out to say hello in person. We walk into the cabana and as the door shuts behind me the mood changes dramatically.

"Leo Bloom? Sir John Isaac? Who are you my friend? Are you actually Philippe?" asked Marco as he walked to a desk he had set up and sat in his chair.

I smiled and took the seat opposite. "I am Sir John, and have known Philippe for many years, although I gather like you have not met him either. I am here with another client, the British Government and the Knights of the Round Table."

"What is this Knights of the Rounder Table?"

"A global community of World Leaders that come together to fight illness; find cures. To date from Russia to China involved and all the many countries in-between. But no sign of the United States of America joining sadly, but we are here to discuss what is happening with the land are we not?"

Marco looked at me and was still unable to relax. "Why has Philippe not delivered the land yet?"

I could sense that Marco was under immense pressure and I was in a dangerous situation. Marco looked as if he was at a point he wanted to kill me to send a message to Philippe that the Family were not happy nothing had been resolved, as well as a message to the Americans he was doing all he could to resolve the situation, and of course let the Family know he was the man and not to look at replacing him.

In these situations Reader one must always remain calm. If they are going to kill you they are going to whether you scream and cry or try to reason. I always try to reason.

"May I?" I asked as I touched the inside pocket of my coat. Marco nodded yes and I took out a mobile I had bought earlier for this very moment. Well to be honest Reader Jimmy bought it and set it up for me when he was out shopping with the ladies. "I have bought this phone for you."

"What is this? Listen no more games, we want answers now!" and Marco thumped his hand on the desk.

"Marco, Philippe is very aware of what you want. Philippe knows about the American, Willis, he knows about the six heads of the Family in America and he knows about the Chinaman. On here is the answer Philippe proposes and also how you can not only flex your muscle in America, but get a piece of the action not just here but in China too."

"So, all I do is take a phone?" asked Marco still pissed, but terrified to miss finding out what was proposed. "What does Philippe say, he going to call me?"

"No. On the phone is a file. In it is the deal that the new President was going to do where his daughter would be sold the land to her company he owns. Of course as President he cannot act in such matters, but through a link Philippe has uncovered the use of CIA and the US Government, that would of led to selling lands and company to Russia in what could be seen as a traitorous act as he also gives them access to agents overseas and even looks to wipe out the Family to be replaced by his own. You see Marco the game has changed and this is what Philippe proposes. On the phone is two mobile numbers. One to the new President private mobile nobody knows he has, actually even he is unaware until it rings, and his daughters mobile. Send the file saying that the land deal is compromised and in order to destroy this file the President drops all charges against the Family, losses all files intended to prosecute with and terminates all dealings in the land in Ghana."

"So I send this and sign it from Philippe?"

"No sign it yours truly Marco. You see Marco you can join us tonight and tomorrow as the new President helps a new initiative sell the land to the Chinese and you will also be part of the deal. You will act as middle man and have access to the Chinaman, China and Ghana."

"But the American here...?"

"Once he sees me leave and shake your hand will presently be on the run. Why not send the file now, but give it a read of course and if OK with you can I use the bathroom?"

"Sir John, of course, but don't go far."

"It's just in the next room and I will be back as would not want to miss this for the world. You see the President is an old enemy of Philippe and even though we will not bring him down this time we will stunt his growth."

I walk to the bathroom and as I closed the door Reader I have to say I needed that loo. For all my confidence and bravado I was truly unsure as to whether Marco would shoot me or not. I wash my face with cold water and exit to a smiling Marco.

"So what next? Oh I send it by the way."

"Well, tonight Philippe has arranged for the land owner to return to his house after being in a coma where he found him and we need to have his partner and Willis found and questioned by local police. Not just for the wife's murder, but a prostitute in the area. Come to the house for seven and introduce you to all the world leaders as the man that helped us find the husband and then have you involved in the deal, so making money for the Family and seen to be the good guys. I am sure you can drop some evidence to the police regarding the partner and Willis and their involvement in the murder of the prostitute, be nice if she was a witness to Willis at the house during the time of murder, and then tomorrow night as you hear the President apologise for his error of judgement, which he will do as at the very least his daughter will be tried for treason under the information in that folder sent, you should hear from your Family, well six major Uncles that they are extremely grateful."

"Who is Philippe?" Marco asked.

"To be honest I think Philippe is an army of Invisible Men that work together to bring a spotlight to those that think that they cannot be seen."

"Tell Philippe that again I am truly grateful and the usual fee deposited by next week, as well as remind him not to be shinning any torches my way." With this Marco laughs and I shake his hand.

"One last thing," I say as I turn in an opportune moment and ask Marco, "why not have the village where the mines will be have a fund given to them, to house and look after the workers, paid for by the company that helps with the deal. A Family undisclosed that is part of the organisation you belong to?"

"I wish I had men like you working for me, tell Philippe he is a lucky man to have you."

"I will make sure I do in my report or when he contacts me next. So shall we do the handshake outside and I'll let you enjoy your weekend and see you soon at the party?"

With this Marco stands and as if a great weight has been taken off his shoulders he smiles. Suddenly the mobile I gave him starts to ring. We both laugh as I say that it'll probably be for you and he has a goon answer and put them on hold.

Outside the cabana we shake hands and I look to Marco as he slaps my face, yes they do this in real life not just the movies Reader.

"Remember Marco, be nonchalant as if you don't care about the six, you have his Presidency, and may be there will be a chance to negotiate more from this at a later date."

"Oh I am already enjoying", he screams at me, I smile, "and that file is a piece of work. I see you tonight."

A goon appears, "It is President."

Marco and I smile and Marco takes the mobile, "Mr. President how nice of you to call, that phone, that phone is yours, you see we wanted you to have the file and... one second Mr. President," Marco cups the mobile with his hand, "Thank you, it seems we are negotiating already, money will be transferred later." Marco walks back into he cabana and I can hear him on the mobile, "Mr. President we have a new agenda so if you have paper and pen I tell you as my family would hate to see your daughter executed as a traitor..."

The door shuts and I see Willis at the bar. Suddenly one of Marco's goons takes my arm. "This way Sir John, I am to make sure you get home safe, your car is this one yes?"

"Yes."

"I like it. Shall I drive?"

"Let me. You may need to be ready in case our Mr. Willis wants to make a move."

"You smart and just to say I am Constantine brother. He had a suspicion you'd be here. He and Margot getting married and I am best man. He makes lots of money from laundry and very happy. He wants to know if you need any more money for Philippe as he sees huge profits and feels that you would want some."

"Tell Constantine that Philippe would want me to tell you to buy you a car like this and use the money to buy a holiday home in Venice for you and all your family to use. I think that is what Philippe would want. Now come on I have got to get back for a party."

With that we raced off to the house and I realised that part one had gone to plan, but still we have the last pieces to put together.

30

I am getting changed in my room and pressing my trousers when in walks Chastity and Quetty, followed by Caitlyn and Stephanie, who was in deep conversation with Ntombi. Behind them in walked Flo who was the only one that realised I was only half dressed.

"Oh sorry Sir John," Flo remarked as in walked the boys who all stood at the door and in silence all looked at me.

"Did we not knock?" asked Caitlyn.

Then in walks Nelson, "The music set up here and have your friends singing arrived and by the pool. Hello, party started, am I over dressed?"

"It's OK Nelson just ironing my trousers as the world descended. So what's up?"

"Caitlyn and I were wondering, well," stammered Chastity.

"We were wondering what you want each of us to do tonight?" stepped forward Stephanie and smiled at me with a mischievous look.

"Well, I thought I was a guest too, but I think best plan is this. Caitlyn, you are the host and greet everyone and you are in charge. Just be the perfect hostess as if your friends have come round to your house. You know who everyone is. Chastity, Quetty, smile a lot, and enjoy yourselves. Robert and Henry, act like lads on holiday and tell awful jokes to the guests and make sure Guinevere, and Elaine are never left alone, Ntombi, you introduce the band and be ready to be just the wonderful guest we know you will be and make sure you have the guests all excited to attend big gala tomorrow, Your party as you and Stephanie will then be the hostesses. Nelson need you to stay behind as want a quick word and can you see Flo has a great night and flirt with her outrageously with her to wind Stephanie up."

"Sir John!" cries Stephanie.

Nelson smiles, "Be my pleasure Sir John. So tonight we call you Sir John?"

"Call me if you need me and one last thing the caterers also, I want them to be involved as if family. I will come see them in a moment, but whatever you do enjoy everything OK? Right bugger off as Nelson is going to help me iron."

"I am? Where do you want the iron burn to be?"

The others exit and I ask Nelson to sit. As I carry on ironing Nelson looks around the room and seems a little uneasy.

"Nelson, I have another huge surprise and want you to know in advance, but tell no one."

"Sure, is it anything to do with ironing," he laughs.

"No Earl will be coming tonight."

Nelson looks to me and suddenly he looks scared.

"It is all OK and if all goes to plan he will find that he and Ben have the protection of a global family and never have to look over his shoulder again. Ben is to arrive from a hospital outside Kumasi, where he has been in a coma since the day before Ben's wife was killed. This as you are well aware is bullshit so need you to believe everything you hear. The story is being corroborated by a doctor and a source from the Family that were sent to kill him; long story cut short we have managed to move the goalposts. You must note Joseph will be here before them so give him a hug, as you obviously know him, praise his work Earl and Ben were working on helping him fund, and ensure Earl is with you during the following moments he arrives. Jimmy will tap you on the shoulder follow him if anything goes wrong and lead you all to safety. Sorry this is obviously a lot to take in, but your mind wants to ask me something else and feel once that is clear we can be confident all will be well."

"Sorry, not sure what you mean, my brother and Ben, here.."

"You wanted to ask me since we first met what relationship Stephanie and I had. Well I was here taking photos, she was the model, we spent three days together, you have seen my cabana, she had one room and I the other, mind you I fancied her like mad, but British and all that so, well we wined and dined together and she is an incredible girl. I met you with her at your club and within seconds realised the reason she did not want me was she is hopelessly in love with you. I think you are hopelessly in love with her and still see you too playing games. Have you had a girlfriend before?"

"Yes," said Nelson defensively.

"She has had boyfriends before too I am sure, but nothing matters as all that matters is you both realise that the future is all about you two now. Listen, she loved this ring at the jewellers when she went shopping. It is white gold and a cluster of diamonds. I want you to give it to her tonight. Whether you give it to her as a present or engagement ring that is up to you as I feel she will say yes before you get to finish asking, and I want you to accept this as a paid bonus rather than tax deductible cash, OK?"

Nelson stands and looks at me mystified and a tear in his eye, "Tax deductible, never heard of that, but Sir John you are a cunnumbdren. When I was fourteen I was at school and Earl was being bullied, but before I could do anything this feisty ten year old jumped in front of the bullies and tore them apart with words. I was mesmerised and we all became great friends. We have been great friends ever since and I have loved her since that first day, but too scared to tell her for fear of losing my best friend. I realise before you say it, that unless I tell her I will regret it for the rest of my life. Yes I am in love with Stephanie and I care not for her past relationships, I watched most of them crash and burn, and realise that she makes me complete. I am grateful, but this ring is too generous and...."

"You are being stupid. The money that bought it came from the fund paying for all this so seemed right. Also tomorrow call the manager at the hotel and arrive early as want to discuss another business opportunity with him and need you to be there as party organiser, but not until twelve as feel you will not be able to get any sleep tonight. I have met Earl and he is as wonderful a person as you are, I call it as I see it and to be honest I think you and Earl will have other big events to plan. Just be by the fireplace when Earl and Ben arrive."

"I still..."

"Nelson say no more, you are welcome and please let me get my trousers on or Earl will not be the only one people will start talking about in men's rooms."

Nelson hugs me and I hug him back as the door opens and it is Stephanie, "Sorry, I am interrupting, and if this is meant to be how you intend to wind me up? And Nelson I think Flo is out of your league so you two better of concocted another plan."

With that Stephanie spins on her heels and exits only to return immediately, "Band want to know what time you want them to start?" And then she exits again.

Nelson and I start to laugh as he starts to exit.

"Thanks again Sir John."

"Thank me in five years if you've managed to stay alive and able to keep up with her. I actually feel happy and sorry for you."

Nelson exits as in walks Jimmy.

"Nice touch with the ring, and Marco is on his way. He has picked up doctor, managed to get photos of the massive car crash he witnessed, even though he wasn't even in the country, and is bringing Ben and Earl himself. I thought he might double cross us, and your new friend, Constantine's brother called to say he would make sure all went to plan. I think GJ Isaac would be proud of this one. Just heard Saudis on their way, as is the new President of Ghana. Oh and put your trousers on, it's not that kind of party."

Jimmy laughed and exited.

As I put my trousers on the door opened again, it was Jimmy, "Almost forgot the Foreign Minister from UK is at his hotel and car picking him up in an hour to take him to the brothel Nelson gave me the address to. Driver is a guy I worked with in Istanbul and has already planned to drug the pillock out and have him in Game of Thrones orgy scene as well as having quite a few press already arrived for tomorrow's party sitting outside the brothel. This guy is so disliked globally as a buffoon that they are happy to enjoy a meal together on us in the restaurant opposite before going in to take photos. They are all excited to come to the party as guests as well. I am really enjoying myself, but this is the last. I have a good life in Venice and the girls need me."

"I know," I said as Jimmy started to exit a second time, "I hear Margot's sister is also stunning."

Jimmy stops and then smiles as he exits the room, "Put your trousers on" he shouts as he walks back downstairs.

31

The party is all ready and I walk into the kitchen to see Arthur already making the staff all feel at ease. As he goes to take another canapé I smack his hand. He turns and laughs, Sir John the wife sent you?"

"Couldn't resist. OK glad you are here sir, OK folks I am extremely grateful that you all have agreed to work with us tonight. There are going to be a lot of guests that are happy to see you too. I want you all to be like our extended family and service with a smile and even come join in on breaks. I will even take trays and be serving you if you are on break chatting. It will be incredibly informal. We are the Knights of the Round Table and all I ask each to remember is when referring to this man here you address him as Arthur. OK?"

All nod.

"Great, now can I have one more of these delicious pastries?" asked Arthur.

"Better check with your wife Arthur," shouted the chef and all laughed.

"I'm doomed, doomed," laughed Arthur as in walked Guinevere and Elaine.

"We all laughing at my husband's jokes?"

"No miss," said one of the waiters.

"This is Guinevere and Elaine," I say before Guinevere interjects.

"His jokes aren't very good I am afraid to say, but he is pleasant on the eye." Guinevere kisses him on the cheek.

"Can he have another pastry?" the waiter follows up.

Guinevere taps Arthur's stomach and says, "He can have all he likes as long as he remembers it comes off in the gym." With that she takes a pastry and feeds it to Arthur and exits.

"Will do Miss, Guinevere," says another waitress and all laugh, including me, and then Arthur looks to all and smiles.

"Well you heard the lady, as much as I like," and the waiter hands a pastry to him on a dish. "Listen I want you all to enjoy as Sir John says and happy to have you chat to your new President with me, is he a good man?"

"He is a great man, he is at last a man of the people in power. We are all here for him," says one of the waitresses.

"Well that is good to know so I want you all out on the floor when we make our announcement later and also want you all to say hello as opportunity arrives. Folks again, thank you for being here and we are truly grateful. I think this is going to be a great night," and Arthur takes another pastry, "Are you guys doing the food tomorrow at the hotel?"

"No sir, sorry Arthur," says the chef.

"Good, so before he says it," pointing at me, "I would like you all to come with your families to the event, just make sure we have all your details and names of those coming with you. I will have the hostess of the evening Caitlyn put up a paper and pen for you to all sign in the kitchen."

There are squeals of delight and Arthur exits grinning at me, "You're wearing off on me."

Before he exits the room I say loudly to the staff, "OK no more pastries for him."

As I exit I can see all the staff so excited and manage to see Joseph and Chenguang deep in each other's company and see Aiguo look at me and grin. Then Guinevere places her arm around Aiguo and leads him off to chat in the main room.

The scene is set. Jimmy is invisible to all but me and reminds me to make sure I am invisible too. For tonight so much will happen and the consequences will reverberate worldwide.

I walk to the pool to meet the band and the singer turns and runs to me with a huge hug and a kiss. Everyone looks in silence and Nelson laughs shouting over, "Any women you do not have that effect on?"

It is Bella. Flo is on the mixing desk and waves, "Thought she would be a great surprise."

"Flo bought me a ticket when she knew she was coming and I hope you are not disappointed. Also I sing with band three numbers. Have you seen who's singing, David Mcalmont. He is amazing." And with this Bella was incandescent, a word I used before and aptly sums up Bella.

"Bella, I am over joyed and you staying with Flo and everyone at hotel where party is tomorrow yes? Well we will have lunch here tomorrow, all of us, on Flo. Only kidding on Arthur."

Arthur looks to me, "What have I agreed to?"

"We are buying everyone lunch tomorrow," says Guinevere.

"Great, I will go talk to the chef now then," he says as he exits.

"Don't eat anymore of the canapés!" Guinevere shouted after him. As Elaine arrives with Arthur passing her.

"Try the shrimp, they are incredible," Elaine cries after Arthur.

"Oh please don't encourage him, now where is that lovely young man Nelson. I believe you promised to make us a truly sensational drink?"

Nelson looked to Guinevere and smiled pulling out a chair by the bar and calling to the barman to take an order.

At the bar are the band and singers as well as our new star crossed lovers are completely engrossed in each other's conversation Joseph and Chenguang. Aiguo enters with all his security and Elaine stands to ask him to join them. Joseph sees him sit and escorts Chenguang to the table and all sit.

Stephany arrives and helps Nelson with the drinks and places them on the table and then sits next to Aiguo. Aiguo smiles and seems a little uncomfortable and Stephany looks to me, and smiles.

"I hear your wife was the most wonderful woman sir," says Stephany.

"She was, and who told you this, my daughter?"

"No your men."

Aiguo is taken aback and looks to them and then relaxes. "She had a way of making everyone relax. She would see the one person that seemed not involved and make them feel that they were the most important person in the room. I love her. She was like you."

"Like me?" asked Stephanie with a puzzled look.

"She was black, well Sri Lankan," chipped in Chenguang.

"She was beautiful," said Aiguo and a tear welled in his eye. This mountain of a force of commerce, brutal in getting what he wants reduced to tears by a woman.

"Well if she was half as lovely as your daughter, sir, then she would have been I agree, wonderful."

Aiguo smiled and his man came forward with a mobile as if he had a call. Aiguo made his excuses and took the call on the other side of the pool. He seemed a little confused then looked at his daughter and came back to the table, "Apologies and will have phone turned off."

"Daddy! Unbelievable, you turn phone off. My word Joseph, alert the papers, my father has turned the phone off to enjoy the night."

"She has my wife's wit too," grinned Aiguo.

Jimmy sidled up to me, "It was Willis. He is on the run… don't look at me like that of course I monitored his call. Willis is going to be down in a town not far from where the Foreign Minister will be waking up in a moment."

It seems Willis is trying to now deal with the Chinese on behalf of the President unaware that things have changed.

Arthur re-emerges as Flo is playing some lovely tunes and a few more guests arrive. Then the Saudi Family and entourage walk in with Chastity and Robert followed by Caitlyn and Henry. Quetty is with Ntombi and the waitresses and waiters with food on trays.

Nelson calls to me from the reception, "Sir John just found another lovely group that have arrived."

I go to investigate and it is Tony and all his family and the owners and staff not on duty at the hotel. "Tony and you have come with your daughter as well?"

"No, Sir John, this is my wife."

"Your wife Tony? May I say what a pleasure to meet such a beautiful lady."

She looks at me and then it dawns on me she does not speak a word of English. Tony translates and she blushes and I walk them all into the pool area and to the bar.

It is a night of people introductions and hand shaking, interpreter's at the bar as all got on so well they decided they would admit they talk English and centre court was Arthur and Elaine. Guinevere was with the band and walks up to the microphone. Friends, Knights, welcome and I feel it is time to introduce our two singers for the night who are going to sing one of my favourite songs, a duet, improvised and well hands together for David and Bella."

All applaud and I notice it is 7:30pm and realise that Marco has not arrived with Ben. The party is a wonderful success as being a Round Table event all are equal. One of the waitresses speaks fluent Arabic and the Saudi's are enthralled and laughing. The chef pops his head out and Arthur calls him over and he bows and says hi, then Caitlyn comes to the door to nod at me. The new President of Ghana has arrived. David, ever the pro sees the situation and brilliant grabs Bella's hand as they sing a line and then as the band play David stands on the Microphone,

"Friends of the Round Table, may I present the New President of Ghana."

All stand and applaud. You could not write this stuff Reader, no one would believe it, but again from going with the flow impeccable timing occurred. As the applause died down and the new President started shaking hands David nods to Bella to take up the song again.

I walk the President to the bar and introduce him to Tony and staff, "Mr. President may I introduce Tony from the hotel that is hosting the event in your honour tomorrow night and his staff and directors of the hotel."

Tony is overwhelmed, as are the staff and Tony's wife steps forward and shakes his hand. The President smiles and in Ghanaian they have a wonderful conversation where she and Tony introduce everyone.

I suddenly see Jimmy make a move to the hallway. He somehow creates a small commotion and everyone looks to see Marco arrive and with him a dishevelled Ben and Earl.

I grab Ben and Earl and say hello as if never met them before. Arthur notes to grab Marco's hand and shakes it, "I believe you are a colleague of Sir John's are you not?"

With the President is Telcom in plain clothes. He is in such shock he cannot move.

Marco moves to the new President, "Mr. President, my apologies for interrupting, we were looking forward to meeting, but found this poor man in a hospital we have been looking to fund, and he has been in a coma after this terrible accident and appears to be a man accused of a crime he could not of committed."

Arthur steps forward, "Hi, Marco is it not, Sir John tells me great things about you…."

"Sir, this is the wanted murderer Ben Timbury," jumps in Inspector Telcom.

"What murder?" asks Arthur.

"Mr. President, this man was tried and convicted of the murder of his wife three weeks ago, and…"

Ben interrupts Telcom, "My wife, what do mean murder for my wife, where is my wife?"

As Telcom tries to move forward to grab Ben the President steps forward and halts his progress. "My apologies sir there seems to be some confusion. It seems your wife was killed and you have been found guilty for the crime. Have you any explanation?"

"I cannot believe…" stammers Ben as Jimmy hands Marco a file and smiles then disappears. Marco on cue looks inside and sees what he has to do.

"Mr. President, I had been reading about this case and it seems this file we have from the hospital seems to explain everything. It seems Mr. Timbury was in a car accident, here are photos of the wreckage and was in a coma at the hospital we are looking to fund, which is why I was visiting earlier today, as Mr. Timbury came round yesterday and so met him. It would appear that it would not be possible for him to of committed the murder unless he was able to do so whilst in a hospital a hundred miles away. What evidence was there on this case to convict an innocent man not actually in the court?"

The President looked at Marco, then Telcom, who in turn looked at the exits and confused. "Mr. Timbury, huge apologies as there has obviously been a huge mistake. I would like to give you complete amnesty from this case and sorry for your loss. Inspector Telcom would you ensure all the evidence is on my desk tomorrow so we can find out what went wrong?"

Telcom nods and exits.

"Mr. President, how magnanimous and an honour to see the intelligent way in which Ghana is now run. I have great faith in this country is now in the right hands," Says Arthur at which point the Chef and waiters cheer. "Sir. John, let us help our guests to drinks at the pool, Our friend here, Mr. Timbury and business partner somewhere to freshen up and time to discuss more wonderful things to hand."

"Please everybody, may I say a few words," says Joseph who is standing next to a beaming Chenguang, "But this ladies and gentlemen are the two men I was talking of that have financed and helped my cancer research here in Ghana. Mr. Timbury I was sure you would not of been involved in your wife's sad demise, she was an amazing woman, but Mr. President and guests without these men my research would never of happened."

"Cancer Research in Ghana?" asks the President.

"Yes, and one of the reasons we came was to meet Joseph," says Arthur.

"And I want the Chenguang Foundation to support the work for as long as it takes," says Chenguang as her father almost spits his drink out.

Seeing Chenguang looking adoringly at Joseph he claps his hands. All stop and look and he smiles placing his arm around Arthur, "I feel as if fate bought us here and I can concur with my beautiful daughter we will help support the work you are doing here in Ghana and what an honour it is to say we do this jointly with the Knights of the Round Table and what an honour to meet an African President the world will see become one of it's greatest leaders," the staff cheer again, "and obviously a man of the people."

All laugh and smile. I see Jimmy whispering in Caitlyn's ear as a moment as all applaud she steps forward, "Honoured guests please join me by the pool, raise a glass and enjoy the food as we listen to our amazing band and the wonderful voice of Mr. David Mcalmont."

And with that all walk through to the pool as I take Ben to his quarters and see Telcom on his mobile outside. Jimmy is listening in and Ben looks to me as if he cannot thank us all enough. I tell him to go get dressed and return to the party with us all. I see Marco talking to the Saudi's and I nod as he leaves them to join me.

"Marco, that was.."

"Inspired?" he interrupts, "so how does your boss now see the rest of the plan working out?"

"Nicely I feel, but it appears our Inspector Telcom is on the phone to CIA man here Willis. When Ben comes down he is going to have you organise the contracts for the mines and also get you in a partnership with Chenguang Foundation, I see China as a golden opportunity for the family. With the President of Ghana turning all upside down and on a manhunt for an ex-CIA agent tomorrow, as well as the file you have already sent, things working out nicely, but we have to get through until tomorrow night. As for tonight let's just enjoy the party and I will have Philippe contact his man to find Willis for us. Now let me introduce you to Chenguang and Joseph then they will introduce you to her father Aiguo via Arthur."

Marco relaxes and smiles, "You know we often do business differently, but I like it this way." Marco walks into the pool area with his men and walks directly to Chenguang and Joseph.

Jimmy explains that Willis has confirmed he is going to disappear, but cleaning his tracks and I was mentioned.

The President appears with one of his security men and I walk up to him. "Looking for the bathroom Mr. President?"

"No, you." He smiles. "It seems all has been incredibly arranged. I have the Saudi's, some Italian businessmen, and one of China's biggest foundations investing in Ghana. I think I may need your people to arrange a few more parties. I had thought the UK Foreign Minister would be here as well, but he seems to of got lost."

"Oh I am sure he will turn up, but before we return to the party can I introduce you to some of your fans?"

The President looks at me quizzically as Ntombi walks into the reception, "If you would like to use the bathroom off the office there will see you here in five?" He nods and laughs then walks to the bathroom followed by his security guard.

"Ntombi, can you do me a favour and round up all the waiters and staff and have Henry and Robert do the bar, you and Stephanie join me and Arthur here ASAP with Chastity and Quetty as need you all to wait. Also have Guinevere and Elaine join me here? OK?"

Ntombi looks at me and grins and rushes to the pool as I walk into the kitchen to see staff and Chef busy plating up food. "Chef, stop what you are doing as need you all to come to the reception area for a photo call."

"Sorry, you want what?" asked the Chef.

Chastity and Arthur arrive followed by waiters and Quetty. Followed by Stephanie and Nelson laughing.

"Right, Arthur you can have this tray, rest of you grab a tray of canapés and all the staff come with me as we serve you in the reception as I would like to introduce you properly to your new President."

The Chef and staff start to wail and cry as overwhelmed.

"Come on you lot pull yourselves together, he is probably as excited to meet you as you are him," says Arthur.

In walks Jimmy with camera and Joseph also holding a camera, "We're ready Sir John," says Jimmy and I usher all the staff into the reception area. Jimmy has them all stand together and Arthur looks to see Elaine enter and tells her that the staff are to be photographed with the President.

"Well everyone over here by the fireplace, it will make a much better picture and, oh my God! Is that a Picasso?" Elaine sees a Picasso above the fireplace.

Suddenly the President appears and Guinevere and Elaine start to clap, and the staff join in, and cheer. The President smiles and is slightly taken aback.

Arthur holding a tray of canapés laughs, "Sorry to startle you, but these wonderful staff, under this amazing chef, have been really excited to see you of all the people here tonight. So I was wondering if you would mind a few photographs and say hello?"

"I would be honoured," and then in Ghanaian he speaks to them all. Jimmy and Joseph take loads of photographs and a wonderful group photo of all the staff with the President and standing next to Chef for a huge photo of all smiling. I laugh, as in the photo are Elaine and Guinevere flanking the President and Chef, and at the sides and in the group are Knights and Arthur serving them food.

As the photos end the President raises his hand and all look. "I would be honoured, if OK with you, Caitlyn was it not, as our hostess, would you mind me making a speech to all the guests and would like the staff to join in too."

"Of course sir that would be an honour." Caitlyn looks to Arthur as if she is amazed as she is recognised as the hostess and a little tear wells up in her eye.

"Mr. President would you kindly allow me to escort you to the pool area?" asks Elaine and also manages to link her arm in is and also into the waiter next to her and effortlessly glides towards the exit to the pool.

Guinevere links her arm with the Chef and a waitress and smiles as she leads then to the pool. I take the tray from Arthur and he walks in with two waitresses followed by everyone else. Ben and Earl appear and I have two waitresses grab their arms and take them through as well.

At the pool there is a rapturous applause for David Mcalmond and he sees Stephanie motion she wants to say something on the microphone. David, the ever professional even manages to introduce Stephanie in his own inimitable style, "Now ladies and gentlemen I believe a few words from the lovely Stephanie, who I am sure you will agree is much easier on the eye than me."

All applaud as Stephanie introduces the President to the microphone.

The President walks onto the stage and waves his hand to acknowledge the applause and then looks to see Ben and Earl.

"Friends, what a great way to start a speech and I feel that after tonight we are all good friends. Now I have just been appointed as the new President of Ghana," the staff cheer and all smile, "and have to say that this kind invitation to meet you all before tomorrows event feels like I am showing you just how amazing Ghana is. This is my country and I am proud to be Ghanaian. I love the country and to find tonight that our Chinese friends will fund with our new Italian friends finding a cure for cancer as well as support hospitals just too wonderful for words."

"We too would like to help fund a hospital here in Accra," said the Saudi's. And Arthur and all applaud.

"Wow, and again I am overwhelmed. I am looking forward to doing business with all of you and look forward to projects that are beneficial to you as well as being the bedrock for a brighter future for my people. And now please thanks to the Knights of the Round Table let us continue to enjoy this beautiful Ghanaian night."

Arthur takes to the stage and looks to Nelson, "Mr. President it has been an honour and I look forward to hosting a meeting where we can all come together on a project to make a difference, but now I would like to introduce our master of ceremonies, another local boy, Nelson, Nelson what have we next?"

Nelson sheepishly steps up to the microphone and Stephanie joins him. "Well, I think a song from a young lady from Poland would be a nice moment and introduce our lovely Bella."

All applaud and staff look as if they should leave as Bella walks on stage, "And to our staff please have a seat and enjoy as this can be your break as we serve you."

Again Bella hops on stage and smiles, "This is a song I love and sing to all here tonight by a hero of mine Bob Marley called Redemption song and love to sing this with David."

All turn to David as he climbs on stage with his glass of wine and looks where to put it down. Stephanie takes it and places it on the table by the piano. Guinevere then walks across the stage carrying beers for the band and then all laugh as she walks back past the microphone, "Well let's hear it for the band." All clap and Arthur laughs as you can see the love between the two.

Jimmy looks to me to get my attention and as the song starts and we disappear to one side, "I have just intercepted a call from Willis and it seems he has been talking to our PM in London and the New Order are also in the mine with American President. Seems this was the deal to cement the New Order moving into America. And also it is now two hours after the paparazzi has been in to visit the Foreign Minister and have a few pics to send to press, which one do you like?"

Looking at a series of photos of the British Foreign Minister looking confused with a stripper naked straddling him and another with her boobs in his face, we ended up sending a collection and realised he will be recalled and not present for tomorrow.

"Well keep an ear out, but we should be fine for tonight. Let's organise a meeting here tomorrow and have cars for everyone to tomorrow night's party from here. Come on Jimmy time to enjoy the night and love to have a coke with you and want you to meet Little Mayo, Flo. She was my saviour in Poland." And with that we walked to the bar.

32

I wake in the morning and find myself asleep on a settee in the office. I have blackout as cannot remember why I am there. I walk up to my room and as I open the door see clothes strewn all over the floor and laying face down on the bed naked one of the Saudi party. I must have offered my room and sort of explained that. I hear the shower turn off and then out into the room comes one of their security guards naked. Just drying his hair with a towel. At first he looks at me unsure what to do then goes into bodyguard mode and thinks I am an assassin.

"Hi, no worries, just me, this is actually my room."

He stops and then smiles holding up his hand to say one second. He goes back into the bathroom as the Saudi mooning me from the bed wakes. I smile and grab some underwear and socks from a drawer as the bodyguard returns. The bodyguard looks at the Saudi, then the Saudi looks at me and I look to both and smile, "Just get my suit and razor and leave you guys to enjoy this lovely morning."

Neither says a word as I fetch what I need and then exit. Shutting the door behind me I stop and laugh as I think that that could have been awkward; then laugh as I thought it could not have been more awkward as cannot imagine situations more uncomfortable.

I knock on Jimmy's room and he opens and looks at me, "The Prince still in yours?"

"Yep, I think the Prince is in the bodyguard in mine." I walk past Jimmy and he looks as if to say 'what' and I walk to his bathroom. "Any updates this morning?"

"Willis is on the run and so is Telcom it seems. Willis has put a hit out on Telcom and he has gone to ground. Prime Minister, well she is more than unhappy with Foreign Secretary, whose picture is all over every newspaper and news of big cancer story about to break tonight in Ghana has seen a mass of the world's press rush to report on. Willis is actually in a house just outside the town and seems to be waiting orders from President. I have unearthed a document where it seems the new President of the States has his daughter coming to do a deal with the Saudi's for the land and was to sell it to them under her new company called Tranvapumi Holdings. It seems he has his children all at meetings and they sit behind him as he says that as President of the United States of America he cannot have a company he is part of do deals on special projects, which he is sure everyone understands, and then looks to his inbred brats behind him. Indicating that companies he will suggest should be the ones to work with, and each owned by him in his kids names. It seems the new President of America is even more crooked than we first thought. Now I have intercepted Willis mobile and sent message to President's daughter to come to party and that he will meet him there. Willis will not make it as once Rudy scares him off we hope to have her there alone."

"Rudy is coming?"

"Yes, you told me last night to tell Rudy to place the prostitutes murder evidence onto Willis and that guy is amazing as evidence already at the police station where Telcom not there to intercept."

"I think I blacked out again. So Jimmy, what is main agenda for today, did we arrange to all meet here before party?"

"Yes we have until 4pm when all will be arriving," says Jimmy who stops as we can hear the bodyguard and the Prince having sex, "It was like that most of the night. Anyway all will be here and thought we would have light lunch with staff and Arthur at twelve noon before all the fun starts."

"Jimmy?" I say from the bathroom, "I want you to know what an honour it has been working with you, but I feel this may be my last hurrah as they say."

"Same here buddy, and I think this could be the one they talk about in the future like the stories of GJ Isaac. I will see you in the kitchen in a moment so don't leave the room in a mess." And with that I could hear the room door close as Jimmy exits.

I notice that the room is immaculate as if no one had ever been there. Dressed I exit and walk downstairs to the kitchen where I find Arthur and Guinevere having tea and toast.

"Morning," I say and grab a cup. In walks Ben and he grabs me by the shoulders and sits me down at the table.

"He is making us all pancakes," says Arthur,

"His mother's recipe," says Guinevere.

"Tea?" asks Ben, "Listen before the next part of the madness begins I just want to say I cannot thank you all enough." Ben becomes a little tearful and Arthur stands and shakes his hand then gives Ben a hug.

"I feel you may be doing us all a greater favour later with this deal and before we all get too emotional I feel you should get those pancakes made."

"Teddy," says Guinevere, "That's my name for Arthur."

"He is right. I am actually enjoying making them, normally Earl does most of the cooking, but he is with Nelson catching up."

In walks Jimmy where Arthur, Guinevere and me all turn and say in unison, "Sit."

"Ben is making pancakes, mother's recipe, now you're here we can start," says Arthur.

I look for my watch still in my room, "What time is it?" I ask.

"Seven thirty, still always early riser." Guinevere looks at Arthur and smiles, "It is as if we are still at number 10, he is like clockwork."

Sat eating the pancakes all sit and enjoy the silence. Just as we are finishing we hear the sound of excited voices coming down the stairs. Into the kitchen walk Caitlyn, Quetty, Robert, Henry, Chastity and Chenguang. They all stop and look at us and Arthur rises, "Looks like the second sitting have arrived Ben. Ben is going to make you all pancakes. I fancy a nice walk. Darling would you join me?"

Guinevere stands and smiles. Ben returns and starts to collect plates, "Take the garden gate exit as it leads down to the beach."

"Thanks Ben and compliments to your mother, great pancakes," Guinevere replies.

"And folks lets all meet in the office here for say 11:30? Just relax and chill by the pool etc. as today will be three days in one I fear." With this Arthur places his hand on Jimmy's shoulder, "Is that good for you Jimmy?"

Jimmy smiles and takes his last mouthful of pancake and nods. The mutual respect they have is great to see and my mind wanders back to Willis. I wonder out to the pool and there I see Isaac lying on a sunbed with an orange juice and toast.

"Isaac, you're here?"

"Yes, I stayed in the pool house, more like a small two bedroom house, you own this?" asked Isaac, "you said I could last night. That was OK was it not?"

I realise I had blacked out and forgotten he had arrived at the end of the party, "Yes of course sorry bit tired."

"Thanks for the loan of the suit and trunks and well just for everything. Abraham has gone from dedicated to his work to love struck boy since I last saw him, mind you that Ntombi is stunning, don't suppose you have any girls to introduce me to?"

"Well it is a long day, but at the end of this you will be one of the most influential men in Ghana. Have you tried the suit on? And what happened to yours again?"

"I do not know, I thought I had it in the back of the car and yours fitted fine. May need to adjust the belt on the trousers, not that you are fat, I mean..." Isaac looked flustered and I laughed as Abraham arrived with Ntombi and Nelson with Stephanie. The brothers hug, and then in walks Earl. Isaac rushes to Earl and they hug.

"Is this the boyfriend?" asks Ntombi.

"No, this is my brother Isaac, you met last night, well the prosecco had taken hold so you may not remember."

"Don't worry Ntombi, I have a few vague memories about last night, but Ben is making pancakes in the kitchen and the others are up and all coming for a swim here and chill until we all meet at 11:30, discuss what we need to discuss, then lunch and start to get the hotel ready for tonight. Most work is done and what is not can be done as needs be. Want you all to relax, especially you Nelson, and after meeting I will come with you to the hotel to meet with Tony the manager."

Jimmy arrives and smiles carrying shopping bags and I look at him as he smiles and walks into the middle of all of us. Placing the bags on the table he holds the first one up, "Nelson, this is yours, Abraham, Isaac yours," and starts to hand out bags, "Ntombi this should be good for you and Stephanie this is yours. And Isaac I have a suit for you coming for tonight. Now I am off to have a quiet read in the study." And with this Jimmy exits.

Ntombi opens her bag and takes out the contents. It is a beautiful bikini and fits her like a glove; she is ecstatic and looks to Jimmy who has gone. Suddenly there is a huge laugh from Stephanie and all look. Stephanie pulls out her costume, "That guy has powers. He has the cup and top size perfect as well as the bottoms. How did he....?"

"He is an amazing man, one of the best men I have ever known." I watch as each has costumes and all look to each other. "Well unless Isaac trashed the pool house I feel you should all pop in get changed, sun is up early and have a wonderful morning relaxing, swimming, enjoying life and there are two bags left is one for me?" I asked.

"Not unless you are called Bella or Flo they're not," laughs Earl, "Guess you'll have to skinny dip." All laugh and I smile and walk to the bar. As I am behind the bar Isaac joins me, "What you looking for, Sir John?"

"Orange juice and checking there are drinks for you all."

"Are Bella and Flo the singer and DJ?" Isaac asks.

I smile and reply that they are and may be he should knock on their door to give them their outfits. I look to Earl and tell him the room the girls are in and to escort Isaac there, if he would be so kind. Earl laughs and takes Isaac into the house clutching the two remaining bags.

"Plenty of drinks folks, and plenty of juice, so it is a long day and what we do not drink we can drink after the party tonight." With this I smile and watch them all run off to change. "Nelson have you got a moment? How did it go with directors at the hotel?"

"They were a little snooty, but fine I think, why?"

"Just I heard you were looking for a place to upscale your club events and talking to Tony there is an opportunity for the new clubhouse by their pool to be taken over. Well I have bought the building as an investment and thought may be you'd like it. We can discuss later so be ready to talk to them later. Go on get changed and join the others have fun and let off some steam as feel it will be full on tonight and you need to relax or you may not make it till the end I fear."

"Why do you do this, may I ask?" said Nelson.

"Because I can." I replied and walked to the house to see Flo and Bella in their costumes looking amazing and jumping straight into the pool. That Jimmy was able to size up more than a situation at one glance I feel.

33

It was 11:30 and we had assembled all the Knights and the team for the event and Ben joined us making tea. I guess he had been hiding for so long it was a joy to be visible. Arthur makes a motion to sit and we all do.

"Well tonight's objectives are to secure the deal for the funding for Joseph's research and to follow up on generous offers from Aiguo and Chenguang Foundation as well as there are deals from the Saudi's and our new Italian friend. This afternoon at 4pm all will gather here for drinks before we all go to the hotel in a cavalcade of cars. We do have a cavalcade of cars do we not Sir John?"

"Actually we organised that Arthur," say Henry. "The President's limo is actually hired and the company that he uses have offered us ten more so we can transport another eighty people if needs be."

"Eighty, bloody hell who is coming with us?" exclaimed Arthur.

"Well," says Caitlyn, "I have the list here typed up. We have Arthur and Guinevere in one limo with Ben and Earl."

"Who am I with?" Elaine asks excitedly.

"You have a mystery man and will be travelling with Chenguang and Aiguo, the limo in front will be his security guards and some of the models from the event last week as escorts. In fact there are models in all cars as extra numbers. Isaac and Abraham with Ntombi and Stephanie, Nelson you will be at the event greeting all as host I hear, Marco and his men in another two cars, The President and his entourage in two other limos, David and band in another, and lastly myself and our staff serving us lunch today in the other."

Suddenly the door opens and all look as Sir Lancelot enters, "Hello, my plane arrived early."

"This is my mystery man, my husband?" laughs Elaine and gets up to kiss him. "Of course I am delighted or is there also another mystery man?"

Guinevere and Arthur stand and laugh. One of the waiters comes in and asks if anyone would like a drink and Arthur shaking Lancelot's hand saying 'later' and asks if his bags could be run up to his room. The waiter nods and smiles, "Welcome Sir Lancelot," says the waiter then exits and Arthur laughs.

Arthur turns to everyone, "Right everyone this is another Knight of the Round Table Sir Lancelot."

"Didn't Sir Lancelot sleep with Guinevere?" asks Ntombi.

"Not unless he wants to find himself six foot under," says Elaine and all laugh.

"Actually you are just in time to join us for lunch, why not refresh in your room and in fifteen minutes I think we should all meet as dinner is to be served, oh and Sir

Lancelot, I think you should sit next to me," jokes Guinevere.

"Can you have him next Friday too as got a bridge night?" jokes Elaine and the two women laugh as Arthur places his arm around Lancelot and says, "This way my friend, I think it is going to be a longer day than anticipated and we can catch up over lunch."

All chat and disperse to their rooms or go to the dinning room area. Caitlyn pops into see the Chef and Arthur catches her arm to hold her back as Elaine takes over leading Lancelot to their room.

"Catch up at the table," Arthur says and then turns to me, and Caitlyn, "let's go see what's for lunch and need to ask you another favour Caitlyn."

As we enter the kitchen Arthur walks up to the Chef, "Hello Chef this all smells incredible, when do you want us to sit?"

"Twenty minutes be perfect," he replies and Arthur walks Caitlyn and I to the study.

As we enter Arthur shuts the door and looks to me then Caitlyn. Caitlyn looks to me a little unsure and for a moment I think she feels she did something wrong.

"Don't look worried Caitlyn," Arthur starts, "I just wanted to thank you personally for an amazing evening last night. I was hugely impressed by the way in which you managed everything and kept everyone happy."

"Well I cannot take all the credit, Sir John helped me..."

"Caitlyn I have to concur, you were perfection. I know you came here to be extra pair of hands and believe you have been helping out part time with the Knights, which is why Arthur asked you to join us and.."

"Nonsense Sir John," interrupted Arthur. "Seems even when he is thousands of miles away he knows what we are doing and he sent me a memo and I am eternally grateful as without a prompt from the great Sir John I wanted him to witness me offering you a full time post with us at the Knights. And with the help of another Knight established your boyfriend works in catering at parliament so thought if you would like the next main event hosting at Parliament want to hire him as main chef if that is OK?"

Looking confused Caitlyn is emotional and looks so happy.

"Right just one more job for you tonight," I smile, "you are to do nothing but enjoy yourself, make your friendships with Chenguang and Joseph lifelong and enjoy the whole night as a guest with access to all areas, plus your boyfriend is in the reception also wondering what he is doing here so feel you should go and tell him."

"What? Michael is here?"

"I am trumped again, now do as Sir John says and I will have chef set up an extra place at the table."

Caitlyn hugs me and then hugs Arthur, suddenly realises she has hugged the ex-PM and jumps back, then I open the door and shout into the hallway, "Michael can you come in here?"

Michael appears and walks in to look shell shocked to see Arthur and Caitlyn.

"Hello Michael, I am Arthur and this is Sir John, Caitlyn can you take Michael into town with Chenguang and Joseph after lunch to get Michael all he needs for his five day stay here with us? You have the Knights credit card I believe, Caitlyn? Come on Sir John, oh and the answer Michael and Caitlyn to your question you want to ask is, because we can, that right Sir John?"

"That is right Arthur, kitchen?"

"Kitchen. See you both in five minutes for lunch. And Caitlyn please have Chenguang also pick out a suit for Joseph on us."

And with that we exited. Both grinning like little schoolboys as Guinevere is waiting for us in the main hall, "What have you two been up to now?"

"Tell you over lunch, darling. Shall we? Sir John please do join us," says Arthur and laughing heads off leaving Guinevere and I standing there to then link arms and she looks at me and grins, "I have no idea who you are, but I see you Sir John, I see you."

I walked into the kitchen and Elaine is handing out plates to be carried in. Before I can say anything I am carrying the vegetables and suddenly realise that she has been cooking with the Chef.

"I now can do roast lamb thanks to this amazing lady," says Chef.

"Nonsense, thanks for letting me get involved, I miss cooking. Plus I had a call from my husband complaining about having to eat foreign food. Man is terrified of doing anything outside his comfort zone. Oh and seems he is in good mood, apparently the Foreign Minister was in Ghana last night and was in a brothel, apparently he has been recalled and Prime Minister is flying out to make amends with Turkey after he caused more problems with things he said whilst being interviewed. The old man is having a ball."

And with that Lancelot walks into the kitchen, "Caitlyn told me to come in here," then sees Arthur, "hello," then sees his wife with the Chef and shakes the Chef's hand, "I hope my beloved wife has not been giving you too much grief, mind you Arthur glad to see you got her working." Lancelot starts to laugh.

"Chef, may I introduce my buffoon of a husband, mind you I would not change him for the world." Elaine kisses Lancelot and Arthur looks to Guinevere.

"Right everyone, grab a dish and take it in, I think we should give my husband the vegetables to ensure they make the long journey to the dinning room without all getting eaten." Guinevere then turns to me, "Sir John, it seems we have the Chinese gang all sat up ready to eat, will you carve as feel Teddy will cock it up."

"No Chef will carve, and also laid up a seat for him and three waiters." Chef looks at me and then at the waiters who seem confused. "In Great Britain this is how the family do get togethers, all eat together."

"I cook not carve great," says Chef.

"I have a better idea," says Flo who has arrived, "I feel that Ben should carve, he can then relax in his old home and be nice for him, don't you think?"

I look at Flo and again she inspires me as Guinevere laughs, "Sir John, how do you keep finding so many quite brilliant women?"

"Standing next to him even the village idiot seems clever," says Jimmy as he passes me with more food in dishes. As he exits we hear him call off from the reception, "Ben, you're needed in the kitchen."

Ben enters and the Chef and three waiters holding four huge legs of lamb look at a confused Ben, "Sir would you lead us into the dinning area and we would all like you to carve."

Arthur re-enters, "Come on folks before it gets cold, hi Ben," he says.

Guinevere grabs Ben's arm and leads him out, "Ben's doing the honours of carving the joint."

"Thank God for that, I find it most stressful. Well come on the Chinese are looking bemused."

With that we all exited to the dinning area where Caitlyn introduced Michael to Chenguang and then made sure the waiting staff and Chef were seated after all gave them a round of applause, with the Chef holding up his hands and he and staff stood and pointed at Elaine before applauding.

The meal was a huge success and Joseph even jokingly offered the Chinese chopsticks and Aiguo laughed saying that he would try to use a fork. It was just a really great place to be and soon it was three thirty.

I looked to Arthur who stood and tapped his glass, "Friends, new and old, Knights and honorary Knights again a great feast has been devoured and before my wife starts to heckle me, I would like to again thank Elaine and the Chef with staff for a magnificent meal, but please note that all staff to leave to get ready for tonight's party and look forward to seeing you there. The dishes will be done by the Knights."

"There are four huge dishwashers so it'll only have to be loaded," said Guinevere, "which is why Arthur has offered I am sure to do the dishes."

All laugh. "Thank you darling, now in thirty minutes we have the Italians and the Saudis coming for a meeting and feel we should make the main lounge ready. Joseph, this will be a major new start for your research and it seems that with Ben and Sir John the mining plots are within our control. With our gracious Chinese friends of the Chenguang Foundation we will mine and help fund many great causes here in Ghana, as well as of course make a profit. We will be mining responsibly and Earl has already forwarded an amazing Donkey Sanctuary we can utilise and so much more. The people will prosper and so will the country. I feel that this initiative will open up major inroads for my Chinese and Italian Knights and be heralded as the new way forward in countries cooperating for the better of all."

Everyone applauds and Lancelot stands. All look to Lancelot as if he too has something to say, "Sorry? Oh I was just going to ask where to take my plates and where is the nearest toilet?"

Earl stands, "This way Sir Lancelot."

Soon everyone is clearing the dinning room and loading the dishwasher. Guinevere and Elaine are with Caitlyn thanking the staff as Jimmy to do the honours with a tip. Jimmy hands each an envelope and smiles.

The staff exit looking a little confused, but all huddled together and then outside I see their faces as they peek inside to see a large cash tip. Then Aiguo comes out and one of the limousines rolls up, "Please have my driver take you wherever you need to get, dinner was wonderful."

The shrieks and giggling heard were a joy and I could see Aiguo's face as he beamed with an infectious smile at his daughter who gave him a huge hug and they walked back into the house.

"Lady Elaine, may I say that the lamb was exquisite, it was one of my wife's favourites."

"Well to be honest Aiguo the choice came from Joseph I believe on what to cook."

"I must thank him too, he is an extraordinary young man, I see that I shall have to watch him, but feel my daughter will be at hand to keep me updated."

"Daddy!" exclaimed Chenguang as another limo pulls up.

"Lady Elaine, what a diplomat you are becoming," whispered Guinevere.

Elaine smiles, "Seems I was told to say this when thought it would be appropriate, strange fellow this Sir John."

Caitlyn and Michael appear. To Aiguo, "Sir, may I borrow your daughter and have her help me shopping," asks Caitlyn.

Aiguo smiles as Joseph arrives. "Joseph would you mind accompanying the ladies with Michael and one of my men shopping?"

"Be an honour sir," replies Joseph.

"Wonderful, thank you, now ladies it seems with the children out we can have an adult conversation in peace."

Guinevere and Elaine laugh and each take an arm and the three exit into the house. The limos exit and Jimmy is liaising with the Chinese bodyguards. As the limo exits we see Marco and his entourage arrive in their cars.

"Ladies, are you coming to the meeting?"

"Why not we are all part of the Round Table," says Guinevere.

I smile as I pass them and I walk out to meet Marco.

34

It is quarter past four as the Saudi's arrived after being held up in traffic. It is like a huge family sat around the reception and sofas and chairs form a circle with room for all. I look to Arthur as he hands Robert a folder he was looking through earlier and starts to welcome all that are there.

"Friends welcome and so nice to see you all here in such a relaxed surroundings. As you are aware we have discussed and agreed to put forward a plan to start building an infrastructure for the people of Ghana and also looking to start to mine responsibly, where the workers are looked after and valued; unlike the practices sadly of many American companies."

All present nod in agreement and I think that the dislike for the USA and their new President is paying dividends. It seems the moron we exposed last year now is acting like a spoilt child that has no integrity or breeding, just money and a dislike of anyone who does not kiss his ass. I tell you Reader not since Hitler has there been such a major threat to the global community, but with more Americans now working against this evil little man and his family, as well as his ability to make stupid seem even more stupid, it has in many ways unified the world in opposition to the USA and sadly making America Great Again has become a look at civil war there. My favourite comment was seeing the headlines after his victory, 'OK everyone turn back the clocks 200 years for the next four.'

Arthur continues as Caitlyn and the rest of the Knights serve tasty titbits and Guinevere and Elaine serve tea. Again I love the way Arthur has diplomatically lightened the mood and created a setting where it is like a family get together and all wanting to be seen as part of a happy family. Just as Arthur is about to speak Lancelot stands and takes a sugar bowl and offers it to Aiguo who gratefully receives.

Lancelot smiles and laughs, "Sorry just feeling guilty not doing more."

"You knights are most gracious," replies Aiguo.

I notice Jimmy slip away and realised that I should do the same. I nodded at Arthur as he noticed us depart and then carried on to seal the following deal:

Ben and via Marco the Chenguang Foundation would buy the mining rights to the area and lands surrounding Isaac and Abraham's family town.

Marco and Chenguang Foundation, along with the Saudi Family would finance and develop the town and surrounding areas. A hospital is to be build for the workers welfare and the town, along with a school and other major amenities, and be named after the Saudi Family.

The Italian Family would supply all imports and help bring an Italian Restaurant as well as Chenguang herself wanted to oversee a Chinese Restaurant.

Ben, Isaac and Abraham would oversee the financial accounts with the Knights so that 20% of profits are paid back to the people and this could also be used to offset any debts they may incur in setting up the new housing projects under a Chinese, Italian, Saudi agreement that will be donated and named after the new President.

There are other parts, but Reader why were all so generous you ask? Well the Italians now have access to China, as do the Saudi's. Aiguo has the mining rights and then will be approached first for all future opportunities upon similar deals. In essence they all benefit not just financially in the long term, but hugely through new alliances and associations.

Lastly it was agreed, as suggested at the meeting by Caitlyn, that Chenguang would make the announcement to the President, and she will also announce the new research grant for alternative medicine research for cancer headed by Joseph. I wish I had seen Chenguang's face as this was the seal on the deal as Chenguang then wanted to offer to a visit to his business empire in China and everyone followed suit.

Jimmy and I had jumped into a car with Earl and headed to the hotel to meet Tony and Femi. I had seen a deposit had been made to my account so on the way we visited a Ghanaian bank and opened an account in Nelson's name. I deposited into this the cash and took a slip showing that €176,000 had been deposited.

Jimmy just sat next to me grinning nodding his head and Earl is sat unsure of what is happening. It is now 5:30pm and we are approaching the hotel to see a huge security presence and more police than expected. Femi was at the entrance and rushed to our car.

"Earl, how good to see you, gentlemen sorry about this but the police are hunting the American as it seems he and Telcom were responsible for the prostitutes death as well as planting evidence incriminating you and Mr. Timbury."

"Come on Femi, jump in the back," I said, "you can drive to reception with us as we meet Nelson there with Tony."

Femi smiles and jumps in, "Sir this is great day, great day, we are all so excited."

"Do you have the staff list for me?" I ask.

"Yes, Manager has them in office, I am so excited, I have been asked to liaise with President's men on security and cannot get over meeting him with my wife last night, this is great day, great day."

I drove past the police as Femi waved them to let us through. Parked we exit the car and are led by an over excited Femi into the reception. Tony is at the desk with Nelson as the owners were in the offices looking as if they were running things.

I smile and we all hug each other.

"Tony, we are going to the main restaurant bar area and if you would let the 'owners' know we would love to see them to conclude business, but not until we all have a quick drink together, on Nelson of course."

Nelson looks at me as Jimmy smiles slapping him on the back, "Thanks Nelson I think I will have a large G&T."

We all enter an empty bar as everyone is flat out getting the hotel ready.

"Well all is ready and the new conference structure that you've had built is a godsend," says Nelson.

"Glad you like it as over next six months going to turn to permanent structure and it is yours Nelson, teamed with a centre for offices and base for Little Feet."

Nelson looks at me and Tony arrives with coke for all.

"American champagne, great," sighs Jimmy.

"Right straight to business as all seems to be ready, it is nearly all ready is it not Nelson?" I ask and Nelson nods yes as Tony asks if the owner of the new building on the land next to hotel would be available to meet up before the event as owners keen to do deals.

"Well, I actually own the land as saw it was up for sale and the access from the far side of the pool is an excellent location for use in conjunction with the hotel. Nelson here will be the new business partner in charge and be setting up conference possibilities and an exclusive club that should not interfere with the hotel guests, who would be offered temporary membership if staying at the hotel,"

Nelson looks at me as if a little shocked, "that is if that is OK with you Nelson?"

"Of course, but... sorry I am not sure if I can buy in at present," says Nelson.

Jimmy is sat next to Nelson and hands Nelson the bank slip. Nelson looks at it and then is speechless as still confused. Jimmy smiles.

"Femi, have you the staff names and details as requested?" asks Jimmy.

"Yes, yes I have it right here."

"Good," I say, "Nelson will as a sign of goodwill pay each staff member working and not on party, I see from this spread sheet 72 members of staff, each will be given bonus of five thousand Ghanaian Cedi, that's £1,000 each. Nelson if you can do the honours as your first official duty? Then I think if the owners want to come out of your office Tony we should have a last minute meeting and discuss tonight's plans as well as the new centre."

Tony stands and exits as Femi starts to get more chairs.

"Can you let me know more on this, I am confused, you own the conference land etc., I must say I did mention to Stephanie I would love.... So Stephanie?" asked Nelson.

"Right, Jimmy has a folder for you and in it are blueprints to discuss with owners and I heard things were always problematic with club venue you have at present. The rest of the cash in the account is for you to set up business with. I think a state opening by your new friend the President could be arranged and go with the flow Nelson as here come the hotel owners."

Jimmy hands folder to Nelson who then nods and departs.
"Afternoon everybody and thank you again for your allowing us to hire this wonderful hotel for our event. Now to speed things up may I introduce Nelson who will be part owner of the new conference venue we would like to discuss a partnership of usage with the hotel. Nelson has plans and I am sure that we can work out some sort of deal that is beneficial to all. Nelson was just saying how he feels we can have the President open the centre when finished."

"Yes, yes Sir John and I feel with time moving on I should really ensure last preparations are finishing up," says Nelson and I smile.

"Of course, Tony, Femi, wonderful as always and please note, that we can discuss all this further during the evenings activities." I look at an excited, but bewildered owners as one steps forward to shake Nelson's hand as he starts to leave.

"I look forward to a prosperous relationship Mr. Nelson," he says.

"Actually, it's just Nelson, but I am excited to as feel that this will be a central hub for all of the best of Accra." Nelson shakes everyone's hand and waves the bank slip at me. "Will take care of this tomorrow OK?"

"We can talk later." I watch Nelson shake hands and leave and then I see Marco at his cabana's entrance. He is talking on his mobile.

"Well looking forward to chatting all later and be great to get the President involved too as Nelson said, so until tonight?" and with that I moved outside to see Marco see me walking towards him and waves for me to join him. He seems in excellent spirits.

He hangs up his conversation on the mobile and embraces me warmly, "My friend, I feel this is going to be the best day of my life. That was a good friend of mine in America, he says that six very important families are very grateful as all seems to of gone away with this new President. I tell you that New President Elect is so crooked he makes organised crime look like angels. It seems Philippe's document you sent to us was more than enough to get a certain pressure relieved and who knows we found out more that means we too may have leverage to help many other family friends. Come have an espresso with me." Marco walks into the cabana and I follow.

"Now to business. You know that Chenguang Foundation is well known for running many activities that do not wait for the legal stamps to be approved, so it seems that his daughter knows nothing of this. My family will ensure workers are well taken care of, as often in Africa workers are used like donkeys and cheaper than the mule to hire. We will make this a totally rubber-stamped legitimate mining and have all finances clean for your contacts. We want to thank you for introduction and sure Philippe would not mind that we offer you personally this small token of our appreciation."

With these Marco hands me one hundred thousand dollars in a briefcase and I smile, at first saying that there was no need and then realising why not as this will be done soon and need to become invisible again.

"I feel that with our new found friend Aiguo there will be lots of trade opportunities within China and the family are very happy, very happy indeed to break into that market at last. A few triads may be upset, but Aiguo seems to of already paved a connection for a link for us all to work in harmony."

"I am glad to note that relations will be fruitful and look forward to seeing you tonight and looking forward to the world press seeing the family helping Chinese and Saudi's with the Knights secure a deal that will start more opportunities in the whole of Africa that the President of the United States would have been ecstatic to of had, but after tonight America will have to make America great again internally and I hear already Tranvapumi Holdings are already shutting up shop as being linked to unfortunate murders here. I believe Philippe is hoping to find their man Willis. I do not suppose you know anything of his whereabouts do you Marco?"

"No, but we are looking. I will send you what we find in the post if you like?"

"Just a phone call would be fine," I replied not wanting Willis's head sent Federal Express to the Knights address in Parliament.

We shake hands and as I exit I see Stephanie hugging Nelson and screaming for joy. On the stage area is Flo with Bella and Isaac. I watch as they pretend to be calming down a crowd of screaming fans and bowing. Ntombi is directing tables and helping young waitress with some plates that looked to heavy for the little girl to carry on her own. Abraham sees me and waves. I look at my watch see the Little Feet banners being erected on the conference centre structure. As I see all going on I do not see Jimmy stood next to me. Jimmy as always invisible and reminds me we need to be at the house getting ready.

Abraham walks over and we discuss that we will be back at the house to return at 7:30pm in the cars. Abraham has arranged for everyone earlier to arrive with outfits and change at the cabana. He laughs as he says that the women have taken over and it is carnage in there.

In the main suite of the hotel is tonight's star John Barr. John is presenting his 'Johnny and Friends' cabaret and has bought over three friends to sing with him. Johnny sees me and we hug and laugh as I make sure everything is OK for him and in true John Barr style he laughs and says, "I am sure we'll get through it and if not no one will know."

I remember seeing him perform at a cabaret club in London and everything went wrong, the sound, the lighting, and he made it the best show ever as he won the audience over. I relax and think that at one moment tonight I will at least listen and enjoy something for me, A Johnny Barr Superstar moment. I exit leaving Johnny to flirt with the sound man and for moments after in the car keep smiling thinking how infectious John is.

35

Driving back Jimmy sees the briefcase. He informs me that Telcom has been found and is saying Willis works for CIA and Tranvapumi Holdings and that he threatened his family unless he went along with story. Telcom, it has been decided, should be moved to an area out of Accra and to be honest neither of us thought he would ever reach his destination. Willis was still being hunted.

"Oh, by the way, the family want you and I to spilt hundred thousand dollars for helping their trade relations."

Jimmy looked at me and laughed, "May be I will buy that little speedboat in Venice as a side line now I am retiring."

"Good for you, good for you," I replied and knew this was possibly my last mission too.

Back at the house I am sat with Ben and Earl. We are enjoying a cup of tea and sat listening to the silence the house provides.

"You have a wonderful place here Ben."

"Had I am afraid to say and not sure what the new owners want me to do. Earl is looking at a legal perspective to see if we can make the sale void as of the circumstances, but it may not be possible."

"Why not just say to the new owner, here is your money back, and he may say OK."

"What just say, 'here is the money back'?" says Earl.

"We cannot release the funds for a month and at this moment are not sure who the owner is," says Ben.

"I accept and I can wait a month," I replied.

"What?" says Earl.

"I bought and Isaac was meant to make sure you could buy back with no loss of money. He never told you? Must have been the excitement, but did we not? Oh well lost the plot myself. The house is yours and after next week all of us will move out."

Earl rushes towards me and hugs me tightly.

"Sir John, I am speechless. How can I..?"

"Ben, let's find the cure for cancer with Joseph and it seems you did so much for others it seemed only right to do this for you, and why. Well we have a saying and that is we do it because we can."

"I am so grateful and heard the Knights say this too," says Ben.

"So all settled, agreed, no more said and move on. Just one thing, what was your wife's name? If I may ask as of course understand may be difficult to talk about, but just to let you know she was actually killed by the river and not in the house. Her death was swift and she would of known nothing." I looked at Ben as Earl squeezed his hand.

"Her name was Jessica, and thank you," said Earl.

I raise my teacup and toast, "To Jessica, a truly remarkable woman."

Aiguo, Joseph, and Chenguang, followed by security guards all in their new linen suits, join us. There is a loud shrill of a laugh and Elaine, Guinevere and Arthur follow with Lancelot raising his hands in the air as if he was the one telling the funny story. All meet and greet each other as the limousines arrive with the Saudis and pre party drinks commence.

I am standing by the river entrance with Jimmy as he says that he has picked up a call to say Willis is looking to find me. I was his new mission. It seems the new President wants to send a message and that my death is his best option. Jimmy then laughs, "Don't worry, it is not me just you. He has seen you, but we must keep eye out for staff at party, he may try to come along."

I was worried I had enjoyed this whole mission so much that I had forgot the golden rule to remain invisible. I smiled at Jimmy and looked down by the river.

I look to the time and make a call from the house office on my own.

"Rudy, hi. How is it going? Listen Willis is still about and just be good if we can make sure he is found. Thanks."

I hang up and I hear the computer on the desk bing, it is a message and been hacked. A picture of me comes up by the pool at the hotel and a message below that reads, ' See you soon, best wishes Willis '.

As I delete the message and turn off the computer in walks Jimmy, "Don't turn it off just yet," he says, "I saw Willis has been in touch, but thought this might cheer you up." Jimmy opens a YouTube video from Ghanaian News. The reporter reporting news just in that a man wanted in connection with the murder of Inspector Telcom has a reward of fifty thousand dollars offered. I look at Jimmy.

"I saw the message, well my mobile is still linked to, anyway, I prepared this and sent out an hour ago when you were with the Italians. Come on it will be impossible for him to even make it through the first wave of security and if he does everyone at the party will have seen his face. Come on you still need to put on your suit for tonight and I have a date with Bella for the first dance."

With that Jimmy exits and I smile as I look around at the office. You know reader I think I would of liked to of taken the money I earned and settled in a house like this, 'house', this is a mansion. Changing into my suit I see my photo of Megstar in my wallet and kiss it before exiting to the guests below and before I know where I am I am say next to Caitlyn as she was the only one from the Knights to return as she forgot her shoes. Michael is with her and I ride with them like a gooseberry.

Our limos are ushered through and we have no time at all to get out before everyone rushes to cheer the new President. He is an extremely popular figure and time Africa had men to lead that look to build their countries rather than rob them blind.

Africa has great wealth, not only in resources, but also in their people and if they can stop in fighting they are the future.

Everyone is having a great time. I see DJ Little Mayo, Flo's new DJ name, on the decks with Bella free styling singing on top of the track with David joining her. Michael and Caitlyn dancing with all the others joining in. There is nothing like a good party to bring people together and it was a great night. Ntombi had managed to get the President to dance with her and Stephany. Isaac and Abraham were with the President's wife and Arthur and Elaine were making seriously fools of themselves dancing like they were at a wedding if you know what I mean.

News arrived from Rudy that a friend had sent a picture of Willis boarding a US military plane with the President's son. I sent him a note to come enjoy the party, but he was in a strip joint with a British Diplomat getting hammered.

I suddenly remembered the Foreign Minister and managed to ask Arthur if he had heard from him to which he replied that this morning Arthur had called the PM to see what happened and that he had been recalled as needed elsewhere. Seems the buffoon is like Teflon, to which Lancelot joined us over hearing laughing, "Come on we all know he is banging the PM."

Nelson had done an amazing job and was sorting out the stage for the news release and looked as if not sure who to reach to get up first. I tap Arthur and Lancelot to follow me and then they motion to their wives. Knights soon see us move and follow. As I near the stage I notice huge screens showing video images of the party and a shot of the President and staff enjoying an informal chat with Isaac and Stephany. Then the President, like old friends, is warmly greeting the owners of the hotel and I call Nelson over. I see Marco and Aiguo chatting, looked more like plotting, as old habits obviously die hard, and have Chastity and Quetty go fetch them whilst Lancelot walks to fetch the Saudi's. Lastly Nelson has Abraham fetch Earl and Ben.

I see on the dance floor dancing as if inseparable, Chenguang and Joseph. I motion to leave them for now. Nelson arrives.

"Sorry, not sure what you want next, we didn't rehearse this." Nelson smiles and I give him some cue cards to read from. He takes it and looks at me and steps up onto the microphone and motions to Flo to take down the music.

Nelson is nervous as I have Stephanie join him for Dutch courage. "Mr. President, honoured guests, fellow Ghanaians.." a huge cheers goes out. " As the new owner of this magnificent site in partnership with my esteemed colleagues of the hotel I would like to introduce a few people of stage. Firstly Arthur and the Knights of the Round Table, Marco DiMarco from our Italian friends," Yes reader who would of thought Marco was called Marco

DiMarco? "Our Royal Guests from Saudi Arabia and our new friends from China, the Chenguang Foundation."

As they all wave and enter the stage area to be seen I see Nelson look to the cards and then at me. I motion to continue.

"Friends I am so proud to be with you today, as a Ghanaian and as an African, next to my beautiful African friend Stephanie. The new conference centre is to also house the new Little Feet Foundation started by this lovely young lady next to me. From the offices here we will look to find our lonely and orphaned children, educated them and help build them into pillars of our society. We will give our children and future children a chance to find their way. (Huge applause) I have been honoured to of met the Knights and their work to find cures for cancer and other diseases backed by over forty countries in the world. They are backing a local man whose work on finding a cure for cancer through natural fruits will soon be available worldwide. Joseph, where are you?" Joseph raises his hand and we see Chenguang cheering and hugging him proudly.

Nelson looks to me and continues, "And he is with the beautiful Chenguang whose father here and their foundation have pledged to mine an area of Ghana splitting profits with the people and workers and build a hospital, a chain of medical centres, and I feel with the President's permission, name after Aiguo's loving wife who was lost to cancer and after Joseph's mother who also lost the fight against this disease. The first hospital to be built for the workers and erected in their town south of Kumasi in

Konongo, so please give a huge cheer for the new Lihua Audrey Medical Centres. Just to say I have since learnt that Lihua means beautiful and elegant and Audrey means noble strength. A wonderful combination to be the bedrock for this wonderful new initiative. And friends, when we say noble strength our noble guests from Saudi Arabia will be funding the building works and building greater ties with our great countries. Last but no least our Italian partners will be providing all the necessary drugs and equipment for the hospitals so that they can be set up to offer free medical help to all. Our Italian and Saudi friends will also be building our towns to bring them into the modern world, the modern Africa and now without further ado, please raise your glasses, cheer, shout in a thankful acceptance and also welcome our new President of Ghana to the stage."

The crowd erupt and Arthur steps forward to take the microphone and shake the President's hand.

"May I be so bold Mr. President and kindly note that my wife is a patron of the Knights and wonder would you mind awfully if I respectfully ask if your beautiful wife Sa'dah be the patron of Little Feet as I believe that translation for Sa'dah to English is Happiness."

There are more huge cheers from the crowd. The President is truly overcome with joy as he looks out over the crowds and smiles.

"My friends and honoured guests, fellow Ghanaians and of course all the hotel owners and staff thank you thank you thank you for such a wonderful night. There is so much to do to make this country achieve it's full potential, but together I believe we can if we all work together. My gratitude to our new friends and allies, as well as look forward to much more business together in the future, to our very own Joseph who shines a light on bringing cancer a cure, to all the good things we have to be proud about and also wish to say that I wish those that had been lost to cancer could have been here tonight with us. I am not going to say much more as I am sure you'll be hearing a lot from me over the coming next months and years, but I find myself as an African, a Ghanaian, a proud man, saying thank you to an Englishman who helped us realise this moment and found us Joseph. A man who truly has inspired so many and I would like to say that a new program I hope to devise with my wife, as new patron of Little Feet, in helping local towns and villages set up schools to help all children study and make our future secure looking after the lonely, the scared and the orphans, open to all. I would like to set up this initiative in a courageous woman's name that lost her life protecting our lands and investing in our people. With your permission Ben, I would like to honour your wife Jessica and name the Little Feet schools all be called Jessica. I feel the children have a name to go to, a school named Jessica so that she will always be remembered and honoured."

The crowd cheer and Ben is in tears as is Earl and well nearly everyone, including Arthur on stage. The President looks to me, and smiles and then takes the microphone and looks to Flo, "DJ, please will you get this party started!"

Flo hits the track and everyone cheers as Nelson sets off confetti and streamers and everyone dances.

I look to see all the groups mingling as one and slowly disappear into the crowd.

One of my favourite moments was seeing John Barr sing to the President's wife who looked in complete awe and it was not until the end of the song that Johnny realised she had not understood a word. Then as camp as Christmas he helped her off the stage leaving her with a look of total confusion.

36

I wake in my room back at the house. It is 11:30am. I had made my way back and blacked out. Next to me is Mary, Isaac and Abraham's sister. I was fully dressed and so was she. As I move she wakes and looks embarrassed. I smile and nod my head as if to say morning before rising to stretch.

"I helped carry you here and then realised I had nowhere to stay and so I hope you do not mind?"

I looked at Mary and laughed, "Well I hope I did not snore."

"Not much," she honestly replied.

I am sat downstairs with Mary making breakfast as slowly the Knights appear worse for wear. No one spoke they just made noises in response or motioned yes or no with their hands.

I see a message delivered to me and as I open it I see it is from Rudy.

'Hi, just dispatched two assassins sent from CIA to eliminate you. Word is more on their way tomorrow. Feel you should use route via Moscow.'

The CIA would not get to me in Moscow was Rudy's thinking, but it was time to leave. I was worried as this time I was visible and told Jimmy he should head home too.

I met Arthur by the pool as he was going over contracts, "Ah, Sir John, last night was an amazing success and the PM is suitably annoyed. Seems that the New Order wanted to infiltrate Africa and our event has halted that in parts, you look like we are going to loose you again."

"Yes, something has come up."

"I have a friend in America, it seems that Tranvapumi Holdings was a company indirectly owned by one of the new President Elect's children, well owned by him and he uses them as a front. Funny how here in Africa, reputed as the most corrupt continent in the world and suddenly that all pales into insignificance once we see this new President of America. Seems he was looking to do a deal with New Order and our hideous crone of a PM was happy to be a pawn in his plans. I trust I can count on you for advice when needed?"

"Of course sir, always. Just be the person with eyes wide open and see what is truly going on. I fear it may be a little difficult for me to be seen as have to ensure that our new American dictator does not see me so I can stay safe."

"I will send out a press memo thanking you for your outstanding work and say that you are in Borneo on a commission for the Knights looking into new cures there. Will that help?"

"Arthur, it has been a pleasure and thank you. Give my love to Guinevere and let the team know I will be in touch soon."

With that I stood, we shook hands and I left collecting my luggage and made my way via the river exit to the town to get a car to drive to Mauritania and then have a friend's yacht to take a long cruise back to England.

I find myself back in England, sat in the Boston Tea Party in Exeter. The lovely Becca makes me a Steamer with a shot of coffee whilst Jessica smiles and says hi. Upstairs international relations university student Clara is not working, but there meeting friend, Greta. Small world, Greta the beautiful Italian girl I met knocking door to door selling charity, sat with the wonderful Spanish stunner Clara. Life is funny as things are always interlinked.

Sat in the corner is Tony. We sit we chat and talk bollocks, it is a great way to spend a morning. Tony then shows me something on his iPad of an event in America that has rocked the world.

I sit watching the President of America spouting rhetoric not heard since the rise of Nazi Germany. He has sacked, removed all liberal, democrat, and opposition and now has built his own New Order. He starts on immigrants and religious groups and on the stage next to him stands the UK Prime Minister looking like a weird family member from the Adam's Family, his right wing ally and far right backers, all looking to hire cheap black slave labour straight out of prisons and then there in clear daylight, new security advisor, Sylvester Willis. This New Order is happening in America. No one outside is affected. No one outside America cares as does not affect them, but there are protests to his new regime and rallies not only in all American states, but also in countries around the world.

He ends his rally in a Washington Square with the chilling phrase that America has more firepower than anyone in the world and that America could out nuke the combined forces of the world.

I am not invisible, chinks in my armour have made me visible, but I know that I have no choice I have to go to America to expose to the American people waving blindly flags that their President is Satan himself.

I decide to go to London to see my twin daughters studying at college one last time before I depart. This is one mission I feel I should not take, but for the love of my children and ensuring a future for them, one mission I will have to take.

Reader, this Journal seems to of come to a sudden ending, but I fear this mission is only the start of the next, which I fear will be my last.

I got a funny note from Rudy as he has moved from Russia to America and is working on a deal between new President Elect and Russian leader that they started four years ago.

Jimmy is getting engaged to Margot's sister and all is going well with Family in all corners of the globe as Aiguo and Marco seal new mining deals in other African countries similar to Ghana where they mine responsibly. It seems that they get such preferential treatment they are able to move around the continent without hassle.

The Knights go from strength to strength and Arthur is able to thwart New Order progression as he has teamed up with the Knights of the Round Table in Europe where all work in unison to combat the far right attempts to gain power.

America, a new dictator awaits and I go to see how to remain invisible in a world that has seen me.